CIRCLE OF LOVE

Also by Syrell Rogovin Leahy

A BOOK OF RUTH

CIRCLE of LOVE

SYRELL ROGOVIN LEAHY

G. P. PUTNAM'S SONS   New York

Library of Congress Cataloging in Publication Data

Leahy, Syrell Rogovin
    Circle of love.

    I. Title.
PZ4.L436Ci [PS3562.E23]   813'.54   79-25439
ISBN 0-399-12475-6

In memory of Robert Funk
Born in Shenandoah, Iowa, October 7, 1919
Died in France, August 27, 1944

Parting is all we know of heaven,
And all we need of hell.

Emily Dickinson

I

May 1945

1

The man on the bicycle ahead of hers slowed down to a stop and looked back, waiting. She drew alongside and rested her weight on one foot, looking at him with a face that showed the worry and the fear of what now almost certainly lay ahead.

"This is the road," the man said, his French accented in a way similar to that of the Alsatians.

"Yes."

"I wouldn't go if I were you." He looked equally worried, a thickish farmer type whose ordinary worries were sun and rain, frost and insect pests. "We can get you back, you know. It's no trouble. I know a small truck that leaves tomorrow." He waited for an answer.

She knew she would be unable to speak and if she tried, if he heard her voice, he might take her back forcibly. So she shook her head and pushed the bicycle one step closer to the road at right angles to their own.

"What do you expect to find?" the man asked, persisting, a hint of anger in his voice. Perhaps he thought it would be on his shoulders if something happened to her. "You've heard nothing, right?"

"Nothing."

"It's the bad news that travels. Go home to Madeleine. At least they will know where to find you."

She swallowed. "Thank you, Monsieur DeLaux. They're my parents. I have to look."

"What do you think you will find?"

11

"I don't know."

"Go back to Paris. Madeleine will thank me."

"I thank you, Monsieur. And your wife. I must go now."

He sighed, took the pack off his back and tied it on hers. "Straight ahead," he said, pointing to the right. "Take care of yourself." He kissed her cheeks. "My wife will pray for you."

She smiled for the first time, waved, and pushed off. What would have to happen for him to get down on his own knees and offer up a prayer? She lifted her hand high so he would see it if he was still watching her.

Perhaps it would all work out. She was sure he would see to it that Madame DeLaux prayed for her.

2

She stopped for lunch at the side of the road after she had been hungry long enough to believe that it was lunchtime. Mme. DeLaux had packed several hard-boiled eggs for her, and she ate one with some cheese and bread, taking her time so that it would fill her. They had been nice people, the DeLauxs, the wife a childhood friend of Madeleine. They were her last contacts on the trip east. From here on she was on her own, traveling entirely under her own power.

She rested for a few minutes, stretching out in the grass. Then she got up, walked the bicycle to the road, and resumed the journey. She pedaled at an even pace and started to hum an old German folk tune that her mother had sung to her years ago. She could still sing the words although it was a long time since she had spoken German aloud.

It was six years since she had left them—her parents, her home, her language—to travel with a family friend to Paris to stay for a few days or weeks with Aunt Madeleine, Uncle Josef's wife, who spoke hardly a word of German. It had been necessary to learn French, and she had learned it well. Apart from the first terrifying weeks when she understood nothing and no one understood her, it had been less difficult than she expected.

What she had not expected was that they would not come. She had looked for them every day for weeks and months, standing in front of the house and looking down the street, certain that each new day would bring them to her, that if they failed to come in the morning they would surely arrive before dark. Eventually, she had grown to understand that wherever they might be, they would not be coming to France while there was a war.

Now that war was over. Approaching from the opposite direction was a familiar jeep with its white, five pointed star. There were two young Americans in it, one of them rather handsome, and they waved and called as they neared her. She kept her eyes on her side of the road. What did it matter which soldiers they were or whether one was handsome? A soldier was a soldier, and Madeleine had taught her to regard them all with a measure of distrust.

But besides Madeleine's rather dogmatic warnings, she had other information, more frightening and more reliable, from a girl with whom she sometimes walked and talked in the afternoon when school was over, Nicole, almost eighteen now and wordly beyond her years. Nicole had spent a night with an American soldier soon after the liberation, and she had explained what he was after and described in rather disgusting detail what he had done to get it.

The jeep passed, the young men calling to her. She turned slightly to assure herself that they were gone, only to see them make a sharp turn in the road, overtake her, and pull in front so that she was forced to stop.

"*Parlez-vous Anglais?*" the nearer one asked in the typical Anglo-French they all learned from the little books they kept in their pockets and consulted during their attempts at conversation.

"No," she said.

"No English?" the driver, the good-looking one, asked.

"No." She had learned to understand much of what she heard, but she was unable to speak the language and would not have if she had been able.

"Hey, Madam-wa-ZELL," the nearer one said, "you understand 'good time'?"

"No."

"Want some chocolate?" the driver asked.

14

"No."

"Hey, I got something you'd like." He reached around to the back seat and took something out of a pouch. "Soap," he said, handing it to the nearer soldier who thrust it at her. "Want some soap?"

It held her eyes almost hypnotically. She craved it as she had once craved sweets, yearned for it as she yearned for her parents. She stared at the outstretched hand holding the precious cake. Without signaling her intentions, she grabbed for it and held it behind her back, triumph gleaming in her eyes.

"See?" the driver said. "I told you I had something you'd like. There's more nice things where that came from. Wanna see?"

"No."

"Aw, c'mon, toots," the driver said pleadingly. "Hop in. Take a ride with us. The bike'll fit."

"No."

The nearer one climbed out. "I'll help you," he said, moving for the bike.

"No," she said loudly, pushing the bicycle onto the grass and starting to feel terror. And then in French, "Leave me alone. Let me go. I'm not going anywhere with you. I'll bite you if you touch my bike."

The soldier moved back, apparently shaken by her near hysterics in a language he did not understand. She pushed the bicycle around the front of the jeep and began to pedal away. She was shaking now and very near tears. She heard the jeep start up in low gear, and she shuddered, expecting it any second to draw alongside again. But it didn't. She chanced a look back and saw it heading safely in the other direction. She stopped the bike and allowed herself to cry for a few minutes until she was calm. The tears helped, but even when she closed her eyes at night, she could see the jeep, the two uniforms, and the faces of the enticers. Lying there she wondered how Nicole had managed to do it.

She spent the first night sleeping under some trees not too

15

far from the road. Her back ached when she awoke, and her mouth was dry, but she shook out her skirt and walked the bicycle back to the road.

The bicycle had been old when the war began, and it had been used almost daily since then. Madeleine had promised that, as soon as the war was over, there would be new bicycles. Now she wished only that this bicycle would last as long as she. Perhaps, she thought, jumping off to walk it up an incline, she should have asked Mme. DeLaux to pray instead for the bike.

At the top of the hill she stopped and surveyed what lay before her. Ahead, still many kilometers away, was Germany, the country in which she had been born, and to which she was now returning against the wishes of her aunt and the judgment of M. and Mme. DeLaux. She sighed, half wishing he had stopped her forcibly when he was able. His wife could have saved her prayers then. What would the trip matter if, in the end, the news were all bad?

She turned and looked back along the road that had brought her here. Somewhere back there was Paris, Aunt Madeleine, and a certain comfort in not knowing. Her eye moved down the incline she had just ascended, the road lying like a beige ribbon between the two rows of evenly spaced trees that marked the better French roads. The Germans had marched west along this road when she was ten. Now something was moving east along it, something long and dark and uniform in color and speed.

She felt a little prickle along her back. It was a military convoy, dull brown and heading slowly her way. It was too far away to detect the white five pointed star of the liberators, but she had had her fill of soldiers. She would not care to be riding along the same road and in the same direction as a military convoy.

Back the way she had come there had been a road off to her left, a dirt road leading to a farmhouse and perhaps not much farther beyond. It would be risky to chance going

16

back. Although the convoy was moving slowly, she was afraid she might meet it head-on. She looked down the hill in the direction of Germany. Not too far, perhaps a kilometer, a road crossed the main road in both directions. With the aid of the hill she could reach it easily. She mounted the bike, pushed off, and began to coast. There was a slight breeze and, together with the speed, she began to feel quite exhilarated. Perhaps when there were new bikes, she and Madeleine would ride out in the country. Madeleine enjoyed that sort of thing. She spoke from time to time of how she and Uncle Josef had ridden together when they were students.

Anna applied the brake gently, slowing herself slightly. She would never ride in the country with Madeleine. Uncle Josef would come back, Anna's parents would come back, and they would be two families again in two countries. Madeleine would have children, and Vati would go back to the university. Life would go back—or forward. Everything would be different from now but the same as it was then.

The crossroad was just ahead. She stopped the bike and looked back. The convoy had not yet reached the top of the hill. Left or right? There had been a road sign here once. She could see the remains of it. Had a French patriot torn it down to confuse the invaders, or had it merely rusted away through neglect?

Down the main road in the direction of Germany, a farmer and his horse were plowing a square of farmland. The crossroad to the left led straight through farmland as far as she could see. To the right, the road disappeared into some trees beyond which she could see nothing. She looked back, but the convoy was not yet in sight. She would prefer the trees, she thought, pushing with her left toe and turning the wheel to the right. Perhaps in the safety of the hidden road she might find a house with a friendly occupant. You couldn't be sure, this close to Germany, how they would respond. Madeleine had warned her. So had the DeLauxs.

17

But it would be nice to use a real toilet for a change; even nicer to wash out the clothes she was wearing and wash her own body.

She rode into the patch of woods and came out to more farmland. The sun was high now, and warm. She took her sweater off and tied the sleeves around her waist. Her legs began to ache as she pedaled along, and she realized that she was hungry. She pushed hard on the pedals, but the bike refused to respond. She felt very alone. It was hard not talking to anyone for days at a time. She didn't want to eat alone again, to squat near some tree, to sleep in these clothes on the ground hugging her possessions.

The bike was impossible. She got off and looked at it, her face, her shoulders, her heart sinking. The rear tire was flat. She had lost her transportation. Where could she find a new one—there weren't any new ones—or someone who could fix this one?

She held back tears. Madeleine had let her go and M. DeLaux had not stopped her despite their fears and misgivings. She was alone because they had had the faith to let her go alone, and she would have to succeed.

She sat down at the side of the road and considered her options. She could go back the way she had come, waiting perhaps till the convoy had passed, and then go down the main road. Or she could continue along this one. She had not yet passed a house. Surely there would be one soon, and she would take her chances that they would help her.

She took a piece of bread out of her pack and stuffed it in her mouth, chewing as she walked. She was tired. The pack was heavy and the bike was heavy. She hated feeling unclean. She had been brought up with toilets and down comforters and silver and china. Even Madeleine, who had none of the beautiful things Mutti had, had a sense of elegance which, she had learned on this journey, was more Parisian than French.

And there was a house. It was on the right side of the

18

road, not too far ahead. She pushed harder, looking through the distance for a farmer, a chicken, some sign of habitation.

The shutters were all closed as though this were a day in summer. It was pleasant out but certainly not hot. She knocked on the front door and called out. There was no answer and no sound from within. She pushed the bicycle around the side of the house to a shed with tools, old tools, many rusted. She left the bike there and continued around, calling as she went.

Behind the house and joined to it by a covered gravel path was an outhouse, the door ajar. She looked around, no longer certain whether she wanted to find anyone, but no one was there. All the windows at the back of the house were shuttered, and the door leading to the outhouse was closed. She pulled open the door of the outhouse. It was clean and didn't smell, giving it two big pluses. She closed and fastened the door and sat on the wooden surface. Next to her on a nail in the wall hung a neat pack of square-cut pieces of newspaper. As she sat, she pulled the top one off and looked at it. It was printed in German, and she shivered slightly at the thought of having it touch her body. Still, it was better than leaves and far better than nothing.

She left the outhouse and continued to circle the house. It was a small house with a garden behind it that had been planted and left untended. Rows of lettuce and peas were partly overgrown with weeds, reinforcing her growing feeling that no one was home. At the far side of the house, under a large tree, was a well.

At least there would be fresh water. Fresh water, a toilet, and an empty house.

She returned to the front door, knocked again, and tried it. It was locked and looked very solid. She went around to the back again and tried the back door. It gave slightly and she pushed it.

It felt as though it might only be stuck, perhaps from

19

paint or the warping of the wood. She leaned against it and pushed as hard as she could. It gave with a lurch, and she found herself in a kitchen.

It was very quiet inside. She closed the door and put her pack down on the table, a chunk of sanded rough wood on handmade legs.

"Hello," she called. "Is anyone home?"

A large, handleless, unwashed cup and a spoon lay on the table. Along the outside wall there was a window and next to it a sink but no faucets. The well must be the only source of water. A door across the room from the sink opened onto stairs which descended into darkness.

"Is anyone down there?" she called, not really wanting to find out.

There was one other room on the ground floor, a living room. The front door led into this room, a room full of worn furniture, an old clock stopped at 2:25 of some day or night past, and a rug that once may have had an oriental pattern on it but which now was worn beyond description.

Between the two rooms a steep wooden staircase went up. She mounted it slowly, fearful of what she might find. There were three rooms upstairs, a large bedroom containing a large, unmade bed with two pillows, a dresser with a pitcher and basin on it, a crucifix on the wall over the bed, and an armoire, open, with clothes hanging inside. A second bedroom was smaller and had smaller furniture. The third room was very small and contained only a narrow bed with a thin mattress without sheets. A pitcher and basin rested on the floor under the only window.

At the head of the stairs stood a cabinet which was locked. That, she thought, was where Madame would keep her sheets and towels. But there seemed no way of opening the cabinet without a key.

She sat down on the top step and tried to think where they might be.

"I want someone to talk to," she said aloud. "I haven't

talked to anyone since I left M. DeLaux." She refused to count the American soldiers as a conversation.

She stood up and went downstairs. Against the wall on the kitchen floor were several empty bottles with German beer labels on them that she had not noticed before. Had they been soldiers? Would they come back?

She checked the door through which she had come in. It had a lock on it, and she used it. Feeling a little safer, she opened her pack, took out some of the food Mme. DeLaux had packed for her, and ate enough to pass for a meal.

Mme. DeLaux had shown her how to draw water from a well, a skill she had never dreamed she would use. Now she went out and found she could do it herself. The water was cold and tasted good. She brought some in and washed her face and hands. She wanted terribly to wash the rest of her body, but it would mean undressing, and what if someone came while she was washing? Perhaps tomorrow. Perhaps she would feel safer then. Certainly before she left this place she would bathe.

It began to grow dark, and she went upstairs to look at the bedrooms again. The thought of sleeping on someone else's sheets was very distasteful. The bed in the second room, she discovered, had a quilt thrown across it but no sheets underneath. There were oil lamps in every room but the tiniest bedroom. She wondered what Madeleine would think of this place, but probably it would come as no surprise to her. Madeleine had been born in a village not far from the DeLauxs' farm.

She could not sleep up here. She took the quilt off the smaller bed and took it downstairs. When it became too dark to see without light, she lay down on the lumpy sofa in the living room and drew the cover over her. In spite of the discomfort, she had no trouble sleeping.

21

3

It was impossible to tell what time it was, especially with the shutters closed. When she awoke, she went around the house opening them everywhere except along the front. If the occupants returned, at least they would not know from the road that someone had entered.

She unlocked the back door and went out to the overgrown garden. Heads of lettuce begged to be harvested. She pulled some weeds to clean out a space around a few heads and discovered the "weeds" were radishes. She picked a few more, pulled a lettuce off its root, and took her harvest inside. It would do for breakfast.

The kitchen had Italian oil—where had they gotten the oil from?—and vinegar. She took some of the bread still left in her pack and made a meal, washed down with well water. It meant she could save the sausage for later. When that ran out, she would be in trouble. The little money she had with her would probably buy nothing in Germany. Before crossing the border, she would have to convert most of her cash into food.

She saw him first through the kitchen window, a man walking down the road from the direction opposite to the one that had brought her here. He was still quite a distance away, so she had time to run if she wanted to, but it would mean leaving the bicycle behind. She watched him for a minute or two, wondering fearfully what his destination was. Perhaps he would continue down the road to the main road from which she had come. Perhaps he would simply dissolve into thin air and she would never see him again.

As a precaution, she shut and locked the kitchen door. Then she stood alongside the window and watched his progress. Even at this distance she could see that she had reason to fear him; he was wearing military clothes. He wore shirt and pants, but no jacket and no hat. Quite probably they were American army clothes, but they were not a uniform. The man on the road was almost certainly a deserter.

A deserter was the worst of all possibilities. He was responsible to no one. Having already broken the most serious of rules, breaking another—like raping a young girl in a farmhouse—would mean nothing to him.

Anna moved carefully away from the window. She gathered up the remains of her breakfast and her pack and went upstairs. Setting down her parcel, she closed all the shutters upstairs except the one in the tiniest bedroom because, if the man outside looked up, he would see her doing it. Then she took up a post next to that window and watched.

He had stopped on the road and was looking at the house, a slight man perhaps Uncle Josef's age. She began to pray, making wild promises to a God she only slightly believed in, promises she would keep forever if the man on the road would continue on his way.

But already he had begun walking toward the house. In a moment she would lose sight of him and his disappearance would mark, in another sense, his appearance at the house.

It happened in seconds. There was a knock on the front door, then another. Then he called in accented and oddly ungrammatical French, "Is someone at home? I would like to come in. Do you hear me?"

She held her breath as the knocking became a pounding and then a rattling of the door.

Suddenly the noise stopped and she heard him say something in another language, not English, not German, something different and unrecognizable.

23

Go away, she whispered. Please. I will do anything. I will go back to Madeleine. Anything. Just go away.

Then the pounding resumed on the back door. She left her window, ran into the largest bedroom, and stood next to the shuttered window, trying to get a look through a crack. Through the shutter she was able to see numerous slits of scenery—the outhouse, the garden, the sky—all in thin horizontal slices.

The pounding stopped, and when he stepped away from the house she could see him. He had a pack slung over a shoulder and resting on his back. He was slim. There was no belt running through his pants. He walked to the outhouse, opened the door, and dropped his pack on the gravel path. Leaving the door wide open, he stepped in and stood with his back to the house.

Anna gasped and turned away from the window. Even if he was a deserter, she had no right to watch. She closed her eyes, waiting for an appropriate length of time to pass.

She turned back to the window. He was coming out of the outhouse, buttoning his pants, and she could see the clothing quite clearly. He was surely an American.

The man walked back to the house, and she lost sight of him. She stayed, watching, and then suddenly she heard him downstairs. The unshuttered window in the kitchen. Her heart was beating crazily now, and she was breathing like a runner at the end of a race. He was in the house, her house, and she had no way out.

Very quietly, she sank to the floor in the little space between the wall and the end of the dresser. If he only looked in the door, he would not see her—if he even bothered to come upstairs, which was not at all certain. He seemed interested in the kitchen. She could hear him banging around down there, opening cupboards, rattling dishes, and made a sound, a small exclamation of pleasure. There was another sound after that, something mechanical which she could not identify. She closed her eyes, visualizing the living room, and she saw it. He was winding the clock.

24

He mumbled a few words in the strange language and went to the stairs. He came up them heavily, his boots counting out the minutes remaining in her life. She stopped breathing as he entered the bedroom, commented to himself, and went on to the other rooms.

Thank God she had closed the shutters. It was dark enough that she might remain hidden. Perhaps he would sleep here, she thought, and she could wait until he snored and then run away. (Her father had snored, and she had once asked Madeleine if Uncle Josef snored too, but she had only laughed.)

The man went downstairs and out the kitchen door. When he returned, she heard water sloshing. He was washing or drinking. She smiled. He was doing exactly what she had done on her arrival a day ago.

He stayed downstairs for a while, making noises as he moved around, sat at the table, probably ate something. Then he scraped his chair across the floor and came up the stairs.

She bit her lips to keep her teeth from chattering. He came directly into the large bedroom, sat on the bed, and stood up again. She saw him stretch, turn, and walk to the windows, so close to her she could almost reach out and touch him. He opened the window farther away from her, unlatched the shutters, and pushed them outward. He inhaled deeply, smiling a little as he looked outside.

It was a matter of seconds now. From where she crouched, aching, he was barely a meter away. When he turned—

She screamed, and he started in apparent terror as he saw her and their eyes met.

He said something in the other language, and she said, "I'm terribly sorry, Monsieur. I am here by mistake—"

But he had begun to speak in French, missing her explanation entirely. "Pardon me, Mademoiselle," he said, standing back deferentially. "I am so sorry. I thought this house was deserted. I regret the intrusion."

He was frightened. Strange, for a deserter. Did he think a

little sixteen-year-old girl could return him to his company?

"I was about to leave," she said rapidly. "Only my bicycle is broken. If you will let me pass—"

"Let me help you." He used the polite form although he was clearly older than she, and she had not come to expect it yet. He extended his hand, and she grasped it while he pulled her up.

"If you will let me go," she said close to tears, "I will be on my way. I meant no harm here, Monsieur."

He stood back. "This isn't your house?"

She shook her head.

"What are you doing here?"

"I—I needed a rest. My tire is flat. I was hungry. I wanted to use the toilet," she added, indicating their ultimate similarity as human beings.

"And no one was here?"

She shook her head.

"I'm not going to hurt you," he said, standing back and still using the polite form. "This isn't my house either."

She edged around the dresser and backed toward the door, keeping her eyes on him.

He stood back as she passed. "I won't hurt you," he said again. "You frightened me too, you know. I thought it was your house. You can go if you want. I won't stop you."

"I wanted to wash before I left," she said, the words coming out rapidly. "I should have washed last night but I was afraid someone would come while I was—before I finished washing. I want to wash my clothes too. But then I have to wait for them to dry. Everything's so dirty. I slept in a field the other night. I really want to get clean." She stopped, hearing herself talk almost uncontrollably. "Excuse me, Monsieur. I haven't spoken to anyone for two days." And then she shot out, "Are you a soldier?"

"A soldier? No, I'm not a soldier."

"Why are you wearing those clothes?"

He looked down at the army pants. "I was detained by the

26

Germans last fall. They took my clothes. When I came out of detention, I was given these."

"Why were you detained?"

"I am very tired," he said.

"Do you have a gun?"

He looked at her with some bewilderment and sat down on the unmade bed. "Mademoiselle, I am very tired. I'm not a soldier and I have no gun. If it doesn't trouble you too much, I would like to sleep."

"The sheets are dirty."

He looked at the bed on which he was sitting, his eyes seemingly somewhere else. "I would like to sleep," he said again.

"I'll go downstairs." She walked to the door, hearing a boot drop behind her. In the doorway she stopped and turned around. He was pulling off the second boot. "Are you a German?" she asked softly.

"I am stateless." He lay down on the bed and closed his eyes.

As she started down the stairs, his voice came after her, repeating the first sentence Aunt Madeleine had taught her to say in French six years before: "I am not a German."

His pack was on the kitchen table, and she sat staring at it, wondering at its secrets. He had been afraid of her. She had never frightened a grown person before, certainly not a man, not a man in a soldier's clothes.

The pack might explain who he was and where he had come from, why his French was awkward and his clothing odd. What did it mean to be stateless? In the back of her mind she saw Madeleine whispering with a neighbor, half-heard words that made little sense, strange things that fit nothing, something about numbers, the women suddenly silent at Anna's approach, then gossiping a trifle too loudly and too mundanely. There were things she wasn't told, things she needed to know because in some still unexplained way they were part of her life.

27

There was no sound from the bedroom. She took her shoes off and went quietly up the stairs. The man lay on his stomach, his face toward the window, his arms spread out above his head, the nearer hand clutching the pillow. His breathing was audible and fairly regular but not deep and restful the way Nicole had described her soldier. This man took short quick breaths, as though every moment he might awaken to ambush or battle. He was a man on guard, alert even in his sleep. For what reason had the Germans detained him?

She returned to the kitchen and opened his pack. He was carrying some food including three American chocolate bars, an army jacket and a very small amount of other clothing, a razor, and an identification card. The card was a travel document for stateless persons issued by the Military Government for Germany and printed in English, French, and German. His name, printed in large letters, was Anton Pietrovic, and he was born in 1911 in a city whose name she did not recognize and could not pronounce.

She folded the card and put it back in the pack.

She went into the living room and looked at the clock, a plain, ordinary sort of clock. It was working, but he had not set it. Perhaps when the sun was overhead, she would set it for noon.

The man upstairs slept for hours. Anna became bored waiting. This was a dull house owned by dull people. There were no books or newspapers, no electricity and therefore no radio. She had not found a pencil or a scrap of paper anywhere. What did they do besides the most fundamental things to keep themselves alive?

She went out and worked in the garden. There were plenty of peas, many pods already bulging too much to be sweet. She picked a bowlful and came in and shelled them, eating them by the handful so that she had to go out and pick more to fill the bowl again. When she was nearly finished, the man came downstairs.

"You're still here?" he said.

"I'm sorry, Monsieur, I didn't know you wanted me to go. I'll get my things together." She put the bowl of peas down on the table, misery welling up inside her. There would be no bath and no clean clothes, and what would she do about the bicycle?

"Wait a minute," the man said, "I don't mean to put you out. I don't own this house either. You can stay if you want."

"Oh thank you, Monsieur," she said gratefully. "It's just that my bicycle is broken."

"I'll look at it for you."

"I know your name," she confessed. "I looked at your things while you were sleeping. I can't pronounce it though."

He smiled for the first time, hesitantly, as though he were unsure it would be acceptable, and held out his hand. "Pietrovic," he said, "Anton Pietrovic."

"My name is Anna, Anna Kleinberger." She pronounced the name in the French way.

"Kleinberjay," he repeated, "Kleinberjay. Kleinberger! You speak German then." He had switched languages on the last sentence and reverted to the familiar form.

"I haven't spoken German for six years," she said, trying out the old-new language.

"Try," he said. "My French is only school-French. I still have trouble making it come right. Your French is beautiful. I wouldn't have known you weren't born here. Are you a French citizen?"

"I don't know what I am, Mr. Petr—, Pietro—."

"Pietrovic."

"I don't really know what I am any more," she said, omitting the name entirely.

"What are you doing here?"

"I'm on my way to Germany."

"To Germany? They won't let you cross the border."

She stared at him, the carrier of bad news, hating him. "You crossed the border, didn't you?" she accused.

29

"I know how to cross borders," he said.

"Well, I'll find a way."

"Why do you want to go to Germany?"

"My parents are there. They were supposed to join me in France when the war started. We haven't heard anything. I thought if I went home—"

"You're young to be traveling alone."

"I'm seventeen," she lied.

"Who have you lived with here in France?"

"My aunt."

"And she let you come alone?"

"It isn't that she let me. I think she knew she couldn't stop me any more. Anyway, it wasn't quite alone until now. I had rides along the way with friends and stopped overnight with people my aunt knew. I only started out on my own two days ago, but then I saw some soldiers, and I left the main road."

"That was a smart thing to do. And then your bike broke down."

"It's the tire."

He went to the door. "I don't know if there's anything I can do for a tire, but I'll have a look."

They went outside, and she showed him the bicycle. He turned the poor, worn tire completely around, and she knew it was no use. The rubber had worn away to the cord, and a rusty nail was imbedded in the surface.

"I had one like this for a while in 1942," he said.

"Where is it now?"

"I don't know. Where is anything now?" He put the bike down. "Don't give up yet." He went into the house, lit a small kitchen lamp, and carried it down to the cellar while she stood at the top of the stairs, waiting. After a minute he whistled. She could see the light moving somewhere below in the darkness. "Our friends must be Germans," he called. "Or else they're friends with the Germans. There's enough German beer down here to keep an army going for a month. There's also a bicycle."

"There is?"

30

"Don't come down. I'll bring it up." He came up the stairs carrying it. It was filthy and made for a man.

"Can you ride with the bar?" he asked.

"As long as it rides. I just want to get there."

"I wouldn't go to Germany," he said, taking the bike outside. "I've just come from there. It's been bombed, you know. There are whole sections of cities where nothing is left but rubble. Everything is chaos."

"Why were you detained?" she asked.

He had been adjusting the chain and his hands were covered with black grease. He took his eyes away from his work and looked at her. "Have you heard from your parents?" he asked.

She shook her head.

"Not in six years?"

"No."

He stood the bike up, moved it back and forth on the grass, and squeezed the tires. He found a hand pump in the shed and used it laboriously, till the tires were firm.

"Are you a bicycle mechanic?" she asked.

"I'm a clockmaker."

"A clockmaker." She smiled, her whole image of the man changing once again. He had been a soldier, a deserter, a German, and a mechanic. Suddenly he was a craftsman displaced by a war in which no one needed clockmakers.

"Did you sell clocks?" she asked eagerly.

"Old clocks, old silver, old jewelry."

"Then where are you going now?"

"To England. My wife and children are in England." He leaned the bike against the tree that shaded the back of the house, stood back, and looked at it covetously.

"Why don't you take the bike?" she offered, seeing the look in his eyes. "You fixed it. That really makes it yours."

"I can walk," he said, looking down at his heavy, worn boots which must already have traveled a thousand kilometers. "Farther than you can, I think. And I can take rides with strangers. The bike is for you."

He looked at his hands. They were terribly dirty and he

31

was being careful to keep them away from his clothes. "Do you have any soap?" he asked.

"There's soap in the kitchen."

"German soap?"

"I don't know. Probably."

"I can't use it."

She looked at him with his dirty hands, standing next to the bike he had fixed so that she could ride to Germany to find her parents, a clockmaker on his way to England to join his own family, a man who had been detained by the Germans. She had wanted to save the soap for her parents. She had no gifts to bring them. Almost nothing tangible had survived the war. There were few things as precious today as a bar of soap.

"I have soap," she said at last, offering her gift. "American soap."

"Thank you," he said. "I'll draw the water."

4

The soap seemed to make a difference. He washed his face, rolled his sleeves part-way up, and scrubbed his blackened hands and arms. Then, as she watched fascinated, he shaved his face, using a small metal mirror she had missed in his bag.

"Are there towels in the house?" he asked, his hands dripping in the basin.

"There's a cupboard upstairs, but it's locked. It's the kind that they would keep linens in."

"Yes," he said with a wry smile, shaking water off his hands, "the keys dangling from her belt and the cupboard locked even when no one else is in the house. You show me where it is; I'll get into it."

He got some tools from the shed, and they went upstairs to the locked cabinet. With a screwdriver he forced the doors open. Inside were the flimsy remains of a paltry linen supply that had survived a long war. There were towels so threadbare they resembled handkerchiefs, sheets once thick and rough now worn almost smooth. He took a towel and mopped his face, hair, and arms.

"Take some along," he said. "We can bathe later."

She carried a few towels downstairs and left them on the kitchen table.

"Where did you get American soap?" he asked.

It was an accusing question. Where did anyone get anything American nowadays? "Some Americans stopped me on the road," she said with some anger. "They wanted me to

33

get into their jeep, but I wouldn't. When they held out the soap, I stole it from them and ran."

"Are you angry at me or at the Americans?"

"Why were you detained?" she demanded.

"You're angry at me, aren't you? I didn't mean to imply you had done anything to earn the soap. My clothes are American. A soldier from New York City gave me this shirt." He reached into the bowl of shelled peas, took a handful, and ate them with obvious pleasure.

"I could give you a cooked egg," she offered. "My aunt's friends gave me ten of them."

"You give me a cooked egg, and I'll give you some very tasty wurst."

They made the exchange and she sat down at the table. "How will you get to England?"

"It looks now as though I'll have to make a detour," he said. "I'm out of money. Do you have money?"

"No," she lied quickly. "My aunt packed only food and a change of clothes."

"I'll have to go to Switzerland then," he said as though she might have been able to finance the journey to England all by herself.

"Do you have money in Switzerland?"

"Yes."

"Enough to get you to England?"

He smiled. "Yes, I have that much."

"Money from your business as a clockmaker?"

"That's right."

She sighed. "My father liked old clocks." The tense came out unwittingly. "We had them in every room in the house. They all chimed at different times. When my father had students staying over, they always said it was hard to sleep at night because of the chiming, but it never bothered me. When I got to my aunt's house, it was so quiet I couldn't sleep."

"Your father was—is a teacher?"

"When I was little. Then he stopped teaching; I don't

34

remember when. Even after that, though, his students would come by. He was so well-liked." She could see him as she spoke, a man with a short beard and dark bright eyes, sitting in a room filled to capacity with possessions he could not bear to part with. "He taught history, but what he really loved was the human side of history—that's what he called it. Folklore, songs, stories. He used to go to the country and take down tales that the farmers knew from their fathers."

Unexpectedly, the man's face had become alive. "Did he teach at Freiburg?"

"Yes!" Her body tensed at the possibility of hope. "You knew him?"

"Max Kleinberger?"

"That's my father. Have you seen him?"

The man touched her hand. "I'm sorry. I never knew him. I read his book in the thirties. It has a chapter on clocks."

"His book." She sighed. It was on the shelf among many others in the overstuffed living room. She had turned the pages a hundred times, looking at the pictures of girls in their native costume, the beautiful colorful clothes of the unmarried girls and brides and the darker, more subdued costumes of the married women. He could look at the dress and tell you married or single, Protestant or Catholic. You see how she wears her hair? he would say. She is Catholic. Now this one, here. The Reformation set its foot heavily in this area. These are Protestant girls, maidens. They'll marry soon, and then they'll wear black. "I took it with me to Paris. It's in my aunt's house now. You have his book too?"

"I don't know. I must look in Switzerland. I don't know what's left of my home any more."

"My father couldn't leave his home. He loved everything so much."

"I understand."

"He would stay until the end of the earth came."

The man closed his eyes, opened them, and asked, "Who took you to Paris?"

"A student of my father's—well, he had been a student

35

before the trouble started. I was in love with him." She smiled, remembering the big, handsome young man who had carried the knapsack on his back while he held her hand. "I was ten, and he was twenty-five. Jürgen. I was sure he would wait for me to grow up."

"Then you're only sixteen," he said, and she realized she had inadvertently disclosed her lie.

"I wanted you to think I was older, so you wouldn't tell me not to go to Freiburg."

"Anna," he said, and she heard it before the words were spoken: "Anna, you said a moment ago he would stay in his house till the end of the earth came."

She nodded.

"Don't go to Freiburg, dear child. Don't go anywhere in Germany. Believe me when I tell you, the end of the earth came. You won't find him in his house."

She got up and ran out of the kitchen and into the garden. It was afternoon now, and the sun had moved from overhead and become quite warm. There were lettuces ready to wilt and go to seed if they were not eaten soon and peas aching to be harvested. In the garden the life cycle completed itself while her own stood still, ending perhaps this very day, before harvest, even before maturity. She was trapped in this house that was in no village and marked on no map. She had had somewhere to go yesterday and no way to get there. Now this man had given her a means of travel and taken away her destination.

And if there was no going forward, she knew there was also no going back.

She was shaking with fright and fury. Her father was indestructible; he was adored. How dare this man imply anything else? Her father had survived all the terrible things that had been whispered about, and he still had his students and friends. And Jürgen, beautiful Jürgen who had taken her to France. For whom else would he have done such a favor?

"Anna."

36

She turned around, glaring at the uninvited guest.

"Go home to your aunt," he said. "Your family will find you there."

"I can't go back," she said. "I can't go back," she said louder. "I can't go back, I can't go back," she screamed.

He seemed startled and shrank in some barely perceptible way at her outburst, but he recovered and put a hand lightly on her shoulder. She remembered he was a father himself, and fathers knew how to comfort even when all was lost.

"Come and sit in the sun," he said, guiding her out of the shade of the large tree. He sat and opened his shirt, positioning himself so that the sun was on his chest. "Your aunt has cared for you for six years. She expects you back. She'll be beside herself if you don't come back."

"She's waiting for news," Anna said. "My uncle is in the French army. His last letter came from Germany. That was weeks ago, weeks before the surrender." She stopped. She could see from his face that he had drawn the only conclusion.

"Yes, I see. Then she let you go to spare you."

"I hadn't thought of that."

"But she'll want you back, Anna."

"He's my mother's only brother."

"We all had brothers once. At least there are children left."

"My aunt has no children."

"I see."

"When I got there in 1939 she was—" She faltered, having lost, or never having known, the word in German. "*Enceinte*," she inserted in French. "She was expecting a child when my uncle went away. But she lost it after I got there."

"Pregnant," he said, supplying the missing word in German.

"I have no first language any more," she said. "I have no country, no religion. My aunt is Catholic. What am I after six years?"

37

"One can survive small inconveniences." He rubbed a palm across his chest, the fingers pushing the dark, curly hair. "I have Polish from my father, German from my mother. My children will speak only English now. Somewhere in a safe in Switzerland I have a Polish passport." He stated the events of his life as though he were reading them from a dull chronicle. "I grew up in Poland. I studied in Berlin. I met my wife there. When the time came, we went to Switzerland. It wasn't her country and it wasn't mine, but we went because we had to."

"I was in Switzerland once. Jürgen took me there on the way to France."

"I had a shop there. Maybe we'll go back. Maybe after I pick them up in England we'll go back to Switzerland." He closed his eyes and put his face to the sun. "I'd rather try Paris, though, something grand like the Rue de Rivoli under the arcades or the Rue Royale."

"That's very expensive."

"It'll be a very expensive shop."

"Can you afford that?"

"I have everything I need in Switzerland, money, jewelry, some fine old clocks." He buttoned his shirt. A cloud had passed over the sun, chilling the spring air.

He was lying to her. None of this was true. He had been upset by her outburst so he had fabricated a story to calm her down. No one had a family in England, a fortune in Switzerland, and walked in cast-off clothes out of Germany a week after the surrender. He was an intruder in her house, *her house*. She had found it, her refuge half-way between what she had fled in Paris and what she would never reach in Freiburg. What right had he to enter her sanctuary anyway? So he had given her a new bike. What good was it if she had nowhere to go?

Everyone had lied to her, lied since she was ten years old, and not stopped. Her parents had promised to come to France, but they had known they would never leave Germany. Even Jürgen would not have been able to guide her

38

mother across an illegal border with all its political and geographical impediments. And Madeleine had kept up a quiet fantasy, letting her stand in the street or sit in that window day after day, month after month, knowing they were not coming today, or tomorrow, or indeed ever. Now there were new lies, conversations with neighbors, numbers, numbers, descriptive phrases of hell, cut off suddenly when she appeared. Sixteen-year-olds are children and can be treated like children. Like ten-year-olds they cannot be told the truth. Make up a fairy tale, something sweet and pleasant. Anna will believe it. Children believe anything.

Only Nicole had told her the truth, and the truth was disgusting.

With a surge of anger, she remembered the chocolate bars. She wanted a piece of chocolate desperately. Her mouth yearned for it; her tongue ached for the taste of it. How dare he keep it from her when she wanted it so much.

"I don't believe any of your story," she said angrily. "You've made it all up. They'll be there when I get there, and if you could cross the border, so can I. The Americans are friendly. Why shouldn't they let me cross into Germany? I was born there. As for you, Mr. Pietr—" swallowing his name, "I hope you find what you're looking for in Switzerland. Money, jewelry, Rue de Rivoli, your family in England. How can I believe you when I see you like this in this place?"

"Pietrovic," he said calmly, standing up. "How indeed, how indeed. Come, it's getting late, and I have a wash to do before I leave."

5

He made a fire in the kitchen stove with wood he found behind the house—the last of someone's woodpile, only bits and pieces left—drew water, and set it on to boil in a pail. While it heated, she went upstairs and made the beds with fresh sheets. Then she found the largest towel in the cupboard, took it into the smaller bedroom, and shut the door. With her clothes off she tried to wrap the towel around herself, but it was no use. The towel was too short and too narrow. She would not be able to wash this dress after all. He was not only an intruder; he was an inconvenience, a spoiler.

She put the dress back on over her bare skin, looking with some alarm at the marks her nipples made through the fabric. She was already bustier than Madeleine, no longer able to inherit her aunt's worn clothes. Pulling at the top of her dress to move the fabric away from the skin, she took the underthings and went downstairs.

He was already at work on his own clothes, standing bare except for a towel around his middle.

"Aren't you washing your clothes?" he asked.

"Everything except this. I have nothing else to put on."

He dropped something wet into the pail on the stove and wiped his hands on his toweled hips. Then he pulled the army jacket out of his bag. "This will cover you."

She shook her head. "I'm not clean," she said. "I can't put something clean on me."

"I'll go upstairs while you wash."

40

She waited nervously until she heard him upstairs before undressing. The soap had a wonderful smell. She threw clothes into the sink to soak and began soaping her body. The kitchen had become warm from the stove, and the pail had begun to boil. She rubbed soap on every portion of her body, scrubbing the long dark hair under her arms and between her legs, letting the rinse water drip into a dirty puddle on the floor which she afterwards mopped up with the damp used towel. She smelled the skin on her arms, loving the cleanness of the smell. She put the jacket on, noting with surprise that it had a zipper. She tried it, couldn't quite make it work, and closed the buttons instead, left over right. The length of the jacket was adequate.

"You can come down," she called, starting on the clothes in the sink.

"It's a good fit," he told her, "that jacket."

"I've never had a zipper before. I was afraid I'd catch my fingers."

She dropped her clothes, a piece at a time, into the frothing pot while the man scrubbed himself, sharing the soap with her, making little sounds of pleasure, his soapy hands working their way down his body, the water dripping onto the towel still tied around his midsection.

"Would you like me to turn around?" she asked.

"Yes, you might do that."

She kept her eyes on her washing—which was almost through—biting her lips together, nervous that she stood barely fifty centimeters from a naked man and aware that she could confirm half of what Nicole had told her merely by accidentally moving her head.

"You can relax now."

She took a deep breath and turned, dropping the last of her things into the pot. His towel was back in place, and he was drying his chest with another one. She watched him because she was curious, because she liked to see how he moved the towel on his chest, on his neck, behind his ears.

41

"You don't know many men, do you?"

She shook her head, watching. "None at all. They've all been gone. There have only been soldiers, first German, then American and French, and as far as my aunt is concerned, one soldier is as bad as another."

"Your aunt is right." Rubbing his damp hair again. "But when they come back, they won't be soldiers any more."

"No." Watching him.

"They'll be young men and they'll go to school with you." Reasonable, the way Uncle Josef might put it.

The towel on a shoulder, down the arm, rubbing, now the other shoulder.

She drew in her breath and moved toward him, drawn by a magnetism over which she had no power, her bare feet stumbling over the towel on the floor, her hands reaching for his still wet arm, the glisten of water on his pale skin and, down below the crease of the elbow, a number.

A number. Madeleine and the neighbor whispering, snatches of forbidden conversation escaping, stories of unimaginable horror, unmeasurable grief. Only rumors, mind you. Who could believe such things, even of the Germans? A reporter's madness, perhaps, each survivor with a number on his arm.

"You lied to me," she whispered. "You lied to me," she screamed, shaking the arm she held in her hands.

He said something which she didn't hear and tried with his free hand to pry her two away.

"You weren't detained by the Germans," she screamed in French. "They didn't take you to the police and question you and let you go with new clothes. They sent you to that hell my aunt talked about, you liar. I'll kill you for lying to me." She scratched at the arm with the number and kicked his legs with her bare feet.

He loosened her grip and took hold of one forearm in each of his hands, pressing his fingers into her skin. "Speak to me so I can understand you," he ordered in German. "I haven't lied to you." He shook her by the arms, and she became quiet for a moment, conscious of the pain he was causing.

She looked up at him, feeling very small, very helpless, her feet bare, a borrowed jacket over her nakedness, her hands incapacitated.

"They're dead, aren't they?" she said in German, her voice shaking. "You knew it all along and you didn't tell me. You kept it from me. That number on your arm. You're one of *them*, aren't you?"

He let go of her arms, and she clasped them, aching, to the jacket while he put his hands on her shoulders.

"I'm so sorry," he said, his hands rubbing her shoulders, "I'm so terribly sorry."

She started to cry and there was no place to go, not west and not east any more. He moved his hands from her shoulders, sliding them across her back so that he held her against him, tightly, like a father or an uncle, while she emptied herself of tears until there were no more.

She was sitting at the kitchen table, a glass of water in front of her, a lamp burning several centimeters away. It had grown dark, and she realized that she no longer smelled the boiling laundry. The man was in the next chair, sitting at right angles to her, telling her softly to drink the water, reminding her that it was evening and she had not eaten.

She knew now why he was here in this house with her, why she had stopped and not continued on her way. The house was indeed a sanctuary, and he was the messenger of truth, the one meant to dissolve the fantasy her aunt had perpetuated these six years, the fantasy of life and family and peace in the world. Truth was always an unwelcome intruder, and she had no choice now but to accept him.

It came to her that she was completely alone now. She had been an only child; now she was an only person. Even Madeleine was related to her solely through marriage. With

43

Uncle Josef gone, what would become of their relationship? Had it too dissolved at the end of April in a burst of German gunfire?

She reached for the water and sipped it, her shoulders shaking with cold.

"I want to go to sleep," she said, her voice strange and uneven.

"You haven't eaten, child."

"I can't eat." She sipped the water again. "The wash."

"I've taken care of it."

"But my things."

"It's done," he said. "Let me take you upstairs."

She pushed the chair back and stood up, her thighs below the hem of the jacket peeling away from the glossy, painted surface of the chair. He put his arm around her shoulders and went up the stairs with her, opening the door of the largest bedroom.

"I want the other one," she said hoarsely, needing something smaller, something more like home, and he led her there, waited while she lay down, covered her with the quilt, and sat on the edge of the bed in the dark.

"If you need me—"

"Thank you."

He patted her shoulder, stood up and left the room, more a vision than a silhouette in the absolute darkness. He was still dressed only in the towel, and she realized she had on his jacket.

When she heard him downstairs, she sat up, unbuttoned it, and took it off. Folding it carefully, she laid it across the quilt, lay down again, and closed her eyes.

There were sounds downstairs, warm, family sounds, dishes, a chair, and then, after a moment, a voice humming a tune, an old tune she had forgotten or nearly forgotten, her mother's song, sweet and comforting. She wiped her eyes on the sheet and turned over, falling asleep to the melody from the man in the kitchen.

* * *

Some time during the night, the soldiers came back. She awoke suddenly, hearing their voices, not in surprise but in fear, having known from the first moment she set foot in the house that there would be soldiers and that they would come back. She sat up in bed, her head clearing quickly from the murky unpleasantness of the night's sleep. Her hands groped along the quilt, feeling for the jacket along the satiny surface. It was gone. She put her feet on the floor, stepping on it where it had fallen. The voices were loud and nearby, and she needed to cover herself quickly before she was caught. She put the jacket on, zipping the front quietly, as though the sound would attract them, as if they might be listening for the sound of a zipper closing.

She sat on the edge of the bed, shivering, her knees tightly together, holding her arms, trying to make sense of it, listening for the words, realizing suddenly with a shock of surprise, relief, and a new kind of fear that it wasn't soldiers, wasn't intruders of any sort; it was the man, Anton Pietrovic, talking to no one in the next room.

She stood up and went to her door, leaning on it to listen. He was speaking Polish, the words making no sense at all, but she understood their meaning. He was speaking in agony, calling out in terror. She opened the door, walked carefully, holding her hands ahead of her until they touched the door of the large bedroom. It was quiet for a moment, and she waited, still shivering in the nighttime chill.

The voice called out again, and she opened the door and found the bed. He had left the shutters open, and in the faint light she could see him, his face wet, his shoulders bare, moving feverishly.

She would gladly have been anywhere else right now. She wasn't a nurse. What did she know of fevers and illnesses? But he was so alone in his misery, so far from his family. She sat on the bed and touched his shoulder.

"Anton," she whispered, "Anton. It's all right, there's no one here."

He gasped for air like a diver surfacing, became rigid,

45

opened his eyes, and turned toward her, reaching with his hands.

"Anton," she said again.

He said a name, a woman's name, a name she hadn't heard for years, the name of a woman her mother knew, a sweet woman who baked cinnamon cakes and who went with her family to America before the trouble started.

"It's Anna," she said gently, touching his wet cheek with the back of her hand. "Anna Kleinberger."

"Anna," he repeated. "Anna. I thought—"

He was shivering, and she crawled onto the bed so that she was close to him, her hand reaching across him to touch a damp shoulder, to warm him.

"Anna Kleinberjay," he murmured, half in wry recognition, half in despair.

"Everything will be all right," she said, an echo of her sweet mother, relieved that the delirium had passed and with it, perhaps, the fever.

He put his arms around her, one hand tunneling under her, and held her tightly, still shaking, as hours before he had held her in the kitchen to comfort her. We take our turns, she thought, caring for him with her nearness, comforting him, her charge, her sweet little baby, wishing she had the courage to speak to him as if he were, to say the words one used with babies, mothers, girlhood friends.

His body calmed and she relaxed. He was warm to lie next to, and she liked it. She had never lain beside anyone before. It occurred to her that she understood now why people married; it was warm and close and protected. Poor Madeleine had had it for so short a time.

He moved and whispered, "Sweet child," and she smiled, thinking that it didn't really matter which was the child as long as he felt better. In a moment she would go; he would sleep, and in the morning the fever would have passed.

He moved again, his legs against her legs, skin against skin, very warm, very—. She shivered although she wasn't

46

cold any more, had even stopped worrying about him. Something else was happening now, something different.

"Anna," he whispered, holding her very tightly and then letting go, his hand pulling out from under her, "Anna" again, and then his fingers reaching for her jacket, his jacket really, and in one ripple pulling the zipper down in a toneless melody and placing his palms, both of them, lightly, very, very lightly on her breasts, which no one, no one in the world (including herself) had ever touched this way, her breasts already too big, too full, and now his hands on them, so lightly, stroking the nipples, producing a sensation that brought forth a murmured "Oh," half pleasure and half discovery, a marvelous sensation that reverberated through the cavern of her body, settling, burning, in one place, a strange place, the most extraordinary place.

Nicole had not been so crazy after all.

His hands touching her back now under the jacket, holding her close so that her breasts were against his chest, his hard chest with the covering of curly hair, a nest for her to lie in, and she knew suddenly, frantically, that she had to get out of the jacket so that her arms could touch him, her skin rub against his warm skin. She pulled away, surprising him, sat up, her back to him, tugging at the cuff and she heard him slide up too and felt him pull it down along her arms, kiss her neck as if it were all part of the same thing, and take it off. She felt a momentary panic at her nakedness, which she had, after all, done to herself—what would Madeleine think?—and turned and found him waiting, a warm shape in the almost darkness.

She lay down with him, waiting for him to touch her again, afraid that he would, and more afraid now that he wouldn't.

"Anton," she said in the half whisper induced by the partial darkness, "I'm very frightened."

He kissed her face, running his hand down her now bare arm. "Not nearly so frightened as I," his shoulders begin-

47

ning to shake again, his whole body pressing against her. She knew now what it was snapping angrily at her thighs. Nicole had missed the point of everything, the anger and the fear and maybe something else. Poor Nicole had spent the night with the wrong man.

She knew what she had to do now, not because of the details but because she understood, it made sense now, and above all she needed to. Welcoming him, she felt his fear invade her, felt his instrument of anger falter as he shuddered, and then his weight upon her and the hurt beginning, the hurt, and again the hurt, but really, not so much a hurt as she had thought, as she had feared, and besides, she had Anton, held him, felt the shuddering in his shoulders, in his thighs, and then his weight, heavy, heavy, and she knew she had been wrong about the anger because inside her Anton Pietrovic was being reborn.

His body melted from her slowly, and she relaxed, staying near him. She knew he was awake because he still touched her with his hands, his hands moving slowly over her body.

The feeling came from nowhere and enveloped her, a mother loving a new child, a stranger, a sometimes ugly thing, something she had never understood before, this feeling of mineness. You are mine because this thing has happened to us, this birth. He was hers now, the feeling of possession swelling in her as she lay beside him.

"I don't sleep well at night sometimes," he said finally.

"I thought you were ill." The familiar pronoun slipped out without her thinking about it, all at once not such a great step after all.

"You were very good to me, to come to me the way you did."

"You belong to me now."

"Dear Anna, I can't."

"But you do. A small part of you is mine, and it will belong to me forever."

48

He said nothing for a while, and she wondered if she had made him angry by her possessiveness, that he would think it unjustified or, worse, unwomanly.

"I thank you," he said finally, his voice wavering slightly. "I know you'll care for it properly, that little part of me. It's good to know after all this time I've fallen into gentle hands. I'll sleep better because of it."

She closed her eyes and moved to make herself comfortable, staying close enough that their bodies touched. She fell asleep quickly, waking only once or twice during the night when he turned in bed, each time coming to rest close enough to touch her. Otherwise, she slept well and peacefully, her mind at rest almost as much as her body. Once during the night, when she felt him turn and place his hand upon her, she had a single thought.

She forgave Nicole.

In the morning he was gone. There was a chill in the bed. It was light and empty in the room, and she was very cold.

They always leave you, Nicole had told her in a voice filled with the acceptance of tragedy, when the pleasure is over for them. I knew he had to be back at dawn, but he could have wakened me to say good-bye. I went back twenty times to that corner where we met in Paris, but he never came by again, my beautiful soldier.

Anna sat up, unwilling to cry and unable to prevent it. There was no end to disappointment, no outer limit to grief. The jacket was on the floor where he had dropped it a few hours ago. Only a few hours. How quickly the world changed. She put it on, drawing the zipper slowly upward, remembering, with a new, sharp pain the sound of it being unzipped. What are the kinds of pain? she wondered, wiping her eyes on the sleeve near the shoulder. Toothaches, stomachaches, a sprained ankle. Tears everywhere now, face, chin, sleeves, pocket. The ache in your side when you

49

run too fast, a scraped knee, a bruised shin, hair being pulled, sitting in a window and looking for your parents who will never arrive.

She stood up, sobbing now, the pain within extending to include Madeleine, poor Madeleine whom she would never see again, who had so much more reason to suffer, having lost so much more. How would she survive?

She walked to the window through which only yesterday morning she had seen him in horizontal slices, a stranger whom she had come to love last night, and saw him through the open shutters, sitting against the big tree behind the back door, all the wash (except what he was now wearing) stretched on a line between the tree and the house.

He had waited for her. Drying her face on the jacket, she ran barefoot down the stairs, through the kitchen, and out the back door where she stopped, waiting for him, not sure what was expected of her on this morning, this very special morning, that had simply come upon her.

He stood up and watched her for a moment. Does a man understand these things? Does he know that it's harder this morning in daylight that it was last night in darkness?

("Not nearly so frightened as I.")

He came to her, put an arm around her, and led her to the big tree. He sat down, leaning against it, and took her on his lap. She rested on him, grateful for his presence, his silence, his arms around her, thankful for his mere existence.

"It's true, of course, what you said yesterday," he said finally. "The languages, the countries, the uprooting. I might have stayed in Berlin if I had had the choice—it was a beautiful city once—but there was no choice. My father had a business friend in Switzerland, and the Swiss let us come. There was work and peace and friends, and my daughter was born there in a clean hospital with a good doctor. When the Polish embassy started to make trouble for us with the Swiss in 1939, my wife was already pregnant with our son. It was a difficult pregnancy, and the Swiss were kind to us and

50

kept extending our stay. My wife and I—these things don't always happen as they're planned, you know."

"I know. My friend Nicole told me."

"You get your monthly periods, don't you?"

She shriveled in embarrassment.

"You've never talked to a man about that, have you?"

She shook her head where it rested against him.

"But you'll tell me, Anna."

It was very painful. She had admitted the truth to Nicole once and to no one else. "I started to have them a few years ago but after about a year they stopped."

"They'll come back again," he said, "now that the war is over. It's happened to other women. Did your aunt take you to a doctor?"

The memory of the visit returned like a bad taste, the imperious, silent doctor with his pursed lips and nodding head, all his questions addressed to Madeleine, his prying, hurting fingers and unreadable face. "He wouldn't talk to me," she confessed. "He made me go out of the room while he talked to my aunt."

"You see, no one wants to look another person in the eye while he speaks the truth, not that doctor, not I, not your parents, not your aunt. But your aunt is your family now, and when I leave, you have to go back to her."

"I'm not even sure she's my aunt any more."

"Because you and she had no common ancestor? Because your uncle may not have survived the war? What about Jürgen? He's not a relative. He's a German. Were your parents wrong to put your life in his hands? Did he betray them? Or you?"

"Someone betrayed me."

"Yes, someone or something betrayed all of us, and we will have to live with the consequences of that betrayal forever. Only the Germans seem immune from the consequences of their acts."

"I could go to Switzerland with you."

51

She felt him sigh, the heaving of his chest moving her body.

"I have a wife, Anna."

"I know, and two children."

"Whom I love very much."

(Three chocolate bars.)

"I could stay in Switzerland. I could get work there."

"Not Switzerland," he said. "It's a difficult country. You have no papers— Are you afraid to go back because of last night? Are you ashamed?"

"I'm not ashamed. It was—I'm not ashamed at all. I was only afraid I had done everything wrong."

"The point in making love," he said, holding her very securely, "is that you do exactly what you feel like doing without wondering or worrying about whether it's right or wrong."

Even Nicole had never hinted at that, that it was something that one did, something one wanted to do and enjoyed doing, not a thing that was done to one before being abandoned. She turned and opened the top few buttons on his shirt, putting her palm in, rubbing his chest through his hair, feeling his whole body respond to it. Nicole had never told her about bodies responding either. She had never dreamed she could touch a man and feel his body move because of it. She longed to stay with him, to make it go on and on, to take care of him if he would only let her.

Instead, he caught her hand and stopped it, holding it against his chest.

"I must be on my way," he said. "Let's put some breakfast together before I go."

She stood up reluctantly, feeling the chill of the morning for the first time. Being alone was colder than being together. It was something one needed to get used to again.

She turned back, but he was still sitting in front of the tree, looking down at something without moving. She took a step toward him and saw a wet patch on the thigh of his pants on the spot where she had been sitting, a wet patch with the tiniest thread of pink in it.

Her cheeks started to burn, and she turned away from him. "I'm sorry," she said in French, half hoping her words were too low to be heard.

She felt his arm on her back but she couldn't look at him.

"You don't really understand, do you?" he asked.

She shook her head.

"Hasn't your aunt explained these things to you?"

"I asked her once, but she wouldn't tell me anything. She said when I got older I would understand. I understand some things, you know, the big things, like why you have to go to your wife and what it means for you to love her. I know because—" She stopped, not wanting to articulate the reason.

"Get yourself dressed, child," he said, "and let's have some breakfast. Then we'll find a sunny place, and I'll explain all the little things to you."

He sat with his shirt open, facing the sun. He didn't look like a man who had somewhere to go, but in the house his bag was packed. He looked down at his hands with long fingers and ragged nails.

"I'm sorry about my fingernails," he said. "I have nothing to file them down with. I wanted to touch you properly last night, but I was afraid of hurting you."

"You didn't hurt me."

"I didn't touch you properly."

She looked away from him, down to her bare legs, her toes in the long grass, the skirt of her dress, a cotton dress Madeleine had stitched up for her from some fabric salvaged from some other use. The dress at least could believe in reincarnation.

"I want to know," she said, "if what happened to you last night will happen to me."

He smiled, closed his eyes for a moment, and opened

53

them again. "You're a very beautiful girl, Anna," he said, looking at her. "I promise it will happen to you. All the young men will be home soon and they'll be looking for beautiful girls like you with dark hair and lovely bodies. When you go to the university, you'll have a lover, a good lover, and then—you'll see."

"Does it happen to your wife?"

"I can't tell you about my wife. I can't talk about her."

She stood up and pushed her feet through the grass, her feelings raw with hurt. She wanted someone in the world who would refuse to talk about her, and she wanted it now, not later when she went to the university.

"He'll be young," Anton said, "and he'll speak French to you."

"Shouldn't you be leaving for Switzerland now?"

"Anna." He stood near her, buttoning his shirt. "You'll forget about me. In a few days, when you're back in Paris and everyone's celebrating the end of the war, you'll forget all about me."

"I'm not going back, and there won't be any celebrations." (And I'll never forget.)

"Would you like to keep the jacket?"

She loved the jacket. It was big and masculine and had a zipper. "You'll be cold without it. It's cold in Switzerland."

"I won't need it after I get there. And you wear it better than I."

She bit her lip and rubbed her foot in the grass. "I lied to you yesterday," she said. "I do have money with me. It's in my pack. You can have some of it."

He hesitated. "Keep your money, child. Your aunt will need it."

"Thank you for the jacket."

He went into the house and came out again with his pack. She stood where he had left her, in the sun, fifteen meters from the door. He waved to her, and she watched him leave, returning in the direction from which he had come. Now at least she knew the way to Switzerland.

54

6

She was alone on an island, and there was no one to rescue her. All around her there were impenetrable borders, borders with mountains, with rivers, with men in uniform, and all the borders were closed to her. How long would the hard-boiled eggs and the cheese last, the peas in the garden, the little bit of sausage? Would the well run dry if she continued to drink from it and wash her clothes in its water?

She sat in the sun on the spot where he had sat, wondering about the woman in England that he had left her for, a woman he had not seen for five years. Did that woman know that even now he was on his way, walking on borrowed soles to reach her?

There was no one walking toward Anna Kleinberjay any more. Some day the people of this house would return and throw her out, or perhaps they would find what was left of her after she starved. Perhaps her clothes would wear out from use, or maybe she would outgrow them again and have nothing to wear. What difference did it make? She had nowhere to go. Why did she need something to wear to get there?

It was cold even in the sun. She would eat less now to make it last longer. She would go to bed earlier and sleep later. Summer was coming and she had the jacket now, so she wouldn't freeze. That at least was something to be grateful for, that she wouldn't have to freeze.

The day wore on. There would be many more like this one. This was only a sample, but she had no choice; she could not refuse it. There was nothing better in the offing.

It grew dark and she ate and washed some clothes. He had left her because she did not belong to him. He was going to his family, to the ones who were his. What was it like to belong to a man, to know that wherever he was, he would come to find you?

She lit a lamp so that she could see. What would give out first, the food, the kerosene, the water?

She took the lamp and went to the cellar door. He had said there was beer down there. Maybe there were potatoes or onions that had been laid by for the future. She went cautiously down the stairs, frightened of the dark and the dank smell. The lamp lit only a small area. She would have to walk through the whole cellar to see what was there. From where she stood, halfway down, it was a jumble—tires, straps, pieces of metal that clearly had a function if only she knew what it was.

She went down another step and stopped, hearing something above. Someone was in the house. She bit her lip and listened. There was a voice, a voice calling her name.

"Anna! Anna, where are you?"

It was Anton's voice, back from the dead, Anton returned from Switzerland.

"I'm down here." Her voice rang with elation. "In the cellar."

He appeared in the doorway at the top of the stairs. "Get up here," he ordered angrily. "What are you doing down there?"

"I thought there might be food." She started up the stairs.

"Stay out of that cellar."

"Why? What are you so angry for?"

He closed the door behind her and took the lamp from her hand. "You could have fallen," he said. "What would have happened if you'd fallen and hurt yourself? Who would have helped you?"

"Why did you come back?"

56

He pulled a chair out from the table and sat down. "I'm taking you back to Paris."

"You came back from Switzerland to take me to Paris?"

"I hadn't gotten to Switzerland. I was afraid of what might happen to you."

"I'm not going back to Paris. I told you that. My aunt doesn't want me any more."

"Anna." He touched her arm. "She wants you. Anyone would want you. You're a lovely girl."

"I don't belong to her. I never did, really. Now—" She shrugged. "I don't belong to anyone now, do I?"

"We'll talk about it in the morning," he said.

He took a piece of dark brown bread out of his pack and started to chew it. It was the kind of bread her mother had served for supper every night, hard and tasty, baked just down the street. Madeleine never ate bread like that. It was one of the things she had missed when she came to France, brown bread and clocks chiming.

"It was nice of you to come back," she said. She walked to the stairs. "Good night."

"Anna."

"Yes?"

He looked down at the table for a monent. "Will you sleep in my bed tonight?" he asked.

"I wish I belonged to you," she said. "You're very nice to me."

She expected to be awakened at daybreak to start the journey back to Paris, but when she opened her eyes she saw that he had closed the shutters part way to shield her from the morning light. There were noises downstairs, and she put on the jacket—her jacket—and went down. He was at the kitchen table with the clock in pieces in front of him. He looked up and smiled at her, and she smiled back. For a little while, at least, she could pretend.

"Did you sleep well?" he asked.

57

She nodded and sat down across from him, looking at all the little wheels that lay on the table.

"Do you want breakfast?" she asked.

"I've had some bread. We'll have to get some food on the way to Paris. There isn't much left any more."

She took some bread and a cup of water. "Is it broken?" she asked, pointing to the parts on the table.

"Dirty. Hasn't been cleaned for years. It's a cheap clock but it can be made to run well." Beside him was a bowl filled with kerosene from several lamps at the end of the table. He reached into the bowl and took out a wheel, rubbed it with one of their washing cloths until it gleamed like gold. "Five years ago," he said, "I wouldn't have wasted my time on a clock like this."

"Why not? It looks like a nice clock."

"It's cheap. It's simple. My time was once worth too much to spend it on something like this. It's not a challenge. My father started me on clocks like this when I was twelve." He put the clean wheel down and dipped a dirty one in the solution. "That was a long time ago."

A very long time. She hadn't been born yet.

"My father cleaned his own clocks," she said. "He repaired them too. In a little room he had upstairs. My mother was afraid to go in there to clean it because it was such a mess." She watched him rub the second wheel. "Not really, you know. He would never have been angry at her."

"I thought he might have done his own work. He seemed to understand clocks, the way he wrote about them."

She could see him if she closed her eyes, sitting on his stool in front of a bench covered with wheels, dirty ones, clean ones, wheels with broken teeth, boxes of screws and nails and salvaged bits of wire. There would be a use for everything one day, he told her. It was wasteful to throw things away when, with a little cleverness, you could make something fit in a new place. He was an inventive man, a man who could reason, who could think his way out of trouble.

58

"You survived," she said to the clockmaker. "Others must have survived."

"Yes, others did."

"How did you survive?"

He dropped a wheel with long, very sharp teeth into the bowl of blackened kerosene. "I became a savage," he said.

"I see." She stood up and walked outside. If that were the way, then there was truly no hope at all.

He didn't come out for a while, and when he did she was able to speak again.

"I've put the clock together," he said. "It needs more work but I can't do it with the tools I have here. It'll run for a while—not long—it needs to be oiled. Would you like to come in and see it?"

"You don't have to take me to Paris, Anton. I'll go myself. I know you want to go to your family. I'll get dressed and I'll start back."

"I can't leave you here," he said. "I can't let you stay alone."

"I wouldn't lie to you. I'll go back, I promise you."

He looked uncertain, as if perhaps he had nowhere to go now that she had decided to go by herself. She wondered why he had delayed this long, why he had fixed the clock instead of waking her up and starting west.

"Are you afraid to go to Switzerland?" she asked. "Are you afraid they won't—that maybe your friends won't recognize you?"

"I don't look forward to it," he said. "I left rather a gentleman. I'm afraid I look now like what I've become."

"You're a very nice man," she said. "I don't think you have to worry. You were good to come back. I wouldn't have gone to Paris if you hadn't come back for me."

"What were you going to do?"

"Wait until the people came back."

"They're not coming back, Anna. They've gone forever."

59

Maybe when she was that old, she thought, she would be able to speak with such assurance. What was it that happened to a person that made him know such things so unfailingly?

"If my aunt doesn't want me—" she began.

"She wants you, Anna. She's waiting for you to come back. She's tried to spare you the agony she's going through now. Perhaps she was wrong to let you go. Perhaps she thinks this is what one should do when you're a mother and not quite a mother. She took you when you were only a child, didn't she?"

Over the mountains with Jürgen, a knapsack on his back.

"What happened in September of 1939?"

"The Germans invaded Poland."

"It's funny that I lived through it and never knew it was happening."

"But they knew, the people who cared about you, and that's why you're here today."

"Yes." But hadn't they cared about themselves too? Where were they, now that it was over?

7

It was a day of pointless lingering. He talked about a past before the war and a future after the war—if not France, then Holland; if not Holland perhaps Switzerland. The war was a great gap in his life that he did not talk about. For her, the war was her whole life. The surprise had been when it ended. It had never occurred to her that it would come to an end one day.

"How did he get you to France, the German?"

"Through Switzerland."

"They let you across the border?"

The *J* in her passport, the gentle, persuasive argument with the border guards, the constant possibility that they would not let her into the country. But Jürgen had assured her: if they don't let us in, there are other ways. One way or another, we will get you into Switzerland.

"He explained to them that it was only a visit, that I wasn't staying. They let us in. We didn't go through the guards to get to France."

"I shouldn't think so."

"I don't remember it all that well. I remember getting up that morning. My mother had all new clothes for me. I don't know where she got them from, but they were there on a chair when I opened my eyes. There was a pleated blue plaid skirt, my first grown-up skirt without straps to keep it up." She saw him smile. "And a white blouse and tan knee socks. The shoes weren't new. My mother made me wear those

61

little half boots—you know, the ones with the crisscrossed laces, because I was going to do a lot of walking. I didn't really understand what was happening. I just put the clothes on. My other clothes were in Jürgen's knapsack. I carried my coat over my arm because my mother said it might be cold. It was, after we got to Switzerland. The coat wasn't new either. It was dark blue and already a little bit short. My aunt made it longer after I got there but by the end of the winter, it didn't fit any more anyway. She took it apart and put it together again as a jacket. That gave me another year." She tried to think what had become of the coat after that, who they had passed it down to, who had remade it, who had worn it through another heatless winter. "Do you remember saying good-bye to your family?" she asked.

He looked somewhat startled. "Yes," he said, not looking at her. "I remember."

"I don't. Isn't that strange? I remember getting up and seeing the new clothes and then I remember being on a train with Jürgen. But I don't remember saying good-bye to my parents."

"Sometimes, if things are very painful, if we're lucky, we forget them."

"What do you dream about when you wake up at night?"

He reached out and touched her. It was the first time they had touched since she had lain beside him during the night.

"I dream about the death of my parents," he said.

"But how do you know?"

"I don't. I can only imagine."

She moved closer to him so that he became her shelter. "Why do you always tell me the truth?" she asked.

"Somebody has to," he said. "I don't think anyone ever has before this."

"You're wrong. Jürgen told me the truth. He said farewell when he left me. He knew I would never see him again. I'll never see you again either, will I?"

62

"I don't think so, Anna. I don't see how."

"Then I'm glad you came back. Even if I have to go back to Paris, it was worth it to see you again."

To her surprise his arm tightened around her, and she heard him sob.

He began to undress after dinner, and she turned away and washed the dishes he had used.

He touched her shoulder while she concentrated nervously on her tiny task. "I want you to look at me, Anna. I want you to see me undressed. You've never seen a man's body before, have you?"

"No." She dried her hands on the thin towel by the sink and turned around, an unreasonable panic moving through her. He was completely naked, and the sight of his nakedness terrified her as the feel of it had frightened her two nights before. She faced him hesitantly, suppressing the panic, and met his eyes.

Looking at him helped. He was less at ease than she, more afraid of being looked at in his nakedness. It occurred to her for the first time that he needed her more than she needed him. He had come back from Switzerland because it was easier for him to solve her problems than to confront his own.

She opened the jacket and took it off, putting it on the back of a chair without turning from him. He would want to look at her too, having touched her, having loved her in the bed, and he deserved it for having returned.

"You're very beautiful," he said. "More beautiful than I imagined."

She walked over to him, one bare foot touching one of his, took his arm in her hands, and kissed the spot with the offensive number. His body shuddered, and she put her hands on his shoulders and let her fingers slide down, down to his thighs, barely touching the hair that she had never known before grew on men too, avoiding the forbidden parts because she still wasn't sure and didn't want to ask.

"I want to wash you tonight, Anna," he said, "with that bar of American soap."

(My mother washed me my last night in Freiburg and I never saw her again.)

"Are you afraid?"

"No. You don't frighten me any more."

But the night frightened her, and his going away. After tonight, he would be gone. She remembered her last day at home with her parents, not knowing it was the last day, the last of all days, the anxious, furtive conversations, Jürgen visiting and visiting again, talk, arguments, her mother's tears. In the evening her mother had washed her body as though she were a baby, scrubbed her hair, dried it and combed it, sat by her bed until she fell asleep. In the morning there were the new clothes and a hiker's knapsack packed for her, and then there was Jürgen. He had brought nothing for himself that didn't fit in his pockets. All through Switzerland and into France he never changed his clothes, never shaved. He grew a little woolly beard all over his face so that when she kissed him good-bye it felt funny.

He had told her the truth. Farewell.

She felt soapy hands working the soap into her neck and shoulders, Anton's hands, gently over her breasts, turning her around and then back again. A feeling of delicious wanting grew in her, swelled. She dipped her hands in the water and soaped them up. Following his example she started at his shoulders. Holding her with slippery fingers he kissed her, rubbed her body, kissed her again. It was different from the bed. It was as if his feeling had finally extended itself outside the bed and down the stairs to where she was. She was the center of it now, not the bed. He cared for her.

She moved her palms down, down his chest, washing the curly hair, feeling the bones with too little flesh on them, the soft, flat stomach that even now he failed to fill completely, down to his hard thighs, knowing that nothing was forbidden any more; she didn't have to ask, she could touch

64

anything; she owned him, he was hers. She touched cautiously with wet fingertips—(I don't know what it's called in German)—feeling it reach out to seek her.

"Anna," a whisper, "Anna."

(Why do they say it's dirty? It's clean, all soap and water dripping down my legs.)

"Come upstairs with me, Anna," such a sweet whisper, "Anna, Anna."

He rinsed her in fresh water, water she had drawn from the well, a new skill she had never thought she would master. It was a time for perfecting new skills.

He dried her as her mother had dried her, not letting her do it, wanting the task for his own.

He blew out the lamp and they went upstairs, leaving the clothes behind and the dirty water, the wet towels, the faint smell of kerosene. He lay down with her, his body cool and damp and sweet from the soap that had not quite been washed off.

"Oh Anton, it hurts," her voice barely a murmur. "Inside where you make love to me. Make it stop hurting tonight."

He was still careful with his fingertips but he touched her this time, softly, lovingly—he could not have become a savage; he was too gentle for that—coaxing, encouraging, the reaction of her body taking her by surprise with its violence, its unexpectedness, its depth. He held her until it had ended, until she came back to life again, a woman in someone's arms in the east of France.

"There's nothing left for you to learn from your French lovers," he said, still holding her.

But it didn't matter. There would be no French lovers. She didn't want any, not French, not German. She knew that for the rest of her life, she would never love anyone else.

After a while, she made an excuse to go downstairs. In her pack were thirty-three francs. She divided them up, sixteen and seventeen, weighing the piles, finally putting the sixteen back in her pack. With a kitchen knife, she cut what was left of the bar of soap through the line in the center and put one half on top of the money. Then she went upstairs and, touching him, went to sleep.

In the middle of the night she opened her eyes and saw him standing near the window putting on his shirt. She lay watching, knowing he was on his way. When he was dressed, she whispered to him.

"Have a safe trip, Anton."

He turned and faced the bed. "I didn't mean to wake you," he said.

"You didn't. I just knew you were leaving."

"I didn't want you to see me go."

"I love you, Anton."

He stood for a moment at the edge of the bed near the windows and then slowly began unbuttoning his shirt. When he had undressed, he came back into bed and lay next to her, his hand rubbing her body, being careful not to scratch with the ragged fingernails.

"I've made you very unhappy, haven't I?"

"No. It's just the other way. You've made me very happy."

"I didn't mean for you to love me."

"I didn't think you would take me seriously."

"How could I not? What's left of people if we don't take each other seriously?"

She closed her eyes. What was left anyway?

In the morning she didn't look for him. She got up and dressed, tears dropping like last night's soapy water, clean, very clean. She left the bed unmade, as she had found it four days before, and went down to the kitchen. His pack was gone and with it the clock. But he had left gifts for her. A small stack of bills lay on the table. She counted them— nine. He had misunderstood, had divided her gift to him in half and taken the lesser amount. And under the notes a chocolate bar.

She used a damp towel to dry her face and started to pack the remaining things when she saw he had left a message. Carved roughly on the top of the table were two French words: MERCI ADIEU.

The bicycle took her west to the DeLauxs'. She told them she wanted to go home, and in two days they put her on a truck driven by a young farmer. The whole distance to Paris, she never spoke a word. When he dropped her off at the eastern end of the city, she pedaled the rest of the way home on the borrowed bicycle.

There were neighbors in the house when she got there and Madeleine was wearing black. The news had come a week ago.

In the evening, when the neighbors had left them, Madeleine told her a letter had come from America, from a cousin of Josef who was, of course, a cousin of Anna's mother. The cousin wanted them to come to America as soon as possible. A member of the Congress of the United States was arranging for their passage. They would go to where the cousin lived, in a town with the unbelievable name of Great Neck, a town, like all towns in America, not too far from New York City. Madeleine had already accepted for both of them. There was nothing left for her in France now, and Anna deserved every opportunity.

When they left for LeHavre weeks later, Anna still had the chocolate bar. On the train, she gave it to a little girl who might have been as old as Anton's daughter.

When they got on the ship for America, she found she had gotten her first period in three years.

II

**June 1947-
August 1948**

1

It was almost three, and the sun had become very hot. She pulled the back of her lounge chair up, shaded her eyes, and looked at the glistening blue pool.

"Do you want to swim?" she asked the girl reclining in the chair beside her.

"Not yet. I need five more minutes on this side."

"I think you're like a steak under a fire."

The other girl giggled and opened her eyes. "I see some-one interesting," she said, "and he has a friend with him. If we play our cards right, we'll both get asked out tonight."

"No, Robin. Not me. I want to stay home."

"Don't be such a stick-in-the-mud, Anna. You should get out more."

"I go out enough."

"But you don't. It's because of school. You really should have accelerated."

"What?" The word had come too rapidly, too many syllables piling on top of each other.

"Accelerated," Robin said slowly. "Uh—"

"Yes, I understand." Her driving instructor had used the word last year when she had taken lessons, and she had asked him what it meant. Give it gas, he had said, push down the pedal, when all she had wanted had been a simple definition. But she had understood.

"You could have graduated this year," Robin said. "Then you wouldn't be stuck with all those drippy little boys for another year."

"It doesn't matter."

"But it does matter. Ooh, here they come."

Robin adjusted the way she was sitting, and Anna looked down at Robin's long, cleanly shaven legs. Robin's influence extended over Anna's entire body, from her hair to her toes.

"Hi, Ray," she heard Robin croon, as though there were some special joke or understanding between them.

Anna looked up. The boys were at least twenty and well tanned.

"Hi," the boy named Ray said. "This is Joel Pratter from Lawrence." He turned toward Anna. "You Robin's sister?"

"No," Robin said quickly, sitting up. "This is my cousin— from Paris, Anna Goldfeder."

Anna poked her cousin and heard the boy named Joel say, "From Paris?"

"Not from Paris," Anna said. "From France. Near Paris."

Ray pushed Robin's legs aside and sat down on the end of her lounge. Joel stood looking down at Anna. Shading her eyes from the sun with his body, he began the usual exchange dictated by the unwritten rules that Robin had mastered so easily—he says then you say then he says. And somewhere along the way the inevitable question—where do you go to school?—and her practiced answer and the raised eyebrows. You don't *look* like you're still in high school.

But how do you know, little boy named Joel with your cultivated tan and tight bathing suit, how do you know *what* I look like? The words flowed easily through her mind in French, and she missed what he was saying.

"I beg your pardon." She was embarrassed. She should have been paying attention.

"Tonight," he repeated. "There's a good movie."

She was aware that Robin was waiting for her answer too. "Yes, thank you, that would be very nice."

Madeleine was pleased that she was going, especially if it was with a boy she met at the club. There was a kind of seal of approval on boys met at the club. Madeleine herself rarely went, although a membership had been given her again this summer by the American cousins. She preferred to keep her skin pale and, Anna suspected, Madeleine was not altogether comfortable at the club.

It was one of those movies in which men sang songs and chased a woman for an hour and a half for the privilege of a single kiss, after which they seemed certain they wished to spend their lives together. Joel took her hand after the first quarter hour and by the romantic end had his arm around her. He was going into his last year at the University of something—she had missed the last word and had not wanted to ask him to repeat it. The boys had driven separate cars, and Anna knew what that meant. She should have stayed home.

After a hamburger and coffee they went their separate ways. Joel had a convertible, and he put the top down. It was the end of June and the night was warm.

He parked the car where they could see the Sound, and he took her hand. "So how come you're still in high school? You look as old as Robin."

"I had trouble with the language," she said, modifying the truth slightly. "They put me back two years, and I couldn't make it up." I should have pushed the pedal down harder, she thought. I should have given it gas.

"Where you going to college?"

"I don't know. We'll talk about it after the summer."

He slid his arm around her and moved from under the steering wheel along the seat, closing the gap. He kissed her once and drew back for effect. She wanted to go home, home where she could think in another language, where she could be alone.

He put his hand on her breast and moved it. It was not an experimental touch; he knew what he was doing, and for a moment she allowed herself to enjoy the feeling.

"Please don't do that."

"C'mon. I think you like it."

73

"No. I want to go home."

He let his hands drop to his lap. "You sure?"

"Yes."

He slid away and put his hands on the wheel. "You're the boss," he said, starting the motor.

In her corner of the front seat, Anna relaxed.

He kissed her once at the door. "Can I call you?" he asked.

"Yes, of course." She put the key in the lock and walked inside the apartment, moving quietly. It was after midnight, and Madeleine would be asleep. She turned on one lamp and put her little summer clutch on the table. The single shaded bulb lighted the room dimly, highlighting the pictures scattered on tables around it, the familiar old sepia-tone photographs of Uncle Josef with his dark, curly hair and big smile. Madeleine had built the room around them and around him too. Josef would have liked this chair, and Josef would have wanted a table here. She lifted each photograph several times a week to dust it carefully, looking at the image and responding appropriately with a small smile or a sigh or a look of sadness. They were her family, her constant reminder that fate would not provide her with such happiness again.

A door opened and a moment later Madeleine appeared in her nightgown. "Anna?" The name pronounced with a slight stress on the second syllable.

"Yes, it's me."

"Did you have fun?" she asked in French.

"Yes, it was very nice."

"He seemed like a very nice boy," Madeleine said. "He was very polite, and he dressed well. I like a young man like that."

The sentences flowed richly like French cream, words and grammar blending mellifluously, nouns and verbs falling into place with such ease, such logic. Anna's mind switched gears, moving a notch higher where it labored less, used less fuel.

"Yes, I liked him," she said, because she knew it would make her aunt happy if she were happy.

"I was only a little older than you when I met Josef." Madeleine picked up a picture, looked at it intently, and polished the glass with her nightgown. "Sometimes I think it was only yesterday, and sometimes I feel as though it were fifty years ago. Well, I shall visit him finally, after I've seen my parents."

Her suitcases were almost packed. The American cousins were sending her back to France next Wednesday, only five days away, to visit her father, who was not well. She would spend the summer and make a trip to the military cemetery where Josef was buried.

"Come, it's late. We'll talk tomorrow." She kissed Anna on the cheek and went back to her room.

Anna waited until the door closed, then turned off the lamp and went to her bedroom. She put the light on and undressed, thinking of Madeleine and the trip she was about to take. She would set foot on the Continent again; she would be free to move about, to see old friends, to visit cemeteries.

Anna took her bra off and hung it on the back of the chair. It was damp with sweat from the hot night, but she was growing chilly from the late hour. She caught a glimpse of herself in the mirror over her dresser. A face much like Robin's but, she feared, not nearly so pretty. A body, she had come to learn, with enviable qualities. She had learned to value her figure. She did not tower over other girls, only over her tiny aunt, and her full breasts were admired. She could tell even when the glances were surreptitious. The boys all wanted to touch, and something in her tore apart when it happened. She wanted to be touched, wanted it in a deeply earthy way that her cousin Robin didn't understand, but she didn't want these boys' hands on her.

She went to the closet and reached all the way to the end of the rod, feeling the object of her search without yet seeing it, taking it off the hanger, the long jacket with the too-long

75

sleeves, putting it on and zipping the zipper. She turned off the light and sat across her bed in the dark, her arms hugging her, protecting her breasts from the Joels of Lawrence, the drippy high school boys she spent her days with who wouldn't have known what to do with them anyway, the boys who from time to time called and with whom she reluctantly went out.

If only she could get back, if she could travel about Europe, visit, ask questions, she was sure she could find him. And finding him she could see him again, talk to him, just simple talk in a language in which the verbs did not wreak havoc on sentences, maybe touch him, a small touch, skin upon skin. She had thought—she had told him two years ago when they were together—that she owned a piece of him. What she had not known then, what she had learned in the intervening time, was that without trying to he had come to own her. She measured all men against her memory of him: these were too fat and those were too tall; these were too shallow and those were without feeling; these were not gentle and those lacked any understanding of human nature. Perhaps seeing him again would free her, but she didn't know, she wasn't sure, whether she wanted to be free.

The American cousins, Robin's parents, were generous beyond all imagination. They had paid the rent on this apartment a year in advance so that Madeleine could get started in her job of teaching French. They gave gifts before they were needed; they had love and understanding to spare. When the telegram came that Madeleine's father had had a heart attack, Cousin Bernie had booked passage for her without even asking if she wanted to go. When she had the ticket in her hand, he told her to make up her mind; whatever she wanted to do was all right with him. Next Wednesday the family would see her off.

The jacket warmed to Anna's skin. Through the darkness she could see another place, half real, half imagined. Time passed backwards and forwards before her, then stopped,

76

like a telescope moving along the horizon, lighting upon a scene, sharpening into focus, holding. A need so great she could never fill it.

The feeling had persisted like an illness, but unlike an illness it had been strengthening. There was someone in the world with whom she had shared herself. Aside from Madeleine, with whom she had talked over almost everything (except that), there was no one else. Her cousin Robin, who was practically her twin in age, looks, and heredity, had become her best friend and confidante in those first few months in America, but there were things one could not express, could not even allude to, even to a loving and sympathetic cousin. Robin's father had made money, much of it during the war. He produced some little tool or part of a machine in a factory he had built on Long Island. He had begun shakily in the thirties; the war had brought him undreamed of fortunes. Although the cousins were careful not to exaggerate their own wartime suffering in the presence of Anna and Madeleine, it was clear that they had felt quite put upon. There had been shortages, ration books, priorities.

Still they had managed to eat in restaurants, buy new clothes and shoes (but not nylon stockings), drive cars (but not buy a new one), and get steaming hot water from the tap in the middle of the night. It was hard to explain suffering to cousin Robin.

The mothers of Anna and Robin had been first cousins. They had grown up together in Germany, the daughters of two brothers named Goldfeder. The parents of the brothers were the great-grandparents of Anna and Robin, the common ancestors that ultimately made them related. After World War I Robin's grandfather moved his family to the United States. He had not been successful in Germany. He thought perhaps his daughter, now a young woman, might marry a rich American. He was no more successful in America, but his daughter was. She married a poor American with a good idea and a dream, an educated man who worked

77

hard. By 1945 he was able to bring what remained of his wife's family to the States and to provide for these in-laws as well.

Anna's grandfather, the second Goldfeder brother, had a comfortable life in Germany. He was a jeweler and he made money. He had a daughter, Lotte, who eventually married a promising young teacher, a man who would be a professor some day, and a younger son, Josef, whose taste for the French led him to study in Paris, become a French citizen, and marry a rather attractive (though underfed looking) girl, Madeleine, the daughter of a country doctor. Why, with such a nice life, would anyone leave the Continent?

Such a nice life. She had heard the story of the Goldfeder brothers and of their daughters, the Goldfeder cousins, many times since her arrival in the States. She had never thought of her grandfather as "one of the Goldfeder brothers" or of her mother as "one of the Goldfeder cousins." But having heard the story, she had pondered her own destiny and that of Robin a hundred times in the last two years. Suppose her grandfather had gone to the United States and Robin's had not. Suppose both Goldfeder brothers had gone. But it always came down to the same end: Max Kleinberger would not have married Lotte. There would have been no Anna. Her very existence depended on the financial success of her maternal ancestor and that existence sealed her destiny. Once born Anna Kleinberger, there was no escaping the trip with Jürgen to France and eventually the trip with Madeleine to America. There was no way that Anna Kleinberger could exist and live her cousin Robin's easy life— born in one country, educated in one language, at home with one family, only her mother's faint accent reminding her that her own destiny hinged on her grandfather's fortuitous lack of business acumen.

Robin had been sixteen, Anna almost seventeen, when they started school together in the fall of forty-five. Robin was a senior, but Anna, still stubbornly tongue-tied in spite

78

of all Madeleine's coaching in English, was placed in a second year class. Only recently had she been able to admit, having sat at Robin's graduation, having read the bubbly letters from Smith, that it hadn't only been the language. It had been the loss, all the losses, the change, the fear, the aloneness. It had been their eagerness to make her happy and her terrible fear that becoming happy meant turning her back on everything she had left behind, the marked and unmarked graves, the man in the farmhouse.

She wanted to see him again, see how he looked, how he had aged, changed, or mellowed, how he had become successful, look at pictures of his children, the boy and the girl with their bright, inquisitive faces. She wanted to sit somewhere quiet and not too well lighted and talk to him, tell him it was working out, that nothing would ever have worked out if she hadn't met him, if he hadn't come back from Switzerland that day to take her back to the only family she had. She wanted to talk to him until she cried, knowing he would understand, he of all the people she knew. He would know that there was no end to the mourning, that she missed them still, her mother, her father, her uncle, that she still woke up sometimes wanting to tell them some little thing they would want to hear, that she knew that no day would come when she could say, "It's over, I've recovered, I can live without them."

And when she had said it she would tell him the other thing, that although she had lost the two years, she had taken one great step on her own last year to confirm that he had been right. She had taken her aunt's name as her own. It was her uncle's name, after all, and her mother's and that of her famous, successful grandfather, so really, it was hers too. And now it was easier for everyone. She was Madame Goldfeder's niece.

Anna stood up and took the jacket off, hung it in the closet and put on pajamas. She had to get back, cross that ocean, visit Paris, look in the shops on the Rue de Rivoli under the

79

arches. And later on, after she had found him, she had to go to Freiburg.

She went out into the hall and tapped softly on Madeleine's door.

"Anna?" the voice called from within, the gentle French stress pleasing her as always. No one pronounced her name correctly—no one since Anton—but the French way was nice. It fitted easily into sentences. It was prettier than what they did in English.

"Yes. Can I come in?"

"Of course, chérie."

She went in and sat on the bed. Madeleine had already sat up.

"Something is wrong?"

"No, nothing's wrong. I was thinking. Next June I'll graduate. I'll be nineteen then, almost twenty," she exaggerated. "I could go back before I start college."

"Back?"

"To France," she said, "and then—and after that—to Freiburg."

"Anna, no, you don't want to go there."

"But I do. I have to. I have to look. I have to—Listen, if I put away my money this summer, I can pay the fare. I can work after school and pay the rest of the way." She paused, waiting for an answer.

Madeleine sighed. "I wish I could go with you but twice in two years, it's too much."

"But you'll let me go?"

Madeleine kissed her cheek. "Let me talk to the cousins about it. After the summer, after I come back. I promise."

"Thank you." She returned the kiss. "Good night."

"Good night, chérie." There was sadness in her voice. She might win a round and postpone the trip for a while, but in the end she knew she would lose.

Anna made her way through the dark apartment to her bedroom. It was a start. She had never said it so strongly

80

before, with a time that she wanted to go and an ultimate destination. She lay down in bed, pulling only the sheet over her. There was a little breeze now through the open window, and the night would be comfortable. It would all happen. She would get back. She would see Freiburg again. She would find Anton.

2

The summer job began on Monday. Anna and Robin had been hired by Robin's father to do office work to replace vacationing employees. They were paid a dollar an hour, and Anna's wages would go, almost untouched, into a savings account.

Among her other duties, Robin was to operate the switchboard. Anna had declined that particular job. It was still hard to understand people on the phone, even harder to formulate quick, fluent answers to their questions. She had never used a telephone before the fall of 1945, and even now its ring stirred apprehensions. She was happier typing letters, filing cards, and filling out forms.

On Wednesday she, Robin, and Robin's father went instead to the pier in New York from which Madeleine's ship was leaving. The pier was as ugly and unpleasant as she remembered the one at which they had arrived, but she didn't want to think about that today. Today was a day of happiness for the departing passengers. There were streamers on the deck, champagne and little sandwiches in Madeleine's cabin. The cabin, small and compact with its own tiny bathroom, was filled with guests. Robin's mother was there, one of Robin's older brothers, two of Madeleine's fellow teachers at the college, and a neighbor from the apartment building.

Madeleine remained nervously quiet during the festivities. Anna knew she was concerned about leaving Anna alone for all those nights of the summer, leaving the car in

Anna's care although Anna was a careful driver, leaving Anna period. The little apartment in which they lived, not as mother and daughter, not as sisters, not as friends, but in some special unique relationship that had evolved between them, was a refuge for both of them, a kind of haven. And although the relationship was unique and did not lend itself to explication, Anna sensed that through her Madeleine retained a living link to Josef, to the wonderful, irreplaceable days that were gone forever.

There had been a party on Sunday, and Madeleine had received gifts for the trip. Between the gifts she had received and the gifts she intended to give, there had been little room to pack many of her own clothes. Now she worried aloud that she had taken too little along, that she would not have enough, but Anna saw that it was merely another kind of worrying.

The champagne ran out, and Madeleine begged Bernie not to order more. They were all tipsy, and soon the call would come for guests to leave the ship. A strange feeling came over Anna, a feeling and a determination. She would say good-bye to her aunt, she would watch her sail away, and in the fall she would see her come back. The spell would finally be broken. She would say good-bye to someone, and she would see that person again. All the rest of them—her parents, Jürgen, Anton—had gone out of her life and never returned. She wanted to know—she needed to know—that it didn't have to be that way. Her parents were gone. Cousin Bernie had written letters and made phone calls, and always the answer was the same. About Jürgen she could not be sure. But she still had so much hope for Anton, hope that he was alive, hope that he was doing well, hope that she would see him again. If Madeleine came back, and she would come back, it would be like a sign.

"Anna."

"Oui."

"Come with me."

They squeezed through the happy group, out into the corridor, and made their way to the deck. It was a sunny, breezy day, a wonderful day to begin a voyage.

"You will call the cousins every night."

"Yes."

"And be careful driving the car."

"Yes."

"I know you'll be all right."

"I will."

"And write to me every week. If you don't write, you'll lose your French."

"I'll never lose it. I'll write. I'll write tomorrow after work. Maybe when you get to Paris, it will be there."

"I'm not worried about you," Madeleine said.

"I know."

"Only concerned."

"I'll be all right." Anna bit her lips together.

"Don't do that, chérie."

"Are you sure you're coming back?"

Madeleine looked astounded. "Am I—" She took Anna's arm. "Of course I'm coming back. What would make you think—"

"I just wasn't sure."

"But now you're sure. Now you're absolutely sure."

"Yes."

A voice came over the loud speaker, the first call for visitors to go ashore. Madeleine's face grew dark.

"We must say good-bye," she said. "The others will be here soon."

Her aunt looked so lovely. Everything she put on benefited from her wearing it. She had on a black suit and black high-heeled shoes. Men turned to look at her, but she never noticed. Now her face was gray with the sadness of leaving.

"Please don't cry, Madeleine."

"No." She kissed her niece. "You will be well, and I will come back."

They started walking slowly toward the stairs that had

taken them to the deck. The deck was beginning to fill, and one or two guests were already making their way back along the gangplank to the pier.

"When you're in Paris," Anna said, "there was a man, a friend of my parents." She was nervous just talking about it; she had practiced many times what she would say. "He sold antiques, clocks mostly. If you could bring me the page from the telephone book where those stores are listed—" She stopped and held her breath, being careful not to bite her lips together.

"Of course, Anna," Madeleine said. She smiled and her face lighted up. She was so young really. When she smiled her youth became visible. It surfaced like a breathless diver. "Next week, in the hotel in Paris. I'll send it in my first letter from Paris."

Anna kissed her again. "Thank you. Have a wonderful trip. Look, there they are."

The cousins, the friends, the neighbors were all emerging into the sun, shading their eyes and searching. Anna waved, and they all got together, hugged and kissed, fought back tears. They then retired to the dock to watch the final festivities, the confetti, the removal of the gangplanks, and the big ship beginning to move toward the center of the river.

Madeleine stood alone at the railing, a small figure in black with the white of her blouse at her throat and the white of her orchid at her lapel. With all the throngs of passengers, she was alone. Confetti fell across her shoulder, trailing to the deck. She saw it and laughed, and her guests waved and cheered, especially Robin, who stood next to Anna and giggled with champagne and excitement.

Finally the ship made its turn and floated out of sight down the Hudson, and Bernie drove them all to the club for the rest of the day while he returned to the office where he belonged.

3

It was strange being alone. In her whole life she had been all alone only a couple of nights, when she had slept in the fields on her way to Germany and the first night in the little farmhouse in France. Then Anton had come, and she had not been alone any more.

It was a different feeling now. This time the apartment was hers. She could walk through it with a sense of ownership, a feeling of independence.

She spent very little time there. Klara, Robin's mother, wanted her to eat dinner "with the family" almost every evening, and weekends Anna went to the club with Robin. But at night and on weekend mornings she had it to herself.

On the first Saturday morning, following Madeleine's example, she found a dustcloth and cleaned all the surfaces in the living room, giving special attention to the pictures. Then, feeling adventurous, she opened the door to Madeleine's room and tiptoed in. She knew the room, but she never went into it when Madeleine was not there. Like its occupant it was austere, nothing out of place, only a few objects visible on the dresser top, one of them a picture.

It was an unusual picture. He had not posed for it. Someone had caught him unawares, naked to the waist, and even the rough lens in the old camera had picked up the glisten of sweat on his back in the summer sun. He was bent over one of those funny old cars of the early thirties, the hood up.

His curly head looked down into the gray blur of the motor.

This was the picture she had chosen for her bedroom—Madeleine, who never looked at men, who discouraged any but the most formal conversation with them. Madeleine was a mystery; perhaps she would always be a mystery.

"*Tag, Josef,*" Anna said softly, speaking German to her uncle, greeting him as she had when she was very little, in the days when he still came to visit. She sat on the bed and faced the picture, waiting for him to answer. "Madeleine is on her way to see you," she said. How long was it since she had spoken German? She knew, knew to the day. "We miss you, Josef," she went on. "Madeleine is very faithful to you. I think she will always be faithful. She's a very good wife."

The young man in the picture concentrated on the car. Why had she chosen this picture, of all the pictures she had, for her bedroom? Usually, people put their wedding pictures in their bedrooms. Klara had one like that, the bride in a long white gown, a swirl of veil, Bernie like a black tree beside her. Her father had scraped together all he had to give her a grand wedding, and the photograph was a shiny memento of his last illusion of affluence.

"I wish you were here with us," Anna said to the picture of her uncle. "But in a way, you were lucky. You died before you found out what happened to the rest of them."

A picture of Madeleine's husband with a naked back and dirt on his arm. Anna stood and walked to the dresser. It was not large, only four drawers, two along the top row, a larger one beneath them and another large one at the bottom. She grasped the knobs of the two top drawers and pulled them open. They were half empty, Madeleine's underclothes gone from the left one and only a little jewelry and a few papers in the one on the right. She closed them and opened the middle drawer. A few neatly folded sweaters lay there, a faint scent of mothballs emanating. She tried the bottom

87

drawer. There were some shirts and other pieces of clothing belonging to a man. Anna knelt and lifted a few things out. They were old and worn and had belonged to her uncle. She touched them reverently, lifted out a woolen scarf that she seemed to remember from long ago. Her mother had knitted it and given it to him once for a birthday. How many years it had kept him warm. It occurred to her that this was the only thing left that her mother had made. Perhaps Madeleine did not even know.

She went to put the clothes back when she saw that she had uncovered a book, a rather large, thick book, something like Robin's college scrapbook. She put the clothes down and took it out. It was filled with photographs. Anna put it on the bed and opened it. The first pictures were from the early thirties, a very young Madeleine and her girlfriends, an occasional young man whom Anna did not recognize. After a few pages, it was the mid-thirties and there was Josef, Josef and Madeleine. Anna turned the pages and stared in amazement, looking at the pictures and reading the scribbled notes beneath each one. Surely it was Madeleine, but it was Madeleine without her cloak of sadness, without her ever-present propriety, Madeleine in summer without white gloves.

In the pictures they held hands, they kissed, they smiled, they laughed. They were in Paris, they were at the sea. Madeleine wore a bathing suit. Josef doused her with water. Her shrieks of pleasure rose from the page.

She was so young there, Anna thought, as young—or as old—as I am now. But it was not just the youth, not just the smiles, that made the difference. There was something else in the pictures, something about Madeleine that she had never seen before, and for the first time she understood the picture of Josef that sat on Madeleine's dresser.

The letter with the pages from the Paris telephone book arrived a little more than two weeks after Madeleine's departure. It was preceded by three letters, written on board ship, that came all at once a few days before. She was glad she had written regularly. Madeleine would not be disappointed. Besides, it was turning out that Madeleine had been right about Anna's French.

For the first time in her life, she awoke, had breakfast, went out to wait for Robin and Bernie, and spoke English first thing in the morning. All day there was only English. Even in the last hour of the evening there was no respite. Only when she sat and wrote the letters to Madeleine did her mind begin to relax. But she knew that by the end of the summer, the language would be hers.

The pages from Paris showed no listing for a Pietrovic. Although she was disappointed, she knew that such shops often had other names than that of the proprietor. She had seen them in New York. Many of them were simply called "Antiques." It was already mid–July, and she had much work to do if she was to locate him by summer's end. She sat down with pencil and paper and composed a letter that she could copy and send to everyone on the list. It was simple and short and formal: Are you acquainted with . . . I am looking for . . . I appreciate your kind attention.

The following evening she began to type the letter, over and over, doing several each night. She bought a large supply of airmail stamps, and each morning she mailed a fresh batch of letters at the corner mailbox before Bernie arrived to take her to work. She forced herself not to believe an answer would come until three weeks had passed. Even then, there was nothing. Four weeks and still there was nothing. Letters arrived regularly from Madeleine, from the little village east of Paris where she was staying, the postmarks indicating that they took no more than a day longer than a letter from Paris.

It was almost the end of August and not one answer had arrived. What was wrong? Had her letter offended them in some way? Had they never heard of him and therefore ignored her query? Or did they know something that they did not want to put in writing, something that would dismay Mlle. Goldfeder in the great United States?

It nagged at her all through August, the fear that something was wrong. It made her happy that her days and evenings were occupied, that there were people around and work to be accomplished. She worked hard so that only a tiny corner of her brain was free to worry.

One morning Anna, Robin, and Bernie arrived at work to find that the switchboard operator had been in an accident on her way to work and would not be in that day, perhaps not for several days. Robin was replacing her father's personal secretary, who was on vacation, and no one else could be spared.

Bernie stood at the door of the clerks' office, his eyes moving from desk to desk, calculating. Ordinarily, his secretary took care of crises like this, but his secretary was away.

"I can try," Anna said, wondering at her temerity.

"Good," Bernie said. "Come this way. I'll show you how to operate the board."

She was amazed. The president of a company and he knew how to work everything, every machine, every piece of equipment in the factory.

It was really quite simple, he told her. You answered on this cord, and you made the connection with that one. When both lights went on, you pulled both cords out, very carefully, he emphasized. Never cut off a call. Then he smiled.

"I know you won't," he said, "and if you do, it's only because you're learning."

The first call of the day came in, and he stood aside while she handled it, looking at him for approval when she was finished.

"Easy as pie," he said. "See you later. It's all yours."

All hers. She had done it to test herself, to prove that she could still get on a bicycle if she had to and travel alone, done it to help out the person who had helped her and Madeleine most, and this morning she could repay the favor

90

slightly. But the job had another effect besides proving she could do it. The switchboard was busy for hours at a time, and she thought of nothing else except the calls and not cutting people off.

In the ladies' room after five she stood in front of a mirror with Robin. The office was empty, but Bernie never left on time, and the girls waited until he was ready.

"How'd it go?" Robin asked, beaming.

"I think it was all right."

"It was terrific, Anna. You made long distance calls all over the country. You were marvelous."

"I cut someone off, you know, that Miss Berry. She was very angry."

"She's an old bitch," Robin said. "Daddy says you did fine. He says he knew you would. He says you can do anything you put your mind to."

She felt a glow and a rush of warmth for her cousins. There were times when she wondered what it would be like to come home and tell your parents you had accomplished this or that, and she knew that Bernie and Klara tried—as Madeleine did, in a different way—to give her that feeling.

"I should graduate last June," Anna said. Robin was looking at her quizzically. "Should have," Anna corrected herself. Always the verbs when she was flustered or excited. How many mistakes had she made on the telephone today? Did anyone care?

"You could have," Robin said. She dropped her comb and lipstick in her bag. "But you didn't, and why cry over spilt milk? You'll graduate next June. Daddy says he wants to do something very special for you when you graduate." Robin's dark eyes were shining as though she knew a secret.

Something very special. Had Madeleine spoken to Bernie before she left? "Your father does many special things for me, Robin."

"Wait and see," Robin said. "Come on. It's getting late, and we don't want to keep the old man waiting."

91

When she got back to the apartment after dinner there was a letter from Paris, from one of the elegant shops not far from the Place de la Concorde.

She ripped the envelope open and read the formal contents rapidly. They had never heard of him. The name was unfamiliar. She had been misdirected if she had been told that the gentleman in question worked in their employ.

Anna read the letter over a second time, and then once again. She was not sure whether the writer was simply very reserved or whether he was annoyed at having been burdened with her question, with the task of writing her an answer. There was a clear sense of dismissal in the letter, a please-do-not-trouble-me-with-your-problems-again message.

Anna looked at the address from which the letter had been sent. If Anton had opened a shop in the part of Paris he had once selected, he was not known to his neighbors. She felt as though she were sinking. He had not made it. His dream had failed, and if it had failed, what of her own? Where would she look to find him?

She put the letter down near a photograph of her uncle and went to her room, taking off the clothes sticky with August sweat. She adjusted the water in the shower and got in. The water ran warmly over her, cleaning away the summer grime but leaving the sadness. It was after nine, and the water was as hot as at noon, an American miracle. A memory came back, the early, confused months after their arrival in forty-five. They had come home late after dinner in a restaurant and a movie and then an ice cream soda, and Anna had turned on the hot water just to see if there might be a little left over in the pipes from the day's supply. The water that flowed from the faucet had been blistering hot, and Anna had called Robin to tell her—nervously—that her father had forgotten to turn the hot water heater down. She hoped he wouldn't be angry when he found out.

And her cousin Robin had laughed. They *never* turned it down. They had lived in the house for years, and she didn't know whether it *could* be turned down. What a thing to worry about.

Anna had been amazed, amazed at the lushness of the country and the complacency of its citizens. She vowed that she would never let it be ordinary to her, she would never allow herself to expect it. She would preserve forever her original amazement, her awe.

She dried herself and got into pajamas. The summer was coming to an end. Madeleine was coming home next week, and the job would be over. In September she would begin her last year of high school and apply to colleges.

She went to the living room and retrieved the disappointing letter. Why had they waited so long to answer? She turned the envelope over and inspected the postmark in the light of the lamp. The letter had been mailed in July. Figuring the duration of its trip rapidly in German—she had never stopped counting in German—she saw that it had taken a month to arrive. She tried to think why. It had been clearly and properly addressed. The stamp was on it.

The stamp. It was an ordinary stamp. The letter had been sent by sea mail. Anna said, "Ah," as she understood. How characteristic of the Parisian shopkeeper. He would not use the phone if he could send a postcard; he would not pay for an airmail stamp as long as the ships were afloat.

She had thought, up until the time she wrote the letters, that she was still one of them, but she saw now that something had changed. The hot water might continue to amaze her, but she had begun to take other things for granted. From her small allowance she would buy airmail stamps, while the rich Parisian shopkeeper saved his pennies. What had happened was more amazing than the hot water; she had changed.

4

Madeleine disembarked wearing a light summer dress and a happy smile. Privately, she admitted it had been a varying experience. Her father was recovering nicely, and she was relieved to have seen him, but she returned with almost no luggage. The black suit had fit her mother with very little alteration. Her sister and sister-in-law had eyed her wardrobe with scarcely hidden envy, and as the summer neared its end, she had parceled out her belongings.

"Even the slips," she said to Anna with a sigh. "And my black shoes. They were such good leather, and there is nothing there to compare. My sister wanted the shoes, but they were too small for her. It broke her heart, but I gave them to Annette."

She had remembered them as proud people, not rich but well-off. Her father's practice had always been successful; her brother-in-law's farm had produced abundantly. But now material goods were hard to come by and harder still to pay for.

When, a few weeks later, she finally alluded to the situation during an evening with the cousins, Klara wept, went upstairs, and fixed a bundle of clothes to be mailed the next morning.

By the last of August two more letters had arrived for Anna from Paris with the same message as the first. They had never heard of Anton Pietrovic. Having received the same message three times over, she was convinced that he was not in Paris. Certainly if someone she had written to had had other news, a letter would have been sent more promptly than these and by swifter means.

On the first Tuesday in September she accepted Klara's invitation to go to New York for a last day of shopping before school. Robin would leave for her second year at Smith soon, and she still needed clothes. Anna went along so that she could visit the library at Forty-Second Street. She had been there before, but only to browse. It was not the books she was interested in now, but the magazines specializing in antiques and clocks. They were full of advertisements with names and addresses.

She read magazine after magazine in French, German, and English. There was no Anton Pietrovic, nothing even similar. She had looked once in the Manhattan directory and found the name—or something similar—but no A. or Anton. There were various spellings, and she had memorized all of them: Piet—and Petr—; —c, —cz, and —ch; v's and w's interchanged. No one with such a name advertised in the foreign magazines.

Hours had passed, and she had to meet Robin and Klara later in the afternoon. She took out pencil and paper and started copying. He had said France, so she took down those addresses first. He had thought about Holland, so she copied those also. His family had gone to England, and there was a chance he might have stayed. They had lived in Switzerland, and someone there might remember him from before the war. The list grew and grew. It would be weeks before she would get through it. She would need to compose a letter in German and, worst of all, one in English.

At five minutes to four she scribbled the last entry on her list, folded the pages to fit in her bag, and left the library. Down the steps she could see Robin and Klara approaching the lion on her left. They were arguing about something, and Anna hesitated, hoping they would stop arguing before she reached them. She had witnessed many of these scenes between Robin and her mother, and they left Anna in a state of confusion. She had often wondered what it would be like

95

to shop on Fifth Avenue with her own mother. What would Lotte choose for her to wear? How would Max react when she brought a new dress home? She imagined herself modeling something for him, watching him smile, watching his head bob in approval. What she could not imagine was turning on her mother with the anger that Robin used against hers. No one in Anna's family had ever shouted. Except that one time, and she didn't like to think about that.

Klara looked up the steps, saw Anna, and waved. "Where did you have lunch, dear?" she asked after she kissed her cousin.

"Oh." Anna felt herself turn red. "I forget about lunch—I forgot. I wasn't hungry. I was busy with the books. Really, I wasn't hungry."

"Oh Anna, I don't know what I'm going to do about you." Klara gave her a hug. "You should have come with us. You need a winter coat, and you're easier to shop with than Robin."

Robin gave her mother a surly look. "You should see what she wanted me to get," she said to Anna. "Long underwear. People don't wear things like that any more."

"It's cold up there in the winter," Klara said calmly. "I want you to be warm."

"But nobody wears things like that. Children wear those. I've been there, Mother, and I know."

Klara took a breath. "Let's get a taxi to the station, girls. If there's time, maybe Anna will have a sandwich and a glass of milk."

Anna reached into her bag. "I have the five dollars," she said.

"My goodness, don't give it back. You'll have plenty of things to buy for school. Come, there's a taxi."

As she turned the key in the lock she heard a man's voice speaking French and a girlish laugh in response. She wondered if she should wait, but Madeleine had heard the key.

96

"Anna?"

"Yes, it's me." She closed the door and went into the living room, where she saw them drinking hot tea on this last hot afternoon of the summer vacation, her uncle's widow and a man.

"Come and meet Richard Michaux."

Reeshar. He was in his late thirties with slightly thinning hair, and Anna liked him from the moment she shook his hand.

"How do you do?" he said. "Madame Goldfeder has told me all about you. We crossed the Atlantic on the same ship." His French sounded different from what she remembered, a breath, perhaps, of the new, postwar Paris.

"I'm glad to meet you. Will you be living near here?"

"Yes, it seems that I will. By coincidence your aunt and I are both teachers of French."

"How lovely. Do you like it here?"

"Well, yes, of course I like it, but it's rather hot. It's very hot. I didn't know it got this hot in America."

"It gets hotter, doesn't it, Madeleine?"

"Well, not so much. Richard will survive. Tell him he'll survive, Anna."

She was being very solicitous. She liked him. Anna made a fist around a thumb, an old habit from her first schooldays. In America they crossed fingers. Maybe something would happen. Maybe Madeleine would love someone again.

She picked up the mail and went to her room, leaving them alone with their tea and French conversation. She wasn't hungry. Klara had made her eat something at the station. Besides, she was excited now. There were letters to write and addresses to send them to. She wanted to find him by spring so that she could see him in the summer. It would be a busy fall, writing letters and doing homework and applying to colleges. After the semester was underway, she would visit Robin at Smith as she had done the year before. It meant spending a weekend with girls her own age, going out with a boy from Dartmouth or Amherst or Harvard who she would never see again and wouldn't care to. The getting away was good. The taste of college life was very sweet.

Later, after Richard left, they had dinner.

"He's very nice, Madeleine."

"Pleasant enough. You can't really tell. You said only a few words to him. You only talked about the weather."

"Yes, but there's something about him very—very—" She sought for the word in French. "*Appealing*," she inserted in English.

Madeleine looked at her sharply. "I don't know. His French is strange. His sentences are littered with words they pick up over there from the military." She meant English. "One feels one should clean it up, like a dirty street."

She was hurt. She had left her niece for one brief summer, and now she inserted Americanisms the way the new Parisians did.

"It's only words," Anna said. "I like him. It must have been very pleasant to have such good company on the ship."

Madeleine smiled. "Yes, it was very pleasant."

It was a week before she was able to mail her first letter. There was a party for Robin the night before she left for school. There was homework. The math especially was challenging. Finally she was learning things she had not learned once before in France.

She concentrated on Holland and France first. Early in October she wrote to addresses in London and a few cities in Switzerland. Each letter cost double postage now. Having learned a lesson from the French, she included international reply coupons in all the new letters. The answers from Paris dribbled on through September and then stopped. Barely half of the dealers she had written to bothered to answer. None had heard of Anton Pietrovic.

In school there was a girl whose parents had come from Poland just before the war. She went to their house one day and talked to the girl's mother. Yes, she remembered some of the large, elegant shops in Warsaw and yes, she would be glad to write letters to them asking after Anna's lost friend. Of course, Poland was not like the west, she cautioned. Letters didn't always get through, but she would try.

In October the cousins talked to her about college. She had visited Smith, and in New York she had seen Barnard. Once they had driven upstate to show her Cornell. They were sure she wanted to go where Robin was, and they were surprised when she told them. She was afraid of the narrow liberal arts curriculum that she saw in the catalogs of the women's colleges. She wanted to go somewhere big, a coed university where she could taste and sample their offerings. It was a dream she had of the Great American University. Something about it fulfilled a promise of her childhood and something else, perhaps, another promise made to her in a farmhouse when her childhood was gone.

They agreed that she must go where she wanted to, but they asked her to apply to some of the women's colleges also; she might change her mind over the winter, and she should not close the door on opportunity. So she began to write letters to the colleges asking for applications.

Soon the first answers to her second group of letters to Europe began to arrive. One from France, two from Holland. Then, a few weeks later, two from England and one from Switzerland, all with the same message. We have never heard--We are not acquainted—

Richard became a frequent visitor. Sometimes he brought flowers for Madeleine. Sometimes she invited him for dinner, and he came with a bottle of French wine. After dinner they would go out and not return until Anna was asleep. When Robin invited Anna to Smith for her birthday weekend, Anna accepted gratefully. She wanted to leave them alone, to give them an empty apartment. Her aunt was at least thirty; perhaps she was more than that. Surely she did not conduct herself with men the way Robin did—a kiss in a car, a polite struggle, an agreed upon victory.

Her birthday, November 12, fell on a Wednesday. The cousins had them both over for dinner and a cake.

"We don't have a lot of little presents for you this year, Anna," Klara said. "But we do have a big one."

Anna looked around the table and held her breath.

"We want to send you and Robin to Europe for the summer, after you graduate."

"Thank you." She swallowed and held her lips together tightly, releasing them when she realized Madeleine was watching. "It's what I want most. It's really what I want."

"I was against it," Bernie said, but there was a twinkle in his eye. "I told Mom here I couldn't spare my best switchboard operator."

They all laughed. It was a story that had been told over and over since the summer, how Anna had saved the day, how Anna had cut off Miss Berry, who had almost had apoplexy. Apoplexy. Anna had never been able to repeat that part of the story.

Of course there were "small" presents too—a cashmere sweater, a silver charm bracelet with one charm and the promise of more, a red leather wallet.

Friday after school she took the train up to Northampton. She and Robin spent the weekend talking about the trip to Europe.

"I can't wait to see Paris," Robin said. "You'll have to show me everything."

"I don't know Paris that well. We'll have to discover it together. We didn't live in Paris, you know. We took a train from the Gare Luxembourg. It was a quiet little town, even quieter than Great Neck."

"I don't care. You're still mycousinfromParis. You always will be."

"Yes," Anna said. "I think I always will."

"Where else will we go? Italy? Switzerland?"

"I want to go to Freiburg."

Robin looked at her with quiet surprise. "You want to go to Germany?"

"Only to Freiburg. Only for a day or two." Just talking about it made her tense. She held her hands in tight fists.

100

"Then I can go anywhere. After I see Freiburg, I'll feel better."

"Maybe you'll feel worse," Robin said in a low voice.

"No. I won't feel worse. After I go to Freiburg, it will be over. It will be behind me forever."

"Anna, sometimes you scare me."

"I'm sorry. I don't mean— If you don't want to go there with me, you can stay in France or Switzerland, and we can meet afterwards."

"Are you kidding? I wouldn't *let* you go alone."

She had not been aware how frightened she was of the possibility. "Thank you. I really want you to come with me."

On Saturday they went into Northampton for lunch, then drifted back and walked around Paradise Pond, talking about small secrets and fragile intimacies.

"Your English is better," Robin said suddenly. "It was good for you to be alone last summer."

"I know, but don't say it to Madeleine. When we came here, she only wanted me to speak good English. Now she only wants me to keep my French."

They sat down and said nothing for a few minutes.

"Are you going to visit anyone in Europe?" Robin asked.

"I don't know. I had a girlfriend in France, but I don't know if we have much in common any more. But there was a young man who took me to France. If I could find him—"

"He probably joined the Gestapo and killed Americans."

"I don't think so."

"Daddy says—"

Anna smiled. Bernie was Robin's god. Whatever Daddy said was true.

"Daddy says scratch a German and you find a Nazi."

Anna held an arm out. "Scratch me."

"You're not a German, cousin. You're an American, a true blue American."

"Not yet," Anna said.

101

"But you will be. You know you will."

She knew it was true, but she wondered what it would mean to her when it happened, whether having the piece of paper, the gray-green passport, would make her feel as though she belonged, whether roots would spring spontaneously into the earth on which she stood.

"You know," Robin said, "I asked you for a special reason."

"Asked me?"

"Who you were going to visit." Robin leaned slightly toward her. "Did you have a boyfriend in France before you came here?"

"A boyfriend? I knew boys, but nothing you would call a boyfriend."

"I mean—like an American soldier."

"Me?" Anna laughed. "Madeleine would never have allowed it."

"You had an army jacket. It used to hang in the closet in our bedroom when you were living with us. I never saw you wear it, but I took it down once when you weren't home, and I looked at it. I thought maybe you had known a soldier."

"No, there were no soldiers. I think I found the jacket somewhere after the war was over. Along the road, I think. I like it. It's very comfortable. I wear it in the winter when I'm alone." The story tumbled out staccato. She had never told Robin the truth. She had never told anyone. She had wanted to many times. Talking about it—about him—would have given it substance, lifted it out of the realm of memory mingled with fantasy. Someone else in the world would know. It would exist elsewhere than in her mind. But she had been unable.

Robin was watching her. The late afternoon sun was starting to sink and it was growing cold. Suddenly she grinned.

"Come on." She got up and brushed her skirt off. "We

ought to get back to the dorm. We'll have to change soon for tonight."

They walked back to the cluster of Henshaw Houses on Elm Street. A blind date had been arranged with a nice American boy from Amherst who would want her to kiss him good night. She had to find Anton. She had to put it all behind her, the way she wanted to put Freiburg behind her. She wanted to be more like Robin, go out with boys and have a good time and enjoy kissing them good night. But that could only happen afterwards. If it could happen at all.

Madeleine met her at the station. Had she had a wonderful weekend? Had she met someone nice? Did he like her and would she see him again? Wasn't it wonderful to be nineteen?

"What about your weekend?" Anna asked. "Did you see Richard?"

"Oh yes. He took me to New York to the theater. Of course, he has a hard time understanding the players."

"That's not important. He understands you."

Madeleine gave her niece a strange look. "What a weekend you must have had," she said. "You've come back a philosopher."

At the apartment, Madeleine handed her a few letters. As she took them, glancing quickly at their corners to note a foreign stamp, it occurred to her that it was strange that Madeleine had given her the mail this way. Ordinarily, she left whatever was Anna's on the desk in Anna's bedroom.

"I think you get more letters from France than I do," her aunt said lightly.

Anna felt her cheeks become warm. "It was those letters I wrote," she said unevenly. "My parents' friend. He had a shop—I thought it was in France." She stumbled over the words, aware that Madeleine was watching her carefully. "I think he isn't there any more. He must be in another coun-

103

try, maybe Holland." The letter she held had a Dutch stamp.

Madeleine put a hand on her shoulder. "You'll find him, chérie. Things are still not straightened out over there. It doesn't mean they're lost. It will take time but many people will turn up."

It was what they did for each other now, hold a hand out with support but make no firm promises, nothing each could not personally guarantee. The fantasy promises had all ended in the spring of 1945.

As Christmas approached, the letters from Europe slowed. Many of her queries, of course, were never answered. The ones that were, were delayed both by the writer and by the carrier. Everyone seemed to write letters at Christmas time. Even those from Madeleine's family took a few extra days to arrive.

On the last day of school before vacation, her friend Wanda, the girl from the Polish family, found her at her locker at the end of the day. She waved a piece of paper as she called hello.

"Your letter," she called. "My mother got an answer yesterday. She's translated it for you."

"My letter? You mean the one she wrote to Warsaw?"

"Yes. You should have seen the answer. It was opened by the censors and resealed with half an inch of glue."

"What did it say?" Suddenly she was trembling.

"My mother wrote you a translation. I hope you can read it," Wanda said. "My mother's handwriting is very old-fashioned."

"Yes, of course I can read it." She took the sheet of paper. "Tell your mother thank you."

"O.K. Merry Christmas, Anna."

"Yes. I mean thank you. Merry Christmas to you too." She watched Wanda leave, unfolded the sheet, and looked at the close, old-world handwriting. It was the translation of a woman who would never master the intricacies of her new language, but the meaning was clear.

104

Yes, the writer had known a Simon Pietrovic (spelled a little differently), but it had been many years ago, before the war. There had been sons in the family, but he didn't know or remember their names. No one in the family had returned after the war.

Anna slid to the floor and sat in the corner formed where the row of lockers met the wall of the building. She felt suddenly chilled. It was the last day of school, and the heat must be down. The letter was a message of immense sadness. As if they had gone away to a better place. As if they had elected to go and elected not to return.

The school was very quiet. They were all gone, gone to have a merry Christmas. Anna sat looking at the translation. Footsteps came down the hall, stopped, and she looked up. The janitor stood at the entrance to the narrow corridor between the rows of lockers, wearing the brown uniform of his trade.

"You put your homework away," he said kindly. "It's vacation time. You go home to your mother and daddy and have a merry Christmas."

"Thank you," she said. "The same to you."

She stood, took her coat from her open locker, closed it, and snapped the combination padlock. The man had gone. She put the letter in her bag and went home.

New Year's Eve was a Wednesday, and she and Robin had their hair done together in the crowded, tinseled shop where Klara regularly went. Anna had a date with one of the boys she had met over the summer, and Robin was going out with a boy she had known since high school. Robin dropped her off at the apartment a little after eleven. Madeleine was out with the car, shopping for the late dinner she would cook for Richard.

The mail had come, and she took it from the box, running through the letters as she walked upstairs. The red, white, and blue edging on familiar tissue-thin paper caught her eye, and she pulled it from the pack of Christmas cards. It was from Bern, and she ripped it open, standing on the stairs, flicking her mind into German. They had never heard of him. She bit her lips together in disappointment.

In the apartment she sorted the mail—Christmas cards, a postcard from one of Madeleine's colleagues now away on vacation, a letter from one of those organizations that always asked for money. She put them down. What had happened to him? Had he opened some small shop in an obscure corner of France? Why had no one heard of him?

She hung up her coat and went into her bedroom to look at her fresh coiffure. She looked older and more sophisticated with her hair done, more worldly, more like Robin. What was it all for, the good looks, the worldliness, if it was all to be wasted on a boy from summer?

She went back to the kitchen and picked up the envelope from the organization that wanted money. Why did they ask her? She had nothing to give. She squeezed out a little now and then from the allowance Bernie gave her each week, and even Madeleine, who used to save up for a favorite saint, now gave to a refugee organization instead.

Everyone gave. Everyone who had lost, who had survived, who had been helped. The organizations knew where everyone was. How could she have forgotten? Bernie had called one after the other in the months after the war trying to find out if her parents were alive.

Excitement took over her body, interfering with the orderly activities of the internal organs, prickling her skin, almost blinding her. The organizations would know. She would find him. It would happen. She would see him again.

She shouted, moved her hands, and scattered the letters on the kitchen counter. They flew like confetti, like the streamers on the ship Madeleine had sailed on, like rice at someone else's wedding.

It was too late today, and tomorrow was New Year's. Friday no one would be open but Monday, Monday she would make some phone calls, get some names and addresses. She would find him.

106

5

It was the longest weekend of her life. On Monday she went to school with a pocket full of nickels. When school was over, she crossed the street to the little coffee shop where groups of students spent their afternoons sipping their lemon Cokes and smoking forbidden cigarettes. There was a pay phone there, and it took only one call to New York to get the list she needed. She hurried home, anxious to write her new set of letters. When she reached the apartment, there was a letter from Basel.

> I am acquainted with the Mr. Pietrovic of whom you write. He was in business with Michael Hofstetter of Zürich before the outbreak of the Second World War. I suggest you contact Mr. Hofstetter, who can no doubt help you to determine Mr. Pietrovic's whereabouts.

Zurich. He had lived in Zurich. She had a name and address now, a person who had known him.

She sat down and composed a letter, mentioning the Basel reference. It was too late, when she was finished, to go to the post office. She needed stamps and an international coupon, and it would have to wait till tomorrow.

After dinner she typed up letters to the most likely organizations on her new list. At the conclusion of each letter, she wrote that she was the daughter of Professor Max Kleinberger, a victim of the war.

She had to stop at ten because Madeleine wanted to go to

107

sleep. For the next hour she read her history assignment, learning nothing from the words. It was something about immigrants, about the early twentieth century. It should have interested her; the stories should have made her tearful. Instead, they washed over her.

She hardly slept. She let the alarm ring in the morning only so that Madeleine would know she was awake, but she had been awake for hours.

"Look at you," Madeleine said over breakfast. "You look terrible. Do you have your period today?"

"No. I stayed up late studying. There was homework in every subject."

"What do you type so much at night? Sometimes I think you're writing a book."

"No. It's just easier than handwriting when I have a composition. No one can read my writing anyway."

"I can read it," Madeleine said with finality.

She went to the post office after school, spending a little extra to send Hofstetter's letter express. If it arrived by the end of the week, if he understood it was a matter of great importance, perhaps she would have an answer sooner.

The days crawled. She had figured it out in advance but still the reality was hard to bear. Even the letters to New York might not arrive until Thursday, not having been mailed until almost four on Tuesday. And how soon could she reasonably expect an answer? People had other things to do than look into the affairs of Anna Goldfeder.

There was nothing during the week and nothing on Saturday. She left Madeleine dusting her pictures, got into the car and drove out of town, stopping at a swamp where cellarless houses would soon rise from the green bilge. In America everything went up, while inside her, everything was sinking. She felt like a swamp, like quicksand.

She was so close to the truth now she wondered if she even wanted to hear it, wondered if she could bear it when it came to her. There was no one she could talk to about it, and whatever the news, she would have to bear it alone.

Robin had gone back to Smith. Madeleine would not understand.

She sat for a long time, until she was cold through and through. She had turned the motor off to save gas, so there was no heat in the car. It was wasteful to sit in one place with the motor running.

Eventually, she went back. Madeleine was out shopping. She looked at the pictures of her uncle, picking up her favorite, taken in the mid thirties, a big grin on his face. It was over ten years since that picture had been taken, another era, an era she had been born in and was still rooted to. And no one she could talk to about it.

She willed the time to pass quickly, but perversely it slowed. She wanted to sleep late on Sunday but she was up before the winter sun rose. She sat in the kitchen and counted slowly to sixty only to find that the second hand of the electric clock had barely passed the fifty-second mark.

Monday was no better. When finally she arrived home only to find an answer from Holland to one of her early December letters, an answer assuring her most sincerely that they had never heard of Mr. Pietrovic, she became sure that that was it, the evil sign she had feared.

She walked home slowly Tuesday afternoon. Tuesday she was alone. Madeleine taught an evening course in conversational French, and she remained at school for dinner. It was nice to be alone one day a week, nicer still when Madeleine returned.

She got the mail and started up the stairs. There was something from France for Madeleine, her mother's handwriting. A letter from Robin, thick. Something from the college for Madeleine. A letter with a Swiss stamp.

She turned it over. M. Hofstetter. She started to rip it open when she heard a telephone. It was theirs. Madeleine would be calling. She raced up the steps, the key in her hand. Why now? Let me read my letter.

She dropped her books on the kitchen table and picked up the heavy black receiver.

109

"Hello?"

"Miss Goldfeder?"

"Yes." And then, very grammatically, "This is she."

"This is Mrs. Morgenstern." The woman added something not entirely comprehensible. It was the name of one of the organizations. "You wrote to us last week."

"Yes." She was almost breathless.

"I'm sorry it's taken us so long to get back to you, but there were some complications. I don't want you to worry, dear. Your friend, Mr. Pietrovic, survived the war."

"I know that. I need to know—"

"I've been asked not to give out his home address but I can tell you where his business is. Do you want to get a pencil?"

"Yes, I have one." Hanging on the wall because Madeleine thought of things like that. "What is it, please?"

"It's on Madison Avenue." She read off the number.

"Madison Avenue where?"

"Oh, I think it's somewhere in the Sixties."

"Do you mean New York?"

"Yes," the woman said. "He's right here in Manhattan. He's been here"—there was a sound of paper rustling—"oh, at least a year now."

She was unable to respond, unable to say thank you, unable to let the woman know she had survived the conversation.

"Would you like me to call him for you?" the woman asked gently after a short silence. "I can do that, Anna, if it'll make it easier for you."

"No." It was less of a voice than a whisper. "No, thank you very much. I think I wouldn't like you to do that."

"Then I won't. Are you all right now?"

"Yes."

"Perhaps we can talk one day soon about you. I don't have you on any of my lists. You wrote that you were Professor Kleinberger's daughter, and I see you've changed your name."

"Yes, we can talk. Not today, please."

"No, of course not. I'm glad we could help you. If you have any other questions, you can call me. It's easier than writing a letter."

"Thank you."

"Did you know Mr. Pietrovic's family?"

"No, only him."

"Fine. Oh, by the way, he's Americanized his last name. It's Peters now, Anton Peters."

"I see. Thank you, Mrs. Morgenstern. Thank you very much."

She hung up, brushed the tears from her eyes, and opened Hofstetter's letter. It said almost the same thing. He did not know Mr. Pietrovic's home address, but he was very clear on where the shop was as he had visited it only last summer. It was on the east side of Madison Avenue and was a brisk walk from the Plaza Hotel, where he had stayed as Mr. Pietrovic's guest.

"Dieu merci," she whispered, thanking them all, the gods, the saints, the magical language. She went to her room, wrapped herself in the jacket, lay on her bed, and cried. He was alive and well and he had come to America. And all this time, all these months, and especially these last few days, she had feared he was dead.

6

"I have MET SOMEONE," the letter read. Robin was always MEETING SOMEONE, and Anna smiled. She was still wrapped in the jacket, nestled in a corner of the bed with a pillow behind her. She had not entirely stopped crying, but she could feel the slow return of normality. "His name is Lenny and he's really terrific. He has those tall dark good looks that I always go for and he's *sooo* nice. He's graduating from Amherst in June, and I don't know how I'll live without him next year. We've already gone out three times."

"I love you, Robin," Anna said out loud, shaking her head.

On Saturday she went into New York, walked across Thirty-Fourth Street, took the bus up Madison Avenue, and got out at Fifty-Ninth Street. Madison Avenue was very fine up here. The people walking the street were well dressed, and Anna imagined they had a great deal of money to spend. Some of them carried bags from expensive stores; others carried nothing. That was because they had everything sent. Robin had pointed out that they were the really rich ones. They didn't have to show off where they had spent their money; looking at them, one could guess.

Anna crossed to the west side of Madison Avenue and walked slowly north, her eyes fixed on the shops across the street. In one hand, sweating inside its winter wool glove, she held the scrap of paper with the address, although she had memorized it seconds after she wrote it down.

112

Somewhere around here—or had it been Lexington Avenue?—she had walked with Robin in the fall of forty-five, discovering a long line of women in the street. They had been nicely dressed, and she had wondered what it was they were waiting so patiently and so long to buy—some special food, perhaps, that the war had kept from them. Eventually they had reached the start of the line, a tiny, narrow store selling nylon stockings, one pair to a customer. Neither the line nor its ultimate pot of gold had surprised Robin.

Anna moved out of the line of pedestrian traffic and stopped. It was there, just across the street from where she stood, a door in the center, a window on either side. There were objects in the windows, but she could not tell what they were.

A peculiar sensation of anxiety crept over her, almost a fear, but what was she afraid of? She was so close; she could walk across the street, open the door, and go inside. She could ask to see Mr. Peters. She could wait until he came out. She could say hello, Anton.

Across the street people walked by the shop, looked in the windows, stopped, went on their way. Someone went in. Someone else came out. Anton was alive; he was in a store across the street from her.

She stood watching for almost an hour. Suddenly a man's voice, close by, said, "Waiting for someone?"

She jumped and looked at him, a total stranger, a man taking advantage of a girl alone. "Excuse me," she said crisply, and walked away, down Madison Avenue, back toward the train that would take her home.

The following Saturday she went back, took the bus again to Fifty-Ninth Street, walked north on the west side of the street, stood and watched. Finally, she walked two blocks farther uptown, crossed to the east side, Anton's side, and walked slowly back, very slowly at the end, stopping at the first window, her breath gone now. Behind the display the window was curtained, preventing anyone from seeing in

113

or out. She edged to the center of the first window. A French carriage clock, its hands pointing to the precise time, stood near a necklace draped over satin.

She walked quickly past the door and stood before the second window. A silver tea set stood proudly before her, a card next to it, neatly lettered, with the name of the silversmith and the year, 1807. How did he know exactly? And in a corner of the window, also neatly stenciled, A. Peters.

It was still before noon, and the sun had not yet reached its highest point. She imagined how the displays would look as the sun reached the western sky and hit the rounded belly of the teapot, how the jewels in the bracelet would glitter. He had told her the truth about himself. Surely if any street in New York had arcades, it would be this one, this very block.

A woman walked by in a fur coat, stopping to look at the window with the clock. She might walk in and just take the money out of her bag and buy it, or perhaps she would go home and tell her husband, "You should see what I saw on Madison Avenue today. I'm sure I won't be able to live another day without it."

The woman walked on, and Anna, taking one last look at the silver tea set, went back downtown to catch the train to Long Island.

She thought about it all week. Was it enough to know that he was here, that he was successful, that he had come out of the war whole? She sat in her classes and agonized over it for hours every day and on into the night. There was an emptiness now to her evenings. The last letters had been written; the search was over. She knew the answer to her question without the agonizing: she had to see him. She had always known that she had to see him. She couldn't really go on like this, traveling into New York, standing near the shop and doing nothing.

On Saturday she waited till Madeleine was out shopping, then went to the telephone. Madeleine would not be back for an hour or more. She could make her call without fear of interruption.

She moved a kitchen chair to the counter where the telephone was and sat down, the phone number in front of her. It was ten-thirty. Any business would be open now. She felt sick. Who would answer? Would they put her through to him? What would she do when she heard his voice?

She lifted the receiver and prayed. Please let him answer. She dialed the number and closed her eyes. A ring. Another ring.

"Four-five-seven-eight." It was a woman's voice.

"Is Mr. Peters there?" Her voice not quite her own.

"I'm sorry. Mr. Peters is not here today. Can I help you?"

The woman's voice was clearly accented. You could hear it in the r's especially and in the tenseness of the vowels.

"No. Thank you very much." Anna hung up before the woman could say anything else.

Had she sounded like a little girl or a grown woman? Would the woman think she was a prospective client inquiring about merchandise, and would she pass along the fact that "someone" had called?

Anna put her head in her hand. He did not come in on Saturdays. She had spoken to his wife. Perhaps that was how they worked it out. He took Saturdays off, and she filled in for him. She had a pleasant sounding voice. She must be a very nice person. Not that that was a surprise. Anna knew that already; she had known it for almost three years.

She sat back and considered what to do. She could call on a weekday, and maybe she would get to talk to him, but after that what would happen? She wanted to see him. She wanted to touch him again.

A French calendar hung on the kitchen wall, a gift from Madeleine's parents. Tomorrow was the first day of February and there were only two holidays coming up. Lincoln's Birthday was a Thursday and that was already taken. Klara

115

wanted to shop with her. Besides, that was so near. It was too soon. She needed time, time to prepare. Just thinking about it made her heart flutter. Washington's Birthday fell on a Sunday and she was visiting Robin for the long weekend. Almost to her relief, she saw that that eliminated most of February. It was absurd to think that she could skip school and get away with it. She would have to wait until Easter. Yes, Easter was much better. March 28 was Easter Sunday, and she had the following week off. It was a long time to wait, but she needed the time. Sometime during that week she would go into New York and see him. She would see him. She would actually see him.

7

Like the way to school, she had learned the route by heart. Every step of the way, from the time she got off the train at Penn Station, had become part of her permanent memory. She got on the bus across the street from the back entrance of Altman's and watched the buildings roll by. It was a clear day, a good day for the end of March, a bright day to settle her life.

She had timed it so that she would arrive at eleven. Eleven would be perfect. It was after opening and before lunch. She would get it all over with before lunch and have the rest of the week to get it out of her system.

She got off the bus sensing uncomfortably that she was early. The train had made good time for a change, and the bus had whizzed up Madison Avenue. She got off at Fifty-Ninth Street and stayed on the east side of the street. She knew exactly how long it would take from here, and it wasn't long enough. She slowed down, the sickness of all the months of waiting rising in her.

Maybe she needed a doctor. Maybe she was just sick enough now that his instruments would detect an elevated temperature, high blood pressure, and severe intestinal disorder. Did she dare pray in French any more? The saints had come through once; was it fair to ask another favor of them? Weren't they busy enough without her?

She was at the last corner now. Hofstetter had written in January the number of paces from this corner to the shop. Perhaps she could take tiny steps and prove him wrong. But

117

it was no use. She was there, she had reached the first window. The tea set was gone and in its place was a pair of ornate silver candlesticks. The lettered sign said: Geo. III. She had arrived. She had only to open the door.

Too sick, she thought. Can't possibly manage it today. Some other time, tomorrow maybe. Someone came from across the street and went deliberately to the door, pushed it open, and walked in. She followed him anxiously with her eyes. As the door swung slowly shut, she glimpsed a woman, smiling, busty, a woman who had borne children, her black hair tinged with gray. How old? Thirty-five? Thirty-seven? His wife worked there on weekdays too? It was possible. But how could she go in in front of his wife?

I am crazy, she thought. This love between us, it was my love, not his. He didn't love me. He was a man married and devoted to his wife. He had children that he loved. Three chocolate bars, remember? He stopped because he was tired. He stayed because he wanted to be clean. He came back because he felt sorry for me.

I am crazy. I have lived a fantasy for three years. I go out with very nice boys and don't like them because I'm preoccupied with a myth, but I have no right to him. I didn't belong to him.

She felt dizzy now and close to hysterics. She was in New York, and she didn't know where to find a swamp to sit and stare and be hysterical. She was stupid. It should have been enough to know he was alive.

She turned back in the direction from which she had come, hurried down Madison Avenue, crossed the street and went over to Fifth, went all the way down Fifth and into the library, the nice, safe library. She had walked over a mile, and she was out of breath, out of breath and miserable. She got a book they were reading for school, and she sat down and tried to read. It was Hawthorne, and the English was archaic and difficult to follow. It took great concentration to comprehend the meaning.

I want someone to talk to, she thought, the book open

118

before her. Someone who loves me, my parents, my father. I didn't know my father. They took him away when I was young. I have no father. I have no mother. I have nothing. I am no one.

She pored over the book as though its message would somehow solve her problems. Like the day she spent alone in the little farmhouse, she felt there was no place to go. Hours passed, and she turned pages. The left side of the book swelled like a filling reservoir or a fat bank account, but it was all a sham. She had retained nothing.

Finally she closed the book and found a telephone. She told Madeleine she was busy reading and would come home after dinner. Madeleine had a meeting tonight, and Anna could come home and go to bed without seeing her. It would be better that way. There was nothing she wanted to say.

She had missed lunch, so she had a sandwich at the station and rode home. Madeleine had left her a note. She hung up her coat, went into her room, put the jacket on over her skirt and blouse, and sat on the bed. She took out the whole folder of letters from France and Switzerland and all the other places she had written to, and she read them over. At ten, she turned the light off and sat in the dark.

She heard Madeleine come home, heard her tiptoe by the dark bedroom, heard her take a shower. It was very dark and very quiet, and she sat without moving on the bed, in the clothes she had chosen to wear to see Anton and in the jacket he had given her when they had had nothing but each other and it had been enough for her.

She needed someone—now—to pack her bag and carry her over the mountain and solve it all for her, someone strong, someone she could talk to. Halfway through the long night she fell asleep, still sitting in her clothes. Her eyes opened to early light. Her mouth felt terrible.

Quietly she went to the bathroom and washed. She wrote a short note to Madeleine, left it on the kitchen table, took her coat and bag, and left. It was very cold out, and she shivered waiting for the train. Inside, the car was full of men

119

commuting to work in the city. This was how they lived, up at dawn, on a train, work all day, back on the train at night. What made them happy? What made it worth their while?

She got off at Penn Station and, like a bad dream, went through it all again, the walk across town, the bus north on Madison, the short walk from Fifty-Ninth. She would be sick again, but she would see it through this time. She had to know, and the only way to find out was to see him.

The brightness of the day hurt her eyes. She was at the last corner on Madison. Like an endless film that ran over and over without stopping, she was always at this point on Madison.

She wished she could stop for breakfast somewhere, but she didn't want to miss him. It was almost eight-thirty. Orange juice. What she wouldn't give now for a glass of cold orange juice. The Americans knew how to start the day. She and Madeleine squeezed sweet fresh juice every morning, still marveling at the wonder of real orange juice for breakfast.

She crossed the last street and involuntarily began to count the paces. The Geo. III candlesticks were still in the window. She went to the door and pushed it, knowing it would be locked, but she had to be sure. Her vital functions were a mess now, her breathing, her heart, her stomach, the constriction in her throat, the pulsing in her temple. Suppose someone else came first to open the shop. She moved away from the door and stood to the side of the far window. There was a different clock in the window now, a very ornate one with nymphs crawling around it. It was 8:43. She checked her own watch—8:41. In a gesture of faith, she reset her watch.

People began to come by, mostly singly. She looked carefully at the men. Would she recognize him if she saw him? She had worried so about whether he would know her; would she after all be able to pick him out of a crowd?

120

Through the window a man in army clothes. I love him. I have always loved him. I will never be able to love anyone else but him. It is my particular sickness.

It was 9:00 now on the ornate clock. A man was coming up the street, hurriedly, from the direction of the Fifties. She put a hand against the brick of the building. He was almost to the first window. Steady. Don't let me cry or die here in the street. He passed, still walking quickly, and she turned, dizzily, and watched him go.

Five after. A rest home. Maybe a convent. Perhaps she could persuade Madeleine to join her in a convent.

A taxi stopped across the street. A man got out, paid the driver, smiled and lifted his hand in a slight wave, then waited for a car coming up the street to pass before crossing. He held a briefcase in one hand and a newspaper in the other.

He had not changed. The cheekbones, the nose, the still slim body in a well-cut suit. He stepped on the curb, shifting the paper to the hand that held the briefcase and put the free hand in his pocket.

"Anton."

He stopped dead and looked around, the hand coming slowly out of his pocket holding a ring of keys. He looked at her, squinting slightly in the morning sunlight, and took a few steps toward her.

"Anna," he said.

A weight lifted. "Yes."

"Anna Kleinberjay."

"I was afraid you wouldn't remember."

A puzzled look passed over his face and then cleared away. "You came to America," he said.

"That same year." She was starting to feel better, as though she might live, as though it had all been worth it.

He switched the briefcase and paper to the hand with the keys and took her arm. "Come inside," he said. "I—please come inside."

121

He unlocked the door and relocked it when they had gone in, leaving the keys hanging from the lock.

"Come," he said, taking her to the back so that the whole shop went by like a fuzzy image.

In the back he had an office, a desk with papers, three clocks on a table, tags hanging from them.

"Sit down." He pulled a chair nearer the desk for her. "It is you, isn't it?"

"Your English is wonderful."

"Some tea, Anna?"

"Yes, please."

He filled a metal pot from a jug of water and placed it on a small electric stand that began to glow red. It was the first she had ever seen like that. Seeing it pleased her. She would always learn new things from him.

"How did you find me?" He seemed excited in a subdued sort of way, or perhaps it was only a touch of nervousness. "I've changed my name, you know."

She pulled off her gloves and stuffed them in her pockets. "Hofstetter in Zurich."

"Michael Hofstetter! But how did you come to him?"

"Someone in Basel said he knew you. Jakob Schelling, I think."

"You actually looked for me."

"For a long time."

He bent his head so that his forehead pressed into his fingertips for a moment. Then he looked up. The water had begun to boil. She watched him make tea.

"Who brought you to the States?" he asked while the tea steeped in an old porcelain pot.

She appreciated the delicacy of the question. "My aunt. We live together now, on Long Island."

"I can't believe this." He looked in at the tea. "I think it's ready now. I'm sorry. I have no milk."

"It's O.K. I don't take milk either."

He poured the tea. "You must have been cold waiting in the street. Why didn't you call?"

122

She put the teacup down and bit her lips together. "I was afraid you wouldn't remember me. I thought you wouldn't want to see me."

"Anna."

She reached out and touched his cheek. It was half of what she had wanted, touching him and talking to him. He took her hand as she withdrew it, and kissed it.

"We have a great deal to talk about," he said.

More than she could ever manage in a whole morning of talking, in a whole week.

There was a sound and he looked up. "I must unlock the door."

He left, and she heard him talking to someone in the front. He came back and sat down, poured more tea but didn't drink it. A phone on his desk rang once, but he ignored it.

"It isn't very private here. Shall we take a walk?" He pushed his chair back. "Look at how beautiful you are," he said. "You must be very happy here."

"I am now."

"Yes. Yes, I am too."

She stifled a yawn, touching her lips with her fingertips. "I didn't sleep last night," she explained shyly. "I was very nervous."

He smiled at her. "I'll let you go soon. Come, Anna."

She held a thumb tightly in a fist. Not too soon. Please, not too soon.

He led her to the front of the shop where a woman was dusting small objects.

"Rose," he said, "I'd like you to meet Anna Kleinberjay from—it's Long Island now, isn't it?"

"Yes."

"My cousin, Rose Farber."

"How do you do."

The woman smiled and shook her hand. It was the woman she had glimpsed yesterday, beautifully, roundly maternal, a woman made to hug little children.

"I'm happy to meet you," the cousin said in her gently accented English.

They walked out into the street and down to the corner, his hand on her arm. Along with her own body, the area had come alive. At the corner they crossed the street, walked to Fifth and crossed to the park. The morning was glowing. They started down Fifth.

"You must be nineteen by now," he said.

"Yes."

"And very busy."

"Not really. Just school."

He stopped at an empty bench, brushed it off, and they sat down.

"I'm very glad to see you," he said.

Something uncomfortable stirred within her. He was about to say good-bye. In a moment, it would all be over.

"I have a little house in Connecticut," he said, "a little weekend house. In the woods." He stopped. "There's so much—Do you think you could get away some Friday afternoon, until Sunday?"

She shivered, and he took her hand and squeezed it. "I can try."

He took a large wallet from his jacket pocket, found a small card, and gave it to her. "This is a private number," he said. "It rings in my office. When I'm not there, no one else answers it. Perhaps the weekend after next. You can call me."

She took the card and put it in her coat pocket without looking at it. "I'll call in a few days."

"I won't be in on Saturday."

Anna looked at him and smiled. "You look very beautiful too," she said.

He put his arm around her and pressed her shoulder. "Let me get you a taxi. I have to get back. My cousin is alone in the shop."

He went to the curb and signaled a taxi, took the wallet out again, and folded her hand around a bill.

"I don't need it," she said as the taxi stopped next to her.

"It's a small repayment of a generous loan."

"No, please."

He opened the door for her, closed it after her, and bent to talk. "I'll wait for your call."

He told the driver Pennsylvania Station, turned back for a moment to look at her, and left. The taxi started south. She looked down at the bill in her hand. It was ten dollars.

8

It turned out that it was Robin who made it all happen, Robin who panicked at the thought but who came through in the end.

"But where are you going?" Her voice came anxiously through the long distance that separated them.

"Just to Connecticut, just to be by myself for the weekend." She had to make it short; Madeleine could walk in the apartment at any moment, and she couldn't be caught in the middle of this kind of conversation.

"Is something wrong between you and Madeleine?"

"Of course not, Robin. You know better than that. But she would never let me go away by myself. If she thinks I'm visiting you, everything will be all right."

There was a long pause. Then Robin said in a low voice, "You're not going to meet anybody, are you?"

Anybody? Just anybody? No, I'm going to meet somebody, somebody very special. "No," she said, convinced that she was at least grammatically truthful, "I'm not going to meet anybody." Stressing the offending pronoun ever so slightly.

"Lenny says it isn't safe for girls to travel alone."

Lenny says. At some time between January and March, Robin had switched almost overnight from Daddy says to Lenny says. Lenny had become very important in her life.

"But I travel alone when I go to visit you."

"Yes. You're right. You're absolutely right." Robin suddenly sounded relieved. "O.K. O.K. Go ahead and tell her

126

you're coming here. Just for God's sake be careful. If anything happens, I'll—"

"Nothing will happen, Robin. Thank you. You'll never know how much I thank you."

It was Wednesday when she spoke to Robin. She waited till Thursday afternoon to call the special number, but no one answered. On Friday morning she reached him.

"This is Anna," she said when he answered.

"Anna, yes, how are you?"

"I'm fine. I've arranged it. Do you still want to go?"

"Yes, of course I do."

"Well, it's all right." She was as nervous as the first time. "I fixed it up."

"You'll take a suitcase?"

"Yes."

"With warm clothes. It gets rather cold up there."

"Yes, that's all right."

"I'll meet you at Pennsylvania Station, and we'll go to my car."

They made the arrangements and hung up. Only after that did Anna tell Madeleine that Robin had invited her to Smith. Only then was she sure he had really meant it.

The train was almost empty. People went home at this hour, happy to be finished with their day's work, looking forward to a weekend with the family. Anna scarcely noticed the few other people in the car. They were mostly women, dressed elegantly for the theater or for dinner in some dark restaurant. Their faces were powdered and their lips deep red.

Anna had prepared too. She had shaved the dark stubble from her legs, although Madeleine still frowned on her shaving. In the privacy of her bedroom, she had rubbed an oily cream on her unblemished skin and then, not too long after, wiped it off, leaving only a faint scent of roses. Today after school she had showered and dressed in a fresh skirt and a clean blouse. She had packed enough clothes for a week, but she usually did that when she visited Smith. Robin always had to tell her that it would be a skirt, sweater, and heels night, or a wool dress and pearls night (although Anna didn't own pearls), or maybe a very informal night when they would wear dungarees and her father's cast-off shirts. There was always an extra one around for Anna.

She sat now among the suburban ladies feeling special, the nervousness of the past few days dissipating as the train entered the long tunnel that marked the beginning of the end of the first part of her journey and the beginning of something else, something as special as she felt now, something she had never dared to hope for.

She followed two women off the train, turned, and went along the platform toward the station. She knew quite suddenly that she had nothing to worry about, that he would be there, that he would take care of her as he had always taken care of everything, that regardless of the obvious complications, she would be happy.

"Anna."

She turned and he was there, waiting, as she had waited for him once.

"I was afraid I might miss you." He took the suitcase, and she tucked her hand in his free arm. "My car is just across the street."

They made their way through the large station and out into the street. It was past six and growing dark. He took her to the car, which was in a nearly empty parking lot. The workday was over, and this was neither the theater district nor a place to find restaurants. He put the suitcase in the backseat of the car and a black briefcase next to it, then helped her in. It was a new-looking car, certainly postwar, and not very large. He came around and sat down, put the key in the ignition, but did not start the motor.

"May I kiss you?" he asked.

"I'd like you to."

Soft and very brief. He turned the motor on and pulled out of the slot, and she looked at his hands on the wheel,

128

long, slender, well-manicured fingers, rather aristocratic looking. His hair was carefully and tastefully cut, his clothes well fitting. There was a clean scent about him, very faint, hardly noticeable, clean and something else. The something else made her tense, set her on edge.

The car moved smoothly into the street and she began, for the first time in a long time, to think about death and love and the man sitting beside her and all the things she had been unable to talk about for so long because there wasn't anyone she could talk to, or anyone she thought would listen, or anyone she could trust enough, or just anyone that wasn't he.

He turned north off Thirty-Fourth Street. "It's about an hour's drive from here. Perhaps a little more."

Because how could anyone know? How could Robin, who had never wanted for anything or wanted anything else in life than to have a Lenny and produce his children, understand waking up on September 2 and leaving your parents forever?

"Did the bicycle hold up?"

"The bicycle. Yes. It got me back. I got a ride in a truck most of the way. I went back to Madeleine's friends, and they found me a ride."

"Is Madeleine your aunt?"

"Yes."

How could Madeleine, whose life now revolved in a tight circle around her niece and her work, ever understand that a life could be shaped by a chance meeting at age sixteen, that it could take her this far, to a house in Connecticut on a Friday night to spend the weekend?

"It was built before the war, my house. I'm still fixing it up. There's no heat, just a fireplace and a stove, but there are trees all around. You can see them from every window."

"It must be very lovely."

"It is."

"Your children must love to play there."

"It's a nice place for children."

129

"You haven't changed, have you?" she said. "I was afraid you might be a different person now."

"I've changed. We'll talk about it all tomorrow."

"I haven't changed." It was only part of what she meant to say, that she still cared, that her body wanted him as much as her mind did—and more urgently.

"You're very lovely, Anna."

"It's nice to hear someone say my name the right way."

He laid his hand on top of hers, and she started as though a loud sound had frightened her. She turned her hand over so their palms touched and their fingers clasped. She looked away, out the window, feeling secure. Would she have grown up to fall in love with Lenny if she had always felt this secure?

When they reached Connecticut, even in the dark the trees were overpowering. The view and the feeling were different on the train. Here one rode low; one was part of the environment.

It was a long hour, an hour during which the pressure built, the tension of sitting next to him, touching. She admitted to herself with some shame that she had wanted more than the talking, that perhaps she had wanted the other more, that she had been unable to plan it all because she had been incapable of admitting it.

"I thought by now you would be at the Sorbonne, living in a little room on the Left Bank with your French lover."

She looked at his profile in the dark. He was watching the road. "My cousin says I run away from love."

"Do you?"

"I don't want to talk about it tonight."

"We're almost there now," he said, slowing the car.

He turned off the road and drove a short distance on a narrow, bumpy drive through the woods. The headlights seemed to burn a path for the car to follow. At one point a small, nocturnal animal that might otherwise have frightened her scampered across the way and disappeared in the

130

woods. She was quite calm. Nothing could frighten her tonight. Nothing would ever frighten her again.

He stopped the car, got out, and came around. It was a
small one-story house with a door near the center. It was
unlike the houses people she knew lived in on Long Island.
It was truly rustic. There was no grass in front, no well-
trimmed shrubs, but the night smelled delicious and cold,
like water from a spring—or a well.

He put the key in the lock and pushed open the door,
switching on a light. They had walked into a kitchen which
opened, on the left, to a large living room with a fireplace on
the far wall.

He took his coat off and went to a closet, and she began to
unbutton hers.

"Leave it on till I get a fire started," he said. "It's very
cold." He hung his coat up and took out a jacket, a sort of
hunter's jacket, which he put on over his suit. "Come." He
took her into the living room where logs and twigs and
newspapers were arranged near the fireplace.

She watched him set them up, watched him squat to strike
a match. She came and knelt beside him, her thigh touching
his, while the paper caught, then the kindling. His eyes
were on the fire, assessing his work. She took his hand and
kissed the palm, then looked up at him.

"My hands are dirty," he said, but something about him
was not quite the same.

He stood, taking her hands so that she stood too, put his
arms around her, around the coat, holding her hard so that
her cheek rubbed the rough wool of the jacket. In school
once she had been asked to write a composition on What
Would Make Me Happy, and she had written the whole
thing in the conditional mood with great difficulty and
some assistance from the cousins. She had pushed her imagination to its limits. Now, suddenly, she had no need of
imagination; it was unconditional; she was happy.

"There's another fire to light."

He walked her back through the kitchen, through a door-

131

way and into a room almost as large as the living room, turning on a lamp as they entered. In the back, against the wall, there was a bed, neatly made up without a spread, a chest, and something that looked like a French armoire. Off to the right, under the windows, was the clockmaker's bench, strewn with parts and tools.

She swallowed. "I haven't seen a bench like that—"

"I know."

She ran her eyes around the interior once again and saw it, standing on the chest near the bed, the clock from the farmhouse in France.

"It's the clock," she said, "the clock you took apart that day and cleaned."

"You remember it."

"You said it wasn't worth your time to clean it."

He went over to it, wound it, and set it from his watch. "I've put a good many hours into that clock. I keep it there for that reason. One doesn't want to forget."

In the far right-hand corner of the room there was an old European stove. He put some cut wood in it and got it going. When the fire was strong, he opened the front and the heat poured into the room.

Anna took her coat off and dropped it on a chair as he did the same with his woolen jacket. Now, in his suit, he was dressed like Bernie, very proper, a successful man. In her dreams he had always looked the other way, and she had lived with her dreams for so long it was hard to adjust to the reality.

"Do you like it?"

"It's wonderful."

She could see that he was watching her, and she thought that perhaps she should have said more, but she had run out of things to say. Perhaps he had said it all for her: one doesn't want to forget. There was more, much more, but the time wasn't right, and there was something else, something that had to be gotten over first.

"I never had anyone but you," she said.

He came over to her. "I know that."

"It was because I didn't want anyone else."

He enclosed her in his arms. "I hope you still feel that way," he said.

Still feel that way—was there any way else to feel? Touching him she felt it all, the need, the awful need that had nipped at her when the tall, handsome boys laid their uninvited hands on her, the old feeling, the symptom of the lingering illness that had left her sleepless and pushed her this far, the need for him, for his body and for the other part of him that she couldn't quite reach yet.

It was as though the body had its own memory, as if once learned, all the little connections automatically could be made again on cue. Everything that joined them began to move and work, harmonize and excite. She wanted to tell him something but couldn't think what, couldn't divert the energy needed to form the words into grammatical English. She wanted to cry, but it was beyond her capacity to love and cry at the same time.

He slid his jacket off, and she hugged him, her hands feeling his body beneath the fine smoothness of his cotton shirt. He unbuttoned her blouse and felt her breasts, sedately held in place by an expensive, minimizing American brassiere, which he reached around and unhooked with some difficulty, laughing and saying something silly before he got it undone and then inhaling sharply as he touched them, her breasts which he loved and which had shamed her once because they were bigger than her aunt's and her aunt was her idol, larger even than Robin's and Robin was the bellwether of fashion.

He turned off the lamp, took her hand, and led her to the back where the bed was, where the old stove glowed and made it very warm, as perhaps it had for other people in distant places and earlier times, because that's what love was, a great warmth, a fire. The bed was made up like a hospital cot, white sheets and a dark gray blanket, a place for rest, please, please, after so long, rest.

She let the blouse, unbuttoned, slide to the floor, and the bra, unhooked, go the same way, and the rest of it all in one motion, the stockings still attached to the ugly, awkward garters.

She sat at the edge of the bed watching the fire, tensely waiting, until she felt his hands on her back, and the whisper, "Anna," and she lay back on his bed, in the warm nest he made for her with his body. He had barely touched her, scarcely brushed his lean warmth against her when her own impatient, bursting body resolved it for her, moving on its own, surging for relief. It became shrilly noisy for a moment, and then he joined her in her pleasure, her relief, increasing it for her by sharing it with her, her hopeless need satisfied, the illness in remission, perhaps even cured at last.

And then, finally, she was able to rest.

Except for the faint glow somewhere off to the side it was dark, and he was close to her. She was under the blanket, and she had a vague memory of having been covered, of hearing a clank as the door to the stove was closed. She kissed him, whatever part of him was nearest, waiting to be kissed, and he rubbed her shoulder lightly and moved closer, as though his own peculiar hunger had yet to be satisfied, its limits still untested.

"I love you, Anton."

He brushed his hand along the side of her face, and she felt the smear.

"Shouldn't cry when you say that," he said.

"I'm not crying."

"We can talk about it tomorrow."

"No."

He took a deep breath, almost a sigh, and said nothing for a long time while she waited. "My wife is alive." His voice faltered slightly.

"I know. You sent them to England so they would be safe."

"Yes. Yes, I did that." He sat up, moved to the edge of the bed and stayed there.

Something chilled her. She pulled herself up, ready to move if she had to. "What is it?"

"They never got to England," he said in a low voice.

"But—"

"I found her after the war, weeks after. The children—the children were gone. Both of them." His voice changed. "My little girl."

An image projected itself on her mind, the picture of this house as she had stepped into it, one bedroom, one bed against the back wall. It was a home for one grown man who repaired clocks in his spare time. It had not been built for children. There had never been any children here.

"You put them on a train," she said. "You told me that." Trying to persuade him with his own words, his own reasonable facts, that he was wrong, that there was a mistake somewhere and it was merely a logical one, if he could only admit it.

"Yes, I put them on a train."

He sat on the edge of the bed with his head in his hands, taking short rapid breaths that she could hear, count if she wanted to, eins, zwei, drei . . .

"Excuse me," he said, his voice awful. He went into the bathroom and closed the door. She made a move to follow him but stayed; one doesn't go into bathrooms with other people. She heard water run, heard it shut off. He came out drying his face on a towel. He sat down, still holding the towel.

"She had only just given birth, you know."

"I know."

"When she came back, when I found her—she was another person. She still is. I thought—I hoped—she would come out of it, she would be herself again, but it's been years now. I had people come and spend the day with her when I was at work. We can talk to her. It's not entirely hopeless," he said with no sign of hope at all. "The hardest thing was coming

135

home each night and finding that nothing had changed. It was as if she had gone away and left this part of herself behind. She had been very beautiful and very happy. We were young together, you know."

"I remember." She said it as though she had been there herself, as if she had seen it, but it was only that he had told her. She felt a kind of envy at what he had said. She would never be young together with anyone.

"She's not at home any more," he said. "It takes its toll slowly over the years. She coughed blood one day, and we found she had tuberculosis."

Anna made a sound, and he turned to look at her as though he had forgotten she was there, as though he were saying it all to himself so that he could renew the pain.

"She's in a sanatorium in New York State," he said. "It's quite far from New York, but it's a good place. She's doing well. At least, she's doing better. I try to visit her once or twice a month."

"Then she'll be home some day."

"Oh yes, yes, I think she'll be home. And we'll make her comfortable. I want very much for her to feel comfortable, to eat well and take warm baths and know that we care for her."

She moved across the bed and touched him, a hand on his thigh. He looked down at it as though it were a strange animal, but after a minute he covered it with his own hand.

"I always think that if I had gone with them—"

"You can't think about that."

"What else is there to think about? What do you think about when you wake up in the middle of the night?"

(I think about you.)

"I should have been there." He rubbed his neck with the towel. "At least she wouldn't have been alone."

"Why did you stay behind?"

"I worked for the Resistance. I built radios. I put together explosives. I wasn't taken until forty-four, towards the end of forty-four. You were in France in forty-four."

"Yes."

"They were to have stayed with my cousin, my wife's cousin, actually. She had no way to reach me, to tell me they hadn't arrived. I had to find that out when I got there, five years later. I was—it was a terrible shock."

Seeing a number on a man's arm and knowing it was all true.

"I can't think of what to say."

"You don't have to say anything. You know what it's like." He put the towel down. It had served its purpose, gotten him through the worst of it, and he didn't need it any more. "I don't remember much about those first months in England. I wasn't well. It comes upon you afterwards, the irony of having protected one's investments and lost one's children, having lost, essentially, one's wife." He put his arm around her. "Would you like some light?" he asked. "I can put a lamp on."

"I don't care."

He stood up and went to the desk. The shaded bulb made her close her eyes momentarily.

He sat down on the chair at the desk, a couple of feet from the edge of the bed. "I'm still not able to talk about it, even now, almost three years later."

"I'm glad you told me."

"I've made a recovery of sorts. You can see that. I have a good business. I've bought some property—here in Connecticut and some in New York—which will probably make me a rich man some day. I've developed a reputation for my work with clocks." He said it as though it made little difference. "At some point—it wasn't long after the war, we were still in England then—I remembered you."

She smiled. He was sitting sideways on the desk chair, looking as tired and drawn as she felt. "What was there to remember?" she said.

"I came across the chocolate bars and a few of the French francs."

"Oh."

"I had forgotten all about it and it came back, those three days, like a calm time between two storms."

"Yes, it was that."

"I wanted to talk to someone who had lived something with me, and they were all gone but you. I couldn't talk to Ella. That's not all of it, of course. I wanted the rest of it too. You were so young then, I felt rather ashamed. It must have been forty-six by then."

"We had gone, Anton."

"I went to Paris and tried to find you."

"I never lived in Paris."

"You said you did."

"I know." She bit her lips together. "It sounded grander to say Paris than a little village no one had heard of. We lived south of Paris. I suppose you'd call it a suburb nowadays. You took the train there from the Gare Luxembourg." MycousinfromParis. She could hardly blame Robin.

"Well, no matter. They had never heard of you. You weren't in any of their copious records." He turned to the desk, opened a drawer, and withdrew a file folder tied together to hold the contents in. He handed it to her. "So I advertised for you," he said.

She untied the bow and opened the folder. There were two manila folders inside, one of them containing torn out newspaper pages. She turned them, one at a time, looking at the dates, the cities, reading the circled rectangle on each page—French, German, English—all amounting to the same thing: Seeking whereabouts Anna Kleinberger, daughter of Professor Max Kleinberger, born in Germany, possibly Freiburg, 1929.

"1928," she said, looking up from an ad. "I was born in November of 1928. Were there any responses?"

"A few. I have them put away. They didn't know where you were."

She wondered who would have responded, who would have remembered her. There was an ad in the *Frankfurter Allgemeine*, the *Neue Zürcher Zeitung*. There were even a few in the *New York Times*. Did her cousins read the personals? she wondered. And who besides them would have recognized the name Kleinberger? She slid her eye down a column of uncircled newspaper ads, all looking for German soldiers last seen on the eastern front. Most of the ads contained tiny photographs of uniformed soldiers, young in the early forties, healthy and friendly looking, now buried in Siberian snow. The pathos of the situation escaped her.

She pulled the second manila folder out and opened it. It contained a handful of letters. She looked through them briefly. One suggested in French that Anton contact a certain agency that might help him. Another asked for money. She looked up. He had put a bathrobe on and was going for her suitcase. She read through another letter, a German one from a town she had never heard of. "Very honored Mr. Peters!" (the German style of correspondence at its most formal and awesome distance) "I have seen your advertisement in the *Frankfurter Allgemeine* and an acquaintance has sent me a copy from the newspaper in Freiburg. I have some information which may be of interest to you in your search. My brother, Jürgen Preis, helped the daughter of Professor Kleinberger to flee Germany late in 1939. I do not know if the child's name was Anna nor what their exact destination was, but I believe they went to France. I am sorry that I have no further information for you, but my dear brother suffered a tragic and untimely death by his own hand in 1943."

"No." The tissue-thin paper rattled in her hand.

"Anna?"

The letter was signed, "Mrs. Irmgard Mann."

"No," while her eyes ran along the last sentence over and over, "*mein lieber Bruder . . . seiner eignen Hand . . . neunzehnhundertdreiundvierzig*," and tears spurted.

"Jürgen—" She held the letter out as though she wanted it read to her, as if he might offer a better and more favorable translation.

"The letters—" He looked confused, opened a desk drawer, and passed his hand through its emptiness. "I thought the letters—" He took his bathrobe off and wrapped it around her shoulders. "I didn't mean for you to see the letters."

"He didn't have to do that," she said, imploring him to reinterpret, to pronounce a second opinion that would save the patient. "He was German, he was blond, he was so young."

He knelt in front of her. "I didn't want you to know," he said.

"My God, what happens to the people I love?"

They sat at the table in the little kitchen with tea and toast unevenly browned in the gas oven. She wore his bathrobe, the sleeves too long as his jacket sleeves had once been at another table in another place. He had put a lighter robe on, cotton or perhaps silk. She had never known a man who wore silk.

"I seem to be a messenger of bad tidings in your life."

"Not all bad. It wasn't all bad, Anton."

"Will you be able to sleep now?" He went to the kitchen window which overlooked the woods at the back of the house. "It's starting to get light. I usually wake up at daybreak."

"I was going to look for him, this summer when I go to Germany."

"I wrote to his sister with my condolences. I told her what I knew. I hadn't remembered his name until I got her letter."

The little meal satisfied her other hunger, and she finished a second cup of tea. A pile of drenched tissues lay near her on the table. She picked them up, found the kitchen trash, and got rid of them. He came over to her, put his arm around her, leaned down, and kissed her forehead.

She would never leave. She would come here whenever he wanted her. The college acceptances would arrive next week, and surely there would be one from New York or

140

New England. Her marks were good, and her teachers all spoke well of her. She could spend her weekends here, keep the little house clean and stocked with food. She would cook him wonderful meals, and at night she would satisfy every physical desire, every longing, he had. She would make him happy. It was warm and comfortable, and they would take care of each other. There was nothing else she had ever wanted. Light was coming through the window.

He took the robe from her, laid it on a chair with his own, turned out the lamp, and smoothed the blanket. She sat down, drew her legs up and slid them under the covers. He got in beside her, put his head on her chest and held her. With her arms around him, she could feel him tremble, like a tree in a storm or the ground at the edge of a fault. When he was asleep, she turned so that he could rest on the pillow. As the sun rose, she slept.

9

She awoke to broad daylight and hunger. Turning over, she saw that he was gone. There were so many old fears . . .

"I'm over here."

His voice came reassuringly from her left. She sat up and saw him, in a plaid wool shirt, turning away from the bench, a tool in one hand, removing glasses.

She smiled at him.

"I won't leave you," he said.

"I know."

"Are you warm enough? I put more wood on."

"Yes. It's very nice."

He came and sat on the edge of the bed. She slid down again and took his hand.

"Did you have enough of me last night?" he asked.

"How could I have enough of you?"

He kissed the hand that held his, let it go and took his shirt off, his belt, his pants. It was daylight. She had never seen him in daylight, never imagined that the sight of him naked could make her want him. She had never seen him grow and stiffen in anticipation, as she herself tensed with the same anticipation. She had not guessed that responding to him would be deeper and sweeter than responding to her own frustrations and memories as she had last night. She had not dreamed, after yesterday, there could be anything better.

The room had become overly warm, and she pushed the

covers down. Beside her his skin glistened, and she licked his arm to taste the sweat. He laughed and kissed her.

"You know," she said, "this is all the girls ever talk about, especially my cousin's friends, how they think it's done and what they think it feels like, and with all the talk I never knew that people did it in the morning."

"Anna, my darling Anna, you make me feel like a lover, and I've never thought of myself as a lover."

"I've never thought of you as anything else."

He stretched and took a long breath. "I suppose that means one of us doesn't know me very well, doesn't it?"

He made eggs and coffee for her and promised to buy some oranges later. She used his little shower and came out with a towel around her.

"Can I wear these?" she asked, pulling the dungarees out of her suitcase.

"Of course you can. I like those. I see the girls wearing them on weekends where I live."

"My cousin and I wear them with her father's old shirts."

"Take one of mine. Open the second drawer over there."

She hesitated.

"Go on. Take whatever you want."

She opened the drawer. There were several clean, starched shirts arranged in neat piles. "But they're not old."

"I have nothing old."

She looked back at the drawer, took one out, and unfolded it, removing the cardboard.

"And do something else for me. Don't wear anything underneath it."

"But—"

"No one will see you but me. I'd like that."

"All right."

143

It was a smaller shirt than Bernie's. Bernie was a heavier man and his shirts were roomier, but this one felt slick and good. She left an extra button open to make it fit better.

When she was dressed, he touched her through the shirt. "You won't ever do this for anyone else, will you?" he asked.

"I won't ever do anything for anyone else."

He said nothing, as though he knew she had promised too much, as though he regretted having exacted too great a promise.

It was nearly noon, and he said he would go out and buy some things for lunch.

"Are you afraid to stay alone?" he asked.

"Not at all. I like to be alone once in a while. I like the quiet."

"I'll be back soon."

He left in the car, and she took her dresses out of the suitcase, shook them out, and went to the armoire to hang them up. Only his clothes were inside, but there was a closet next to the bathroom. She went there and opened the door. It was practically empty. There were no women's clothes there either. His wife had never stayed here. On the floor stood a pair of heavy brown boots. She picked them up and inspected them. They were a rough suede with a leather cuff that buckled. The heels were worn thin, and there were scuffs on the raw suede. On the rod was a single hanger holding an American army shirt and a matching pair of pants. She closed the closet door and hung her things next to his in the armoire.

One doesn't want to forget.

When he came back it had begun to rain. They sat before the fireplace and ate oranges, the zest of the peel permeating the air.

"You must be at the university now," he said, and she shook her head. "Has something happened?"

"I wouldn't talk when we came here. I wouldn't speak

144

English to anyone except my cousin. Madeleine was beside herself. The cousins did all they could, but the school put me back two years—as if that would make a difference. After that they wouldn't make a change. It was my fault. I could have gone to college with my American cousin." She sounded as regretful as she had come to feel. Only this year had it begun to mean something to her, the waste of those years, the absence of girls her own age to talk to.

"You have a cousin your age?"

"Yes. Her name is Robin. Isn't that lovely? Imagine being named for a bird." She looked at the fire. "Imagine being named for a bird and never being free for one moment in your life." It came to her as she said it—Daddy says, Lenny says. There was Robin living her prescribed life at Smith, home each evening by curfew, falling in love just the way she was supposed to, and here was Anna in a little house in the woods in Connecticut.

"I'm glad it's raining," Anton said. "It will give you a reason to come back, so that we can walk in the woods."

"I would have come back without a reason," she said. "I don't need an excuse."

"No." He collected the orange peels. "But perhaps I do."

After the orange, she didn't want lunch. He took her for a ride in the rain, showing her some large houses set well back from the road and a small town with one of everything at its center. When they came back, she went to get a towel for her hair, and there was the suitcase on the floor near the bed where she had left it.

She stopped, rain water dripping down her neck. "Could you put it away for me?" she asked. "Somewhere where I won't see it?"

"Of course I can. Is something wrong?"

"I don't want to wake up in the morning and see it."

He looked at her for a second, then took the suitcase out of the bedroom. She heard him open the closet near the front

145

door. Then it closed, and he came back. She was still standing where he had left her.

"Are you all right now?"

She shook her head and started to cry. He took her to the
bed, sat her down, and rubbed her head with a towel, then
her neck inside the open collar of his shirt, then her face.
More than anything else now, she was ashamed. She had
felt rather grandly adult when she had met him in Penn
Station; now, suddenly, she was only a child full of a child's
unreasonable fears.

"I should have thought of that," he said.

She shook her head again. The tears were almost gone, but
she couldn't quite catch her breath. "It wasn't even a suitcase
that first time," she said. "It was only Jürgen's rucksack. I
dream sometimes that it will all happen again, that one
morning—"

"It won't happen again."

"I know. But I dream."

"We all dream," he said.

She leaned against him till she felt better. She could hear
his heartbeat, strong and even. He had survived, and she
had survived because of him. He could take care of her, take
care of both of them, Ella and Anna, and neither would take
from the other. After this weekend, how could there be anyone else?

"Come and look at the clock I'm working on."

They went to the bench and he showed it to her—the rec-
tangular gold and glass case, the blank face, its hands off to
one side, the dozens of wheels and screws and springs. It
was a French carriage clock, a very delicate one that repeated
the hour for the waking traveler. It needed hours of work,
hours he didn't have in the city but that he made for himself
out here because it was a special clock and he wanted to be
the one to put it in order.

"I'm going to take you out to dinner," he said when she
had looked at all the pieces, at the piece in the vise that he

146

had been working on this morning while she slept. "You'll have to change, you know." His eyes were smiling at her.

She looked down at the shirt. "I'll change. I'm all right now."

She had a new silk organdy dress, printed all over with little flowers, the sleeves full but light as air, and a wide, shiny black belt. He held an umbrella over her as they went to the car.

The restaurant was small and French.

"Do you like a drink before dinner?" he asked.

She flushed. Robin had told her what to order if she came to a point where she had to, but she had never enjoyed the taste of whiskey. "I only drink wine," she admitted.

"Good. We'll have some wine with dinner. I always heard those girls from France had good taste."

They sat at adjoining sides of a small square table and talked quietly, touching fingers.

"You said last night you were going to Germany. I suppose you want to visit Freiburg."

"Yes."

"Don't you think if a small thing like a suitcase near your bed can make you so unhappy, you should put off Freiburg for another time?"

"There won't be another chance for a long time. The cousins are sending me as a graduation gift from high school. Besides, I won't be alone. Robin is coming with me."

"Your cousin Robin, the unfree bird."

Anna reached into her bag and took out her birthday wallet with its pictures. She spread them out on the table in the space between them—herself, Robin, Madeleine, Bernie and Klara.

"Your aunt is very beautiful," he said.

"Do you think so?" She was pleased. She was thrilled at his assessment.

"Yes, indeed. Look at the cheekbones. What a delicate, aristocratic face she has."

147

"She doesn't photograph well," Anna said. "Not now, at least. I used to wonder about her and my uncle. He was such a joker, that one. I remember his visits when I was little. I never stopped laughing until he left. I think he drove my father crazy, but my mother loved having him there. My mother was such a quiet little person." She paused, regretting the second adjective. "She said she always wondered where he had come from, that he could be her brother. When I met Madeleine, she was different, so drawn and nervous, I couldn't believe this was my uncle's wife. Then, last summer, when she went back to France, I looked through her album of photographs. There were pictures there taken in the thirties when she and Josef were going together." She turned to look at Anton. "All of a sudden, I understood." He touched her hair. "But it will never happen to her again. I think she won't let it happen."

"But you will, won't you?" Anton said.

"What do you mean?"

"I mean—" He picked up the snapshot of her and Robin and touched the image of her face as if it were warm skin. "I mean that when you go to the university in the fall, wherever you decide to go, you will live the kind of full life that I'm sure your cousin lives, only fuller because you're freer."

"I can't talk about next fall."

They had finished their main course, and she felt she couldn't talk about anything. He touched her hand and all the fears, the reasonable and the unreasonable, departed.

Two and a half years before, Klara had taken Anna aside to explain "certain things" to her the night before her first date in America. It was Christmas vacation, and Robin had arranged the date with a boy returning from college.

The explanation was totally new, centering on the desires of married people to have families and then diverting for no obvious reason to a modern, scientific discussion, with diagrams from an anatomy book one of Klara's older children

148

had used in college, of how one's insides worked, how male and female parts came together in certain places and at certain times, for a very specific reason, how under the best of circumstances a new human being might develop. It had taken Anna a minute or two to equate the content of her cousin's little lecture with what she had experienced in a farmhouse in France only half a year earlier. She had started to laugh about it with Robin the next night when they came home from the basketball game and the hamburgers and coffee at a very famous New York restaurant where someone had a late evening radio show, but Robin had not seen the humor in it. Instead, she had begun to talk about boys and what they wanted, especially older boys like those they had been out with that night.

Robin had not understood hunger, any kind of hunger, the hunger that pushed you from the dinner table before dessert, the hunger mysteriously connected to Klara's anatomy lesson.

But Anna understood it now even better than she had then, and he would see, after the summer, after she came back from her trip, that he could not do without her. He would see.

They arranged their departure on Sunday so that she would arrive at home as if she had left Northampton in the afternoon. He wanted to drive her all the way to Long Island but she refused. It was far out of his way. Penn Station was fine. She enjoyed the train, the tunnel with its mystery, the city, the changing landscape. She watched Connecticut slip away as he drove south.

"Did your monthly periods come back?" he asked.

"Yes, the day we got on the ship."

"I haven't been very careful this weekend."

"It's all right." She had given it some thought before Friday. "It's a long way off. It was just over a few days ago." That was not exactly true, but one of Robin's friends had said you really only had to worry on the fourteenth day—

149

and a day before and a day after for good measure. Anna had several days for good measure.

He drove to the side entrance of Penn Station and turned the motor off. She had told him not to park the car. The suitcase wasn't heavy, and it was a place she knew well, safe and full of travelers on a Sunday evening.

"You'll come back?" he asked. "In two weeks?"

"Yes."

"You'll call me."

"Yes."

"I don't have your number, Anna. In case something happens."

She wrote it down with her address, then looked up at him. "I changed my name," she said. She had forgotten to tell him. It had been a long time, and everyone who knew her knew about it.

"You're not Kleinberjay any more?"

"The cousins wanted to adopt me. It was 1946. I know they meant to be kind, but it didn't seem right, to Madeleine I mean. It would have left her so alone. I remembered what you said about families, about the common ancestor. So I told them I didn't want them to do it, and I changed my name to Goldfeder. It was Josef's name."

"And your mother's."

"Yes, and what difference did it make, really, whether I had my father's name or my mother's? It was Madeleine who was important. She was my family more than the others."

"It was a good decision."

It was time to go. From the station she would call Robin to tell her she was safely back.

"Good night," she said.

"I'll wait for your call. Call me whenever you like. Call soon. You know I won't be there next weekend."

"I hope she's feeling better, Anton. I hope she comes home to you soon."

He put his arms around her. "I love you, Anna. I never wanted to tell you that."

What a funny thing to say. She had wanted for so long to tell him.

She got out of the car, taking the suitcase, and hurried to the station, looking back once and waving. He was waiting, watching for her to disappear in the giant building. Inside, she called Robin, then made her way to her special railroad and sat down near a window. An hour later Madeleine was giving her a hug and asking her how the weekend was and had she met anyone nice.

10

She came home from school, and the envelopes were all fat. Robin had told her that fat was good, and thin was bad, and it was the only time in your whole life you would ever be able to say it.

Wellesley turned her down, but she was neither surprised nor disappointed. They had asked her for the "church of her preference" on the little application cards, and she had had a feeling that it was not the place for her. She had written that she had no preference whatever. She had applied only because it was near Boston, and she liked Boston.

But there were other criteria to be considered now, one very special one in particular. Pembroke had accepted her, and Rhode Island was as close to Connecticut as she could hope for. Some of the great Midwestern universities had accepted her too, the places she had most wanted to go to, and she felt an unfamiliar tug of regret as she planned to turn them down. There was something magical about those places: they were so big, they taught everything.

Madeleine came home from teaching and walked into a living room strewn with the contents of all the envelopes. She stopped and gave a little shriek.

"They all accepted you?"

Anna grinned up from the rug, where she was sitting amidst the litter of proof that she had not failed. She had not stopped feeling happy since Sunday. "Most of them," she said. "Almost all."

Madeleine dropped bag and books, knelt on the rug,

picked up one pile of papers, and read the top, neatly type-written letter.

"Dear Miss Goldfeder: We are happy . . ."

She looked up from the letter. "Oh Anna, they would be so proud."

Anna's smile faded. It was rare that Madeleine talked about *them*. It was as though she feared to conjure up their images, as though their images might renew sadness.

"What about those big ones?" she asked, regaining her normal *joie*. "The ones halfway across the world. Did they accept you too?"

"Yes."

"Good. Now you know that they want you, and the others want you, and you have proven you can do anything, but you won't go too far from home, will you?" Her voice pleaded. To Madeleine there was an ocean between New York and everything west of it. The great universities lay somewhere on its distant shore. If Anna chose one of them, she would never return.

"I was thinking," Anna said carefully, "of going to Pem-broke. It's not very far. I could come home some weekends, and it's a very good school."

"Yes." Madeleine wrinkled her forehead. "Yes, I remember. Klara's friend's daughter goes there, the pretty red-head?"

"That's right."

"Yes, that's a good choice, Anna. You leave the distant places for later, when you have a husband. Let him take you. Now you stay close to home." Her face was glowing. "I must call Richard. Have you told Klara yet?" She raised herself nimbly off the floor.

"No. I've been looking over—"

"We must tell them. I must call my friend Gladys." She clapped her hands together. "A party. We must have a party tonight. Richard will bring champagne."

Anna started to laugh. "I think you've gone crazy," she said.

153

Madeleine was already in the kitchen, but she came back. "I think this is the happiest day of my life," she said.

They poured into the apartment after dinner—Richard and Gladys, Klara and Bernie, two of the neighbors, and somebody's cat, which slipped in the open door and refused to leave. Richard brought champagne, and Bernie sent out for more when he saw how many people had arrived. Klara brought cold cuts, although everyone assured her they had already eaten. Still, when the evening was over, nothing was left but a few pieces of rye bread.

It was the second time the cousins had met Richard, and Bernie spent a great deal of time off in a corner talking to him. Anna had seen Bernie do that only once before, between semesters when Robin brought Lenny home. It had made Anna think that perhaps Lenny was more than another SOMEBODY, although at the time Robin had known him scarcely a month. Now it made Anna wonder again, whether perhaps Madeleine were more serious about Richard than she admitted, whether it was all appearances, the coolness, the seeming lack of caring.

Before the evening had ended, there was another, more startling, discovery. In a snatch of French conversation between her aunt and Richard, Anna distinctly caught the little pronoun *tu*. She almost stopped breathing. It had been many years—late forty-four or early forty-five—since her old confidante Nicole had told her the secret. A grown man and woman would begin to *tutoyer* one another after they had done *it*. The apartment had been empty this past weekend and perhaps . . . It was possible. There were the pictures in the album of a young and passionate woman. Her aunt was not old and she was certainly attractive.

When they had all gone, and the dishes and glasses had been put away, Anna went to Madeleine's room and stood at the still open door.

"It was lovely," she said. "It was as if I had graduated."

"That will be the next one," Madeleine said, brushing her hair. Her pale face was still slightly pink from the evening

154

and the excitement. "In June, just before you and Robin leave. Then, in a few years, an engagement party, and later a wedding, and then you will give me grandchildren."

"Grandchildren!"

"Well, godchildren then."

"Madeleine, you'll have your own children."

"Never." She put the brush down, twisted, and unzipped the zipper on the back of her dress but went no further. She never undressed before Anna. "If I couldn't have Josef's child, how could I have someone else's?" As if that single miscarriage in 1939 or 1940 had been a death knell for her reproductive system. "Besides, I don't want anyone else's child."

Anna walked into the room and looked at the photograph on the dresser, her uncle peering into the motor of the old car, his skin glistening. Inside her, sensual echoes of recent love trilled in little chambers.

"Do they have a cure for tuberculosis?" she asked offhandedly.

"Why? Is something the matter? Do you have a cough?" Madeleine's face became very severe.

"No, we are talking about it in school."

"I don't think so." She relaxed. "They go away where the weather is dry, and they rest. Rest is everything. A friend of my mother's had it. She went somewhere high in the mountains."

"But they get better."

"Yes, if it's not too late, if they're not too old. My mother's friend got better. It was before the war. She's home now."

"Is thirty-five old?"

Madeleine laughed. "I hope not."

"Is Richard going back when the year is over?" She felt she could come back to her main point now that she had successfully diverted from it.

"How should I know?" Madeleine shrugged and sat on the bed. "I'm not his keeper."

"But you're his friend."

155

"Yes, I suppose I'm his friend." Madeleine glanced at the clock on her night table. "Look at the time! You, my little one, are still a pupil in school, and if you don't go to sleep in five minutes, it won't be worth your while closing your eyes." She stood up and gave Anna a kiss on the cheek.

"Thank you for the party," Anna said.

"Thank yourself. Now go!"

She called Robin, who was thrilled at all the acceptances but a little disappointed that Anna had elected not to go to Smith. But it had never been Anna's desire to go where her cousin was. As long as they could not start together, she felt she wanted to do something completely on her own.

She reached Anton on Thursday and told him the news.

"You see, it was worth the extra years," he said. "In the end there was no waste."

"My aunt is very happy. I think she was worried and didn't tell me."

"There will be nothing to worry about after this. You'll do very well in your studies. Have you decided where you'll go?"

"Almost. The cousins want to talk to me about it this weekend."

"Can I meet you for dinner some evening and give you my opinion too?"

"I couldn't get away in the evening, Anton."

"Perhaps you could come in after school tomorrow. I could meet you at the station, about four-thirty. We can have a glass of wine together."

It sounded like something she might do in Paris, at a little café near the Gare Luxembourg. "Yes, I'll be there."

She had to carry two schoolbooks with her, and Madeleine wanted to know why she wore stockings to school. Was she meeting someone special in the library after school?

It was the start of the Friday evening rush when she arrived, but he was there. He kissed her, and they went to a

156

dark bar in the station where she was the only woman. The waiter seemed to think there was something strange about two glasses of wine, but he brought them and set them down on little napkins.

"It's nice to see you like this," he said. "Even for a little while."

"I thought you'd be on your way to see your wife."

"No, I'll open the shop in the morning and then leave. It's a long drive. I won't be there till afternoon."

"I brought something for you to give her."

"For my wife?"

"Yes." She took a small package from her bag. "It's perfume. My aunt brought it from Paris last summer, but I never opened it. I was saving it for something special, but I can get more in July." He was looking at the package, the rather plain wrapping of the store in Paris. "I think she'll like it, don't you? It's very good. Madeleine only buys the best ones. It really makes you feel better to use good perfume."

"Yes, I'm sure it does." He took the package. "That's very kind of you. I know she'll like it. She always used good perfume. I think she may have neglected to take some with her." He was speaking very slowly, as though reflecting on something.

Anna sipped her wine. At the bar a group of men laughed loudly.

"I think I've forgotten what I wanted to say about your college." He pulled his watch out of its little pocket, opened it, closed it, and put it away. "Are you planning to go far away?"

"No."

He put his hand on her shoulder. It was a tiny table, and they were quite close. "And your aunt is happy?"

"Yes. She was afraid I'd go to the Midwest, but I don't want to any more."

"Will staying close spoil your plans?"

"No." She looked away. "Will it spoil yours?"

He shook his head. He seemed to have become very

157

depressed. Somehow the perfume had saddened him. "Tell me about your trip," he said. "You and your cousin. When will you leave?"

"June 16. We're sailing on a little student ship. It's Dutch. We'll have a room for four."

"It should be a fine summer."

"What's the matter?"

He looked at his watch again. "Are you in a hurry? Do you have time for a walk?"

"I have lots of time. I just got here."

He stood up and helped her on with her coat. "Let's go outside." He pulled her hand through his arm and kissed the hand. "I wanted to tell you to go far away to college. I thought about it for a long time last night. I'm glad you came in today. It was my daughter's birthday yesterday. She would have been ten."

They went through the door into the brisk April evening. Their lives would always be full of sentences with unfinished promises: he would have, she would have. They would have been so proud.

"Does your wife remember?"

"She writes it down on little pieces of paper. I find them sometimes in the apartment. Are you cold?"

"No, it's very nice."

There was a hotel across the street. She had always wondered about people who went into hotels, made love on strange beds, and then checked out. Suddenly she wished he would suggest it, just so she could be close to him, so she could hold him. Of course he had thought about her college for a long time last night; he had not slept. It had been his daughter's birthday.

"I feel the wine in my legs," she said.

"In your legs?"

"Yes. I'm not sure they're both there."

"Well, you're here. I'm glad you're here. Ella will like the perfume, Anna. It was very thoughtful of you."

At the corner he turned so that they were headed back toward the station.

"I don't want your aunt to worry," he said.

"My aunt has nothing to worry about. I'm always on time, and she has a good man who loves her."

"Is that all it takes?"

"I don't know." She smiled at him.

He bent and kissed her lips. "I hope so," he said. "Let me know someday." He stopped at the line at the ticket window.

"I have my ticket back."

"Then let me pay for it."

"No."

"But I invited you."

"Please don't give me money."

He brought his hand, empty, from his jacket pocket. "All right."

He left her at the train, and she rode back with all the men in their perfect suits and white shirts. Did they wear wool shirts over the weekend and make love to their wives on Saturday morning? she wondered. She would go to Pembroke and she would have nothing to worry about. She would be on time and she had a good man who loved her.

The cousins were very pleased with the Pembroke decision. They had never liked the idea of a large university with ten thousand or more students. It was not a place for a girl like Anna. After dinner on Sunday at Klara's, Bernie wrote a check, and Anna was pleased with their acceptance.

Robin was dismayed at the Tuesday evening call. "Again?" she asked in disbelief. "Anna, where are you going?"

"To the same place. It's just as safe and just as quiet as the last time."

159

"God, what are you getting yourself into? What am I getting myself into?"

"Nothing. I promise you."

"Please be careful."

"I will. How is Lenny?"

"Wonderful. I think I'm in love. I think I really am this time." Robin's voice contained a note of sadness. It was funny about love. In the best of circumstances, it made even Robin sad.

She met him on Friday and they drove north.

"My aunt thinks I have a new boyfriend in Massachusetts," she told him.

"Does she approve of that?"

"Yes. If my cousin introduced us, it's respectable. She thinks all my cousins have good taste."

"What does Robin think?"

"She's worried, but she won't tell anyone. She's very loyal."

"Ella was very pleased with the perfume. You were right that it would make her feel better. I never thought about it. I only thought about books and magazines and things to eat."

"Madeleine says you can't feel like a woman without a few essentials. Most of her essentials are very luxurious."

"Shall we stop to eat on the way—speaking of essentials?"

"No."

"You may be sorry later."

"I won't be sorry." He had taken her hand.

"Have you gotten your period yet?"

"It isn't due till next week, Wednesday or Thursday. It's not very regular."

He glanced at her. "You must call me when it comes."

"Robin calls it the curse."

"When it comes, it's more of a blessing."

The blessing was seeing him. The blessing was feeling the room warm up to her own accumulated warmth. The blessing was beginning to believe that this was hers—this man and this place and these woods and this feeling. Being here was a promise completed. She would never have to think—I would have or we would have when she thought of Anton. It was here and it was true and it belonged to her.

He had brought a carton of food, and after love he made her eat. It was a light, uncooked supper. In the cupboards there were cans of salmon and sardines and herrings. In the refrigerator were cans of juices, especially pineapple; he had never tasted pineapple until he came to America. Neither, of course, had she. In the cabinets on the floor there were bottles of wine. They ate salmon and olives and fresh celery and drank white wine. Years from now she would think that that was the way to love, to satisfy one hunger and then another, to take care of the most essential first, to wash it down with white wine.

"Are you thinking sad thoughts?"

She looked up. Robin always said you could tell what Anna thought by watching her face. She nodded.

He touched her arm across the table, pushing his fingers up the loose sleeve of his robe, which she was wearing. "Whatever happens—"

"Don't say that, please. Don't say 'whatever happens.' "

"We're very lucky, Anna, you and I. We could have gone through a whole lifetime in the same world and missed each other, not once but twice."

She started to cry, and he came around and sat next to her, letting her put her head against him and feel, for a little while, secure.

He was working on the French carriage clock when she awoke the next morning, and she watched him for a while before he knew she was up. Finally, he glanced her way and put his tool down.

"I want to show you the woods today," he said.

She sat up. "When will you finish the clock?"

"Not till fall. When you leave for Europe, I'll get down to business."

161

She got out of bed, washed, and dressed. He had put her suitcase away as soon as she had unpacked it last night. The room had lost its only resemblance to a hotel and become a place to stay. She wanted to stay forever.

After breakfast they went for a long walk, more of a tramp, through a forest of trees almost ready to leaf out. Next weekend it would be May. The smell of spring was all around them.

"I made an excellent purchase this week," he said.

"For your shop?"

"Yes, from an estate. They must have been lazy fellows. Whenever a clock stopped, they put it in the cupboard and bought a new one. Some of them only need a good cleaning. They'll fetch a good price when we're finished with them. The heirs were happy to get rid of them."

"If I had anything of my mother's I would never get rid of it."

"But others do. Many others."

It was nearly two when they reached the house.

"Is that a telephone?" Anna asked as they approached the door.

But he was already on his way inside and listening intently when she arrived. It had been there all along, a telephone at one end of the kitchen counter, thrust away in a corner. He said "Yes" several times and "Could you say that again?" once and "I understand." He was pale when he hung up, and he looked at his watch before he spoke.

"Ella has wandered off," he said. "She walks a great deal—they all do—but she didn't come back for lunch, and it's two now. Someone saw her at eleven, and no one's seen her since. There are woods all around, and she may have become confused. I'll have to go. I'll take you to the train first."

He had begun to move, to the closet, to the chest.

"I can't go back today. I'm not expected until tomorrow night. I can stay here."

162

He looked up from the bag he was rapidly packing. "I can't leave you here alone, Anna."

"I'll be all right. You can call me here when you've found her." She wanted to sound certain. If they just looked hard enough, they would find her, but they would have to hurry. It was still April, and the nights were cold. It could rain at almost any time. In the mountains, there was still snow.

"We have to find her before tonight," he said as though Anna had spoken aloud. "I can't get there until tonight." He stopped packing, found his wallet, and took two bills out. "I'll give you the number of the taxi. They can take you to the station. This is the train schedule. You needn't go to the nearest station; they'll take you anywhere." He spoke rapidly, an instructor briefing his troops.

"It's too much." They were twenties.

He was opening a map of Connecticut. He looked up. "Please take it."

She tucked it in the pocket of her pants. He studied the map carefully, then folded it with the inside facing out, uncertain lines in red and blue curving this way and that along the surface.

"You're sure," he said.

"Yes."

He snapped the bag shut, carried it to the front door, took the heavy jacket out of the closet. "There's a key where the spoons are. Lock the door and take it with you. Take care of yourself."

"I'll be fine."

"I'll call in the morning."

She stood at the door and watched him go, down the long drive through the trees. Before he reached the road, she could no longer see him, but she heard, in the distance, the car turn onto the road and accelerate.

She went back inside and locked the door. It wasn't even two-thirty yet. She washed the dishes and the sink and cleaned up the kitchen, then took some paper towels and walked around dusting. A woman alone in the woods, a sick woman, a woman whose only memories could break your heart, a woman whom Anton loved, who had given him two lost children.

She kept herself occupied through the afternoon, cleaning, tending the fire, looking at the parts of the French clock but not touching them. She pulled open a drawer in his chest so that she could dust the edges and found his shirts, all clean and pressed and stacked. She lifted one out and smelled it, holding it to her face, feeling his nearness in his absence. Another drawer was filled with underwear and pajamas. The pajamas were a puzzle and then a shock. She had modeled her whole concept of physical love on her experience in the farmhouse, the warmth of his body, the feel of his skin, equating the joy of physical union with the nakedness of the joining bodies. For the first time it dawned on her that his nakedness those nights had been a chance accident, all his clothes washed and on the line, her model built on a fluke, on a false premise. She wanted to know more about him, to ask him forbidden questions, questions about Ella, Ella who was lost in the woods.

She went to her bag and found the ten he had given her on that day in March and which she had never spent. She pushed it in the drawer, sliding it down along the front. He would find it some day and think he had left it there as a reserve. Madeleine did it all the time. Even if the banks closed, if the checks failed to come, if the government collapsed, there would be money for food. Madeleine had learned all of life's lessons well.

There were still the twenties. He kept giving her money and not understanding why she could not accept it. The image was as clear as if it were still before her, the pile of French banknotes on the table, the half bar of soap she would never deliver to her parents. He perceived it as a debt, had said as much at the taxi that first day in New York, but if it were a debt she didn't want the books closed. She

164

wanted them open, wanted him always to owe her another sou so that he would need to see her again.

She would leave the twenties in the desk, in the drawer with the folders. She took them out and read through the newspaper clippings again. There was something so desolate about them, a man looking for a girl, mothers looking for sons, even German sons. A man looking for a woman lost in the woods. She took out the letter from Jürgen's sister. It was Jürgen they needed now. He knew the woods, he was afraid of nothing, not the border guards or the snow. He was strong and sure, and he could carry you over the mountains and make you safe.

Surely it wasn't true. Of all the people she had known as a child, only Jürgen had had a bright future. He could have survived anything. He would be almost as old as Anton now.

In another drawer there was another folder. The letters inside came from across Europe, with a few from America. Hesitantly, she opened one and read it, then another, then all that were written in one of her languages. One group expressed condolences on the loss of his children and the illness of his wife. Another group thanked him for gifts of money. Her eyes widened as she read the signatures. The names were known to her. They had been discussed heatedly by Robin's parents and friends. They were the names of terrorists, Nazi seekers, killers, people for whom law had a new meaning or no meaning at all. Even now some of them were being sought in America and in England. A man could live simply in a little house in Connecticut and quietly pay for the deaths of those who had murdered his family.

"Your generous gift has allowed us to continue our work." "Thank you for permitting us to call upon you once again." "I have seen our friend and he has given me your kind and generous remembrance."

It was six, and she had not eaten since breakfast. In the refrigerator were steaks he had brought in the car. She broiled one and ate it, missing his company. He would have

165

opened wine. He would have touched her breasts under the shirt. She would have felt the quiver of his body when he held her.

She put the key in her pocket and went outside. It was already becoming chilly. Ella would have a shawl or a sweater or a coat, but Anna sat in front of the door with only the shirt on, Anton's shirt. She wanted to feel what Ella was feeling, the onset of night in the woods.

It became very cold but she didn't move, just huddled within herself for warmth. To whom would she pray for Ella's life? She had told Wellesley she had no preference, and Wellesley had rejected her. It was funny that when she thought of God, which was not very often, it was not in terms of a Catholic God or a Jewish God but as a German, French, or American God. It was the German one who had abandoned them all, the French one to whom she had always addressed her prayers. She had never asked the American God for anything, perhaps because he was the one who had given her everything—hot water, all those acceptances to college, maybe even Anton.

"You can't let her die," she said out loud in English, trying to keep herself from trembling, and she realized she had already made a mistake. She was ordering him around. Madeleine would be furious. One asked; one didn't tell. "Please don't let her die," she said to the dark woods. "You've read those letters in his desk. She's lost everything, even her husband because she can't be a wife to him any more. Don't let this happen to her. Let them find her. Please."

It was suddenly as cold as winter. It was dark now too, the only light coming from the kitchen behind her, an oblong piece of ground illuminated near her feet. She had never imagined it could be this cold a week before May. But she would stay and bear it. When she gave up, when she went inside to be warm, it would be the end. It would be the end of Ella.

Nearby, she became aware of sounds, night sounds, rus-

166

tlings, whinings. She had not thought about animals, about the natural dangers of the forest. Only this morning Anton had told her that there were raccoons in these woods, raccoons with black faces and dangerous teeth. What else might there be, what predators lusting for human blood?

It was past nine, and she had never been so cold in her life, not even those nights long ago in Switzerland or in France when the fire went out. Her body was shaking with cold, and she wanted desperately to go inside, to stand before the wood-burning stove and ingest its heat, but something told her it all depended on her staying here. If she could bear this cold, if she could take it on her shoulders, Ella would live.

The intense complications of her life seemed suddenly overwhelming and endless. She should have been born Robin. Life was so easy when you were Robin. It ran along an even line. The ups were lower and the downs were higher, Lenny always said, and the events of your life followed a reasonable pattern: you were pinned, you were engaged, you were married. Your mother and father were always there.

The rustling was closer. Could you tell the difference between man and animal, and which was more dangerous?

"Stay away," she said to the noises in the woods. And suddenly she knew who was making the sounds. "Listen," she said to the American God lurking in the forest in his top hat and red, white, and blue shirt, "you can't punish him this way. He doesn't deserve this. Whatever he's done, he loves her."

The rustling stopped. It was after eleven. She should have put her coat on but she was afraid to go in now, afraid she might break the bargain.

Behind her, the phone rang shrilly. She leaped up and ran inside.

"Hello?" It was so warm. Heat from the bedroom flowed into the kitchen and through her.

167

"Anna—are you all right?"

"What happened?" She could hear the near hysteria in her voice. "Did you find her?"

"Yes, it's all right. Just before I got here. She lost her way, but she's all right."

"Oh thank God." She started to cry, something beyond anything that had ever happened to her, torrents of tears. There was no sound from the other end of the line, but she knew that he could hear. She rubbed the sleeve of his shirt across her eyes, blotting the tears.

"You shouldn't have stayed alone," his voice said from far away.

"I'm O.K. I was just—"

"I know. Make yourself some tea, Anna darling, and go to sleep. I didn't think you would still be up. I just wanted to hear your voice. I haven't slept yet. Will you go to sleep now?"

"Yes."

"It's very empty here without you. Is the fire still burning?"

"Yes. Please don't worry."

"Call me next week."

"I promise."

She hung up. He wouldn't sleep tonight. He was alone. It would be a bad night. I love you, she said in her head. I love you more than I have ever loved you before.

She opened the front door, and the cold of the forest blew into the kitchen. "Thank you," she said, and closed the door again. Then she turned off the light and went to bed.

11

Her period came with suddenness and no pain on Sunday evening, several days early. On Monday afternoon she called his number.

"It came," she told him when he answered. "My blessing."

He laughed. "It's good to hear from you."

"I thought I was dying. It's the first time it came without any pain. I didn't know what it was."

"It means I'm good for you."

"I knew that," she said. "I knew that a long time ago."

"Now the rest of you knows it."

"How is she, Anton?"

"She's all right. I'm sorry you were so worried. She lost her way and sat down to rest. They found her about a mile from her cottage. A state policeman found her and brought her back. They're keeping her in the main building for a day or two, and then they're making a new arrangement. There's an older woman patient there who speaks German. They're going to put Ella in her cottage. I think that will make everything much easier."

"I hope so."

"Will I see you again in two weeks?"

"Yes."

"We'll have to be very careful."

"I know."

What she didn't know was how one went about being care-

ful. She knew about the things the boys in high school carried in their wallets, creating an oval mark in the leather to
impress the girls, but Robin always said that most of the
little rubber objects either rotted or fell away to dust. She
didn't know whether they worked or not, but they didn't
appeal to her. She stopped in at drugstores after school and
walked up and down aisles of toothpaste and shampoo and
nail polish, looking for a clue to something that would let
her "be careful."

But looking failed to turn anything up. Either nothing
existed or it was kept well hidden.

On Sunday there was a call from Robin.

"I have to talk to you," her cousin said in a strained
voice.

"Yes, what is it?"

"Not over the phone. I have to sit down and talk to
you."

"What's the matter? Are you in some kind of trouble?"

"No. Well, not exactly. Anna, listen, I'll pick you up at the
usual time on Friday night."

"Not this Friday?"

"Yes, it has to be. Just a minute." There were muffled
sounds in the background.

"Is something the matter with Lenny?" Anna asked.

Robin exhaled. "Listen, we'll talk about it when you get
here."

"I'll just stay Friday night."

There was a moment of absolute silence. "You're not
going to that place again, are you?"

"Yes."

"Oh God." It was almost a wail.

"I'll see you Friday night," Anna said.

She consulted the train schedule and called Anton. He
told her where he would meet her on Saturday.

"Do you think you'd like to spend the weekend with your
cousin?" he asked.

170

"No. I'd never be able to make an excuse two weekends in a row."

"Then I'll see you Saturday."

She was packing Thursday evening when Madeleine knocked on the open door and came in.

"I have some news for you," she said with a little smile.

Anna turned away from the open suitcase.

"It's about my friend Richard."

Anna held her breath. All the weekends alone, the long talk with Bernie.

"He's planning to stay another year."

"That's wonderful, Madeleine."

"I think it's very nice too. You're right, he is a good friend."

"Give him a kiss for me this weekend."

Madeleine slapped her hand playfully. "You're a fresh girl. How could you have grown up in my house? Go back to your packing for your mysterious young man in Massachusetts."

Robin met her, and they went back to the dorm, where she would sleep in the bed vacated by Robin's absent roommate. It was always late when Anna arrived and usually, in the past, they sat up past midnight exchanging gossip.

Robin closed the door and sat down on her bed, pulling off her shoes.

"What's it about, Robin?" She had gone through everything she could think of in the preceding week, from the ridiculous—that Lenny had left Robin for someone else—to the impossible—that Robin was pregnant with his child.

"It's about me and Lenny and you, and it's just a mess."

"I don't understand."

"Oh God, here goes. Lenny says I can't go to Europe this summer."

"Lenny says—" She was stunned. She said it over in her head: Lenny says you can't go to Europe this summer. There was no sense in it. "But why?"

171

"Because we're in love." Robin looked miserable about it. "We're going to get engaged next spring."

"That's wonderful, Robin."

"But he says it just wouldn't be right for me to go away for the whole summer. He says we'll go when we're married. He says he has to see me this summer. I'm so crazy about him, Anna."

"I see. Have you told your parents?"

"I haven't told a soul."

"Do you think—do you think they'll let me go alone?"

"Would you want to go alone? Wouldn't you be afraid?"

Anna smiled. "I'm afraid of everything, Robin, but I do it anyway. How else could I find out that there's nothing to be afraid of?"

Robin blinked and shook her head. "Sometimes I envy you. I don't know why, you've had such a crazy life, but sometimes I really envy you."

He was standing on the platform when the train arrived, his eyes searching the incoming train. It was like the first time she saw him, almost exactly three years before, through the kitchen window as he stood on the road, privy to the best and the worst news of her life. The train slowed, and she kept her eyes on him, saw him smile as he caught sight of her and begin to walk in the direction of her car. He would always be there, waiting when her train pulled in. He had to be. She could no longer imagine a station at which he was not waiting for her.

Kisses were so sweet when they were hello.

"Tell me about your cousin's problem."

"Lenny won't let her go to Europe this summer." She was more upset about it than she had realized, than she had let on during her visit.

"Ah. He's clipped her wings."

"Mine too, I'm afraid."

"Let's go to the car, and we'll talk about it."

172

It was afternoon and sunny, the kind of May day they had had in France a hundred years ago.

"It's three years," he said when they were driving.

"I know. I watched you from the train window the way I watched you that day from the kitchen window."

"I didn't know you'd seen me coming."

"I watched everything you did. I was afraid of you. I thought you were a deserter."

"I suppose I was in a way. We both were."

"You have no idea how much I looked forward to this summer," she said with anguish. "At first I thought I'd find you there. Now I just want to see it all before it starts to change. I want to see it while it matches the pictures in my head."

"You're talking about Freiburg."

The little house, the flowers in the window boxes. The window on the top floor where the books lay open, the clocks dismembered.

"I really wanted Robin with me when I went to Freiburg. She would understand. She's family."

He put his hand on her thigh. "Perhaps I can meet you there for a day or two."

"In Germany?"

"I was planning a business trip in September. I might manage to leave a little early. Would you like that?"

"You know I would."

"Let me look at my calendar when I get to the house."

They lay in the sun in a clearing in the woods where, next summer, he planned to have a little garden. It was hot, and she had opened the shirt into which she had changed. Next summer Ella would sit here and rest in the newly planted garden. Ella would get better here.

"I wish you would make love to me here," she said. Her eyes were closed, but she lay where she could touch him. "I wish you would make love to me in every beautiful place in the world."

173

"We have to be careful this weekend."

"I know."

"I have something back at the house. I'll show it to you later. We can come out here tomorrow."

"Is that what happens to people? Do they start being careful, and then everything is different?"

"Not everyone has to be careful all the time."

But we do. "Wouldn't you like to have another child?"

Beside her, his body stretched, tightened, and relaxed. "Shouldn't we talk about something else?"

"I want to know everything about you. There's so much to know about you, and so little to know about me."

"That's not true. Why do you say that?"

"They can give me a summer or take it away, and there's nothing I can do about it. It's like everything else. They pack my suitcase and they send me over the mountain."

"It won't always be that way."

"You didn't tell me not to go."

"I won't ever tell you, Anna darling. I won't send you over a mountain, and I won't tell you not to go yourself. I just ask you, when you go, not to hurt yourself on the way."

"Will Ella have more children?"

"No." A very rapid, quiet answer.

"Do you—when she's home—do you still—?"

"Not any more. Not since the war."

"Will I see you after the summer?" She opened her eyes and rolled on her side to face him.

"I don't know." He flung an arm over her. The tips of his fingers wanted her. His bare toes wanted her. "We'll have to see. You have a whole new life starting in the fall."

"No."

"New friends, young men."

She could feel him through his pants. It was two weeks since the last time. He unzipped them.

"Who will I talk to if I don't have you, Anton? Who will you talk to?"

174

"You'll always have me to talk to. You have my number. Whatever happens—"

She pressed her fingers against his lips. "Do you promise that? That we'll always have each other to talk to?"

"I promise."

She wriggled down to where his zipper was open, and now his belt, and kissed him softly. He tensed and leaned toward her.

"Do that for me, Anna," he said.

For a moment she wasn't sure what he wanted. Then she opened her mouth and experimented gingerly with her tongue, with her lips. It was easy to see what he enjoyed, easy to feel what he wanted more of. She lay with her arms upon him, feeling all the hard bones and muscles of his body tense and move beneath her. It ended quickly, much more quickly than she would ever have imagined, a burst of life-making fluid spilling harmlessly, safely. So precious, and all such a waste.

They went out to dinner and came back, and the house was chilly, even though it was May. He started a fire in the bedroom stove to take the chill from the air. From his briefcase he took a bag from a pharmacy in Manhattan and gave it to her.

Inside was a a long, slender box. She sat on the bed and opened it, slid its contents out, looked at the items distastefully and then up at him. A tube and a long, clear plastic gadget with a gold stem inside ending in a black tip.

"There are other things," he said, "but you'd have to see a doctor."

She unscrewed the tube, squeezed it gently, touched its contents, and smelled it. He was laughing.

"It was easier when I was a little girl and didn't get my period. I begin to see why all of Robin's friends are virgins."

"There's an alternative," he said. "If you prefer, I can use one of these."

Through the wrapper she could feel the little ring. "I'd

175

rather—I'll try this. I wish it were all less complicated."

It made her nervous, knowing the gooey stuff was there, knowing it had to be and why, knowing there were more effective things that she was unable to acquire without a visit to a doctor, which was out of the question. The nervousness spoiled it for her. It was the first time, and it came as an unwelcome revelation. She had trusted her body's ability to be satisfied, having faith that like blinking and swallowing, these more mysterious mechanisms were also automatic reflexes. That they might not always respond in the desired way was achingly disappointing. What was more disappointing was that he knew. It hurt her to think that in some way he might feel responsible.

"You were my only virgin," he said, rubbing her shoulder, her arm.

"I don't believe it. Ella was a virgin."

"I don't think so. She had a—a friend when I met her, a handsome fellow in his late twenties."

"She must have been very beautiful."

His hand continued to move along her skin, but he said nothing. After a few minutes, he said, "Let me wash you the way I did that time."

They went into the bathroom, stood on the mat, and shared the soap, and when she was wet and slick and her disappointment almost gone, something deep and anguished inside her wept for Ella.

She had come to think of Ella as a part of the general family, a young aunt or her own older sister, someone warm and beautiful and loving, someone hurt as only those years could hurt people, someone around whom the family members would gather to give comfort and sustenance. In some inexplicable way she believed that her own well-being, her happiness, was woven in with Ella's as surely as Anton's was. Having experienced the intense cold of that Connecticut night two weeks ago, she worried that they would not look after Ella properly, that they would let her get away

176

again, that they missed the essence of Ella's sickness. She wondered if it was possible that Ella had been looking for something in those woods in upstate New York, or for some- one—for the husband she had married in the thirties when they had been so young, or for the children she had borne him.

Madeleine picked her up at the station and kissed her. Her face had the drawn look that indicated the news had come down from the north.

"You've heard from Robin?" Anna asked.

"She called Klara a couple of hours ago. She said you were on your way back, and she wanted us to know."

"What do you think?"

"I think she's young and foolish, and she'll have a million boyfriends after this one, and she should go with you this summer."

"I think you're wrong. I think she's very serious about Lenny. He's very nice, Madeleine. He's very kind to her. He's not just another boyfriend."

Madeleine parked the car, and they went upstairs. It was funny that she failed to notice the change in her niece, Madeleine who could spot an irregular hem at a distance of half a block or detect the lack of a delicate herb in a stew. She found nothing remarkable about Anna, whose pores were filled with the scent of Anton, her mouth with his taste, her small, still untested cavity with his seed.

"It's still a mistake," Madeleine said, closing the door and pausing to look a second longer than usual at a smiling Josef.

"What I meant was, do you think I can still go?"

"You want to go alone." She said it as a little declaration of defeat. There was no surprise at all in her voice.

"I just want to go. Robin will never go with me now. You know I can take care of myself." She wanted to say, I did it once before, but she couldn't talk about that. After Anna had returned, Madeleine had never mentioned the time that she had been gone. It was as if those days had dropped out of the calendar, as if they had died with Josef.

"It's too late tonight to talk about it. You have school tomorrow. We're having dinner with Klara and Bernie tomorrow night. It will all be arranged then."

Klara was exceptionally cheerful at dinner. She could talk about hundreds of things and manage to be interesting. There was always a little experience or encounter that had just happened to her that she could relate, captivating her listeners. Bernie teased her about the experiences. He said she should wear a bell so that people would be warned, but it was clear that he enjoyed listening and approved of the behavior that produced the delightful anecdotes.

They waited till dessert to broach the problem. Klara had bought a cake at the local bakery—always a surprise and disappointment to Madeleine, who bought nothing but bread and rolls, baking everything else.

"Well, our Robin has made a mess of things," Bernie began.

"I understand how she feels," Anna said. She was sure they had been angry with her over the phone.

"They hardly know each other," Klara complained. "She's much too young to promise herself to anyone. She won't be twenty till next year. Twenty is time enough." Klara had been twenty when she had "promised herself."

"Let's not go through all that again," Bernie said. "The question is Anna, not Robin."

Anna looked quickly at Bernie and then down to her half-eaten chocolate cake. She knew she would cry if they didn't let her go, and she had never cried in front of the cousins. Robin often screamed at her mother and wept to her father, leaving Madeleine to wonder at American upbringing. More than anything else, Anna did not want to disgrace her aunt.

"I gave it a lot of thought last night," Bernie went on. "I know how much you want this trip and I think I understand

178

why. Madeleine," he turned to his right, "before I make a final decision, how do you feel about this?"

Madeleine caught her eye fleetingly and looked back at Bernie. Her face was composed. She was prepared for the question and prepared with an answer.

"Anna is very responsible. She goes into New York alone. She goes to visit Robin alone. She stayed alone last summer, and when I came back the house was cleaner than I had left it. She speaks all the languages. If you agree that she can go, I will certainly not worry."

It was clear from Madeleine's face that it was a lie, that she would worry every day of the summer, but it was clear too that she would not be the one to say no.

Klara said, "Oh my," and Bernie looked at her sharply.

"I feel the same way, Madeleine," he said. Bernie always made the effort to pronounce the name in two syllables, although the vowels came out distinctly American. "In fact," he turned to Anna, "I felt right from the beginning that you were the one watching over Robin. Do you think you'll be too lonely watching over just yourself?"

Anna shook her head.

"Well, go and have a good time. Just come back single, that's all I ask."

"I promise." She was amazed. She had been so sure they wouldn't let her go, so ready to cry at her disappointment, that the tears came anyway, and Klara, who cried at everything, came and hugged her and cried too.

When they got home, Madeleine looked at her very severely. "I lied for you tonight, may God forgive me."

"I know."

"I'm going to worry myself sick."

"I'll be all right."

"If you don't write me every day—"

"I will, I promise."

"It's on my shoulders."

"No, really, Madeleine, it isn't. It's on mine."

Madeleine kissed her cheek. "You grew up too fast," she said, but Anna knew it was only a small part of the truth. The time between Madeleine's then and now had grown too great. The distance had become more than she could bear.

Anton didn't answer his phone on Tuesday afternoon, but she reached him on Wednesday. He listened to her news and waited a few seconds to answer. It made her wonder. He would never tell her not to go, but perhaps he would quietly hope that someone else would.

"We'll meet then," he said finally. "About the middle of August. I'll go there directly. Afterwards I'll take you to Switzerland for a few days."

"That would be very nice."

"And I'll see you again, Anna, weekend after next?"

"Yes. I'll write to Robin."

Robin didn't answer until the night before she was to leave. Anna was packing the little bag when the phone rang.

"Anna, I've been thinking about it all week," Robin said. "I've talked to Lenny about it. I hope you don't mind."

"I don't mind."

"You have to tell me where you're going and what you're doing."

"I've told you."

There was a silence. "Is Madeleine around?"

"Of course."

"Lenny thinks you're having an affair. I told him it was impossible, but he said what other reason would you have for going away like this?"

She could feel Madeleine's presence behind her in the kitchen. "I like Lenny very much. You're lucky to have him, Robin. I'll see you both tomorrow night." She hung up quickly and turned around.

"There's trouble with Lenny?" Madeleine said. "It will all be over and she'll have the whole summer to regret it."

"It's nothing serious. They have little disagreements but

180

they're not important. I think he's good for Robin. He sees things she doesn't see. It's good to have a man like that."

Madeleine raised her eyebrows and gave Anna a strange smile.

In the early hours of Friday morning Anna awoke with the familiar crampy aches that signaled the onset of her period. Two days early again. She knew she would not sleep. There were pills from a doctor in Great Neck in the bathroom, but getting up would awaken Madeleine, who was a light sleeper. She turned from side to side, trying to alleviate the pain. At breakfast she would take one of the pills, and by the time she reached school she would feel better. It was only the first day that made her feel like this.

In the absence of sleep her mind worked frantically. Exams were coming soon, and she would leave for Europe in less than a month. Images of recent purchases materialized and then quickly dissolved—traveling clothes and a little iron, a roomy shoulder bag and good walking shoes. Right now she would give up the trip if the pain would go away. It was five o'clock, and she had another hour before she could decently make noise.

She began to think of Ella. Did Ella suffer these pains as well as all the others? Did her period still come regularly, reminding her that once she had been fertile, that Anton had made love to her and given her babies?

Anton. Anna twisted on the bed. She was to meet him tonight. This was their weekend together, their beautiful days. She would not be able to go. What would he want with a girl having her period?

The disappointment was as sharp as the pain and more lasting. She would have to call him and make an excuse. She would have to stay home and miss him.

The pill worked as usual, and she got to school already feeling much better. It was nearly noon before she was able to phone.

"I can't make it this weekend," she said when he answered.

181

"Is something wrong?"

"I just can't come."

"Are you ill? Is your aunt ill?"

"Maybe I can come next weekend."

"Anna—have you gotten your period? Is that what the problem is?"

She sat in the booth biting her lips very hard, her neck and face growing uncomfortably warm in the small, close space. She hadn't wanted to lie to him, and any excuse would have been a lie.

"I want to see you, Anna. Are you listening?"

"Yes." It came out in a whisper.

"I thought we understood each other. Who will I talk to this weekend if I don't see you?"

"If you're sure," she said shakily.

"I'll see you this evening."

She hung up and opened the door of the booth. Girls told you about boys, and women told you about reproductive systems, but only men told you about love. How lucky Ella had been to have had him as the last man to love her.

The ordinariness of the weekend came as a surprise. He took her to a country auction, and when she told him she liked a brass rail headboard, he let her bid for it. The price started at four dollars and rose two or three dollars at a time. When someone else bid twenty-five, she sat back, resigned that she would have to give it up. Anton leaned over and said, "Twenty-seven," in her ear. "Twenty-seven!" she shouted, and the auctioneer, surprised, banged the gavel and cried, "Sold to the little lady with the big smile!"

She was thrilled at the purchase, delighted that he had bought it for her, amazed that he had spent such a fortune. It was in wonderful shape but needed a good polishing. They tried to get it in the back of the car, but it didn't fit, so they tied it to the top and drove slowly. He stopped once to buy some polish at a hardware store and came back with polish

182

and two ice cream cones. They sat in the front seat licking down through two enormous scoops and then crunching the crisp, sweet cones. Maybe they could be young together after all.

At the house they spread the kitchen floor with newspaper and polished the brass, turning it a bright, burnt gold as their hands became black. When they were finished, they moved the bed and pushed the new headboard between the bed and the wall. It didn't attach to the bed frame, but he said he would make something that would hold the parts together. In the meantime, the bed would keep it in place.

It changed the whole room. When you entered from the kitchen, the gleam of polished brass caught your eye. She was pleased that he liked what she had chosen, that she had made a contribution to his home.

At night they lay awake and talked. She told him about the house in Freiburg, about the living room and the kitchen, about the smells of pipe smoke in one and cakes baking in the other, about the room way upstairs where her father worked on the things he loved, and how she had tried so hard but could never remember that last moment, the parting, how one moment she was there dressing and the next she was holding Jürgen's hand at the station. And he told her about his father, whose name had been Simon; how he had taught his sons early how to handle the clockmaker's tools, taking apart the simplest clocks (in English, Anton said, they were called "timepieces" when they had no striking mechanism); how they cleaned these timepieces and repaired the worn spots and oiled the pinions with French oil; how they progressed to more complicated clocks, finally to the most delicate, the French. Every piece of the French clocks fit perfectly, but without immense care the delicate, brittle arbors might snap. He talked about his father's patience (and his occasional impatience), about his brothers and their wives and their children, and then he stopped.

183

Always there was this unspeakable end, this vast hopelessness, the generations that were forever lost, his first brother's, his second brother's, his own, Uncle Josef's, Jürgen's. He lay beside her quietly.

"When you go to school in the fall," he said finally, "you'll meet someone. You're old enough now, and you'll meet the best young men in your college."

"I don't want to meet anyone."

"I know you don't, but you'll change your mind. You'll need someone one day, the way you need me now, and someone will be there."

"Please stop."

"You must have children, Anna, many children. So many are gone."

"I don't want a stranger's children."

"You'll change your mind. He won't be a stranger any more. I can't be a husband to you. You know that."

"It doesn't matter. I don't want anyone else."

"It matters." He held her very tightly. "I don't want anyone else either."

She felt him swell against her. She moved her hand down to touch him, but he took the hand away and kissed it.

"Not tonight," he said. "Not this weekend. Will I see you again, once more, before you leave?"

"I think so. Robin wants to stay up there to be with Lenny. Lenny thinks I'm having an affair."

"Does that bother you, that he thinks that?"

"No."

"It's a very good affair. That's what you'll remember a long time from now, how good it was. None of the other things will matter." He rolled over, lifting her on top of him, holding her with his arms, with his lean thighs. "I always want you most when I can't have you."

She tried to laugh. "What are the other times?"

"When I leave you on Sunday night. I want to take you home with me. I watch you walking away, and I want to

184

keep you another night. I like to look at your back and your beautiful hair. I always wonder who else is watching."

"I told you it doesn't matter," she said. "I don't want anyone else."

12

It was the first time he had ever been late. Usually, when she got off the train he was waiting at the nearest point beyond the passengers' entrance. Today he was not there.

Calmly she moved to a location where she was easily visible but where she would not impede the rushing commuters. It was the first Friday in June, and they seemed more anxious than ever to leave the city.

A half hour passed. Something had held him up in the shop, and since she was on her way, he had been unable to warn her. Another half hour and a small ripple of discomfort. Had it occurred to her sooner, she might have telephoned, but now it was too late. No one would answer. The fear that something had happened to Ella took shape between six-thirty and seven. She had gotten lost again. She had suffered a setback. They had called him, and he had to drive upstate.

It was necessary, then, to form an alternate plan. It calmed her to see how clearly and methodically she could plan in an emergency. There was a Y somewhere not too far from here. The telephone book would tell her where. She could spend the weekend in the city, call the shop tomorrow and leave a message, perhaps learn where he had gone. But she knew where he had gone. He had gone to save Ella.

She would not see him again before she left. Like other good-byes in her life, this last one (which she could not remember) had been a final one, at least until August. She tried to recall it, what they had said sitting in the car outside the station, probably things that had no meaning now—see you in two weeks, call me.

The rush of travelers petered out, and she was almost alone. Ella would be alone too, looking through the woods for her children, for the generations she had borne and lost. What greater loneliness could there be for a woman? And for him . . . Like herself, he had survived all the losses, with Ella the one remaining link, the last member of the family.

For the first time she began to realize how difficult things had become for him. She had thought of herself as the one who gave him a rest, a diversion from the concerns of business and the apprehensions about Ella. But it hadn't turned out that way. Instead, she had become yet another concern for him, another burden. When the call came to go to Ella, he knew that someone was waiting for him at the station, someone who was also his responsibility. Instead of subtracting from his worries, she had inadvertently added to them.

She decided she would wait until ten and then leave the station. If it was too late to find a room, she could spend the night in the waiting room. People did that sometimes. She had endured worse; she had slept under trees. The situation might be complicated or difficult, but nothing was frightening any more. You always knew that the worst was behind you.

Unless you were Ella. If you were Ella, the worst was with you, all the time, sleeping or waking. It was all around you.

"Anna!" He ran across the empty vastness of the station and put his arms around her. "I'm so sorry. I thought you would be gone. I'm so sorry."

"Is she all right?"

"Yes, it was nothing, a call from the doctor, and I couldn't leave until he called back."

187

"Would it help if you went up there?"

"I wish it could. It's all right. I promise you." He picked up the suitcase. "I'm glad you waited."

The parking lot was almost empty, but the sky was still light. He drove quickly through deserted streets and up onto the highway.

"In my briefcase," he said. "There's something there for you." He indicated the back seat. "I wanted to give it to you tonight, but it's late now. I want you to have it."

She pulled the briefcase forward and opened it.

"A small box. Down at the bottom."

Her hand found it, a maroon velvet box. Inside was a ring, three small green stones in a row with flashes of light around them as the last sunshine hit. "It's very nice." She wanted to say something more eloquent, but she was uneasy with eloquence. She slid it on her little finger. "Thank you. I've never had anything before, anything real." She stretched out her fingers and watched the glitter. The flashes of light were tiny diamonds. She leaned over and kissed his cheek.

"They're emeralds," he said. "It's not very old, sixty or seventy years. You can tell your aunt you got it in Europe. It won't be a lie."

She watched the ring until all the light was gone. "I would have understood if you hadn't come," she said. "It must be very hard for you."

"It isn't hard. It'll be much harder after you're gone."

That would be Sunday.

The imminence of the parting hung over the weekend. He had booked passage in August, and he wrote down where and when he would meet her, but it was over two months and three thousand miles away. If anything happened, she was to call. He listed the numbers where she could reach him—the shop, Connecticut, and another number starting with ACademy where he lived. He would take her to Switzerland, he said, to the Engadine. They would walk through the ski country. She must remember to take along the things he had bought her last month, so that he could make love to her in Switzerland. It would be beautiful in Switzerland in August.

He stayed close to her as if he knew that she needed him near, or perhaps he needed her now just as much. He made love to her on Friday when they got to the house and on Saturday before she dressed and in the evening when they should have been out to dinner, snatches of intensity that relieved only the sharp, temporary pain while increasing the other, lingering one, the one that would be with her long after Sunday.

On the last morning they took sandwiches and cold cans of juice out to the clearing, the clearing where he would plant his garden next year. She was wearing her dungarees and his shirt with the sleeves rolled to the elbow. They sat on a blanket in the sun at the edge of the clearing. It came to her that her whole life would be full of gardens that she would neither sow nor reap. There had been that other one . . .

"I gave your chocolate bar to a little girl on a train," she said.

He looked startled, as though his mind had wandered too, but in a different direction.

"What will you plant here?"

"Peas, lettuce, radishes. Spring vegetables."

"Like our little garden in France."

"Anna, darling, it's not forever. I'm going to see you again."

But he looked lonely, lonelier than she had ever seen him.

"I wonder what became of the people," she said, "if they ever came back to that little house."

"They never left. They were buried in the cellar."

A prickle crossed her shoulders. "That's why you were so angry at me that night."

"I was never angry at you."

189

"That night you came back and I was down in the cellar."

"I didn't want you to find them."

But like all the other buried secrets, she had found them eventually.

He parked the car and walked her into the station, holding her arm too tightly.

"You'll call before you leave."

"Yes."

"You'll take care of yourself abroad."

She nodded.

"If anything happens, you'll call me."

"Nothing will happen."

"But you have the numbers."

He let her cry on his shoulder before he put her on the train. There was no chance of stretching out the evening. She had to get on this train because it proved she had gotten off the other, the one from Northampton. He was a truth, like other truths in her life, that she could not share.

"I'll write to you," he said.

She nodded. "Thank you for the ring."

He kissed her. "Switzerland will be beautiful."

"Take care of Ella."

"I love you," he said, and he left the train.

13

The cousins made the usual wonderful fuss when she sailed. Lenny came with Robin. Richard came with Madeleine. Klara came with Bernie. It was a neat, symmetrical world.

She had spoken to Anton the previous week, but had not been able to reach him yesterday. Today was Tuesday, June 16, and the ship sailed in the afternoon. Early this morning she had gone to the bank with Bernie and gotten travelers checks for more money than she would need if she circled the globe.

Madeleine fought tears, occasionally turning toward Richard, who moved her protectively away from the group. Lenny and Robin held hands and looked at each other a lot. Robin gave Anna a present, a little cosmetic case to hold all the traveler's needs.

Klara cried, but Klara always cried. Bernie said it revived her.

It was almost a relief when they left, when she stood high on the deck and waved to them, her orchid fluttering at her cheek. When the tug had pulled the little ship out of its dock, she went down to her cabin, shared with two other girls and an older woman who introduced herself as an English teacher, and changed her clothes. She pinned the orchid to her pillow and washed her hands and face. The change made her feel fresh and independent. She was on her way.

She opened the little kit Robin had given her. It had packets of soap, a box of talcum powder, a bottle of shampoo, and

191

other useful items. From her suitcase she took the box with the tube and the applicator and put them in the kit, all the necessities of her life now neatly packed together.

There was a knock at the open door and a steward walked in, his face almost hidden behind a mass of flowers.

"For Miss Goldfeder," he said.

"Thank you." She felt bubbly, as though she were still drinking champagne. "Please put it here."

The card was in his writing, pleasing her immensely. He had done it in person, not on the phone. Pinned to one of the flowers was a note: "Deliver after sailing."

Her cabin-mates were delighted with the flowers, especially the teacher, who had taken an interest in Anna's accent. Her name was Miss Sternberg, but she wanted to be called Frieda. None of her three younger companions seemed ready to take the step.

A bell rang for the lifeboat drill, and when it was over Anna signed up for her meals. There were three sittings, and she chose the second. Then she went up on deck with a book, watched the Statue of Liberty fade from view, and sat down to read. It was sunny and warm and Anton had sent her flowers. She felt very happy.

On Wednesday morning she went up on deck with Rita, one of her roommates, to play shuffleboard. They quickly added two young men, and the four played until the boys heard the call for first sitting. An hour later Anna went for lunch, and then she went back on deck to find a lounge chair and relax. Relaxing was too easy. Reading to the gentle sway of the ship, she fell asleep and woke up hours later. The book had slipped off her lap, and she twisted down toward the deck to find it.

"You're pretty when you sleep."

"What?" It was the person on the next lounge chair.

"I was watching you. You're very pretty. You sleep like you don't have a care in the world." He looked as though he were describing himself. He was big and blond, and his face was as free from care as a baby's.

192

"I'm looking for my book."

"I picked it up." He handed it to her.

"Thank you."

"Like to stretch your legs?"

"I don't know. I really have to read my book." She wished she could think of a believable excuse. Robin would have. It would have tripped out with tremendous sincerity, unquestionable regret, and absolute finality.

"Come on. After a nap there's nothing like a walk."

"Yes, all right." She put the book in her bag and stood up, almost losing her balance as the deck shifted beneath her. He took her arm and held it to steady her. "Thank you."

"I'm Bill Henderson," he said, offering his hand.

Bill Henderson. He was Robin's true-blue American. "I'm Anna Goldfeder."

They shook hands.

"Hi. That's pretty, Goldfeder."

It's my mother's name. I took it to honor my aunt who has cared for me for nine years. My parents are dead. They were killed by Hitler. Do you know who Hitler was, blond boy with slightly pink cheeks?

"Thank you."

"Like to go to the bar and have a drink?" They had reached the stern of the ship and were curving around toward the other side.

"I don't really drink." Just wine sometimes with a man I love, a man I have had an affair with, a good affair. Years from now I will remember only that it was a good affair. Right now I know only that I want to be with him.

"You can have a Coke."

She allowed herself to be guided indoors, into the large ballroom with a bar at one side. They sat on high stools, and he ordered one Coke and bourbon and water.

"You on a tour?" he asked.

"No, I'm traveling by myself."

"No, kidding." He seemed impressed. "Your folks're letting you go on your own?"

193

She translated "folks" into unemotional English. "Yes, my family said I could go myself."

"Where you headed?"

Home. The place that I remember best. The place where I last saw my parents. "All over," she said lightly. "Back to some places I remember from when I was a child. A town in Germany called Freiburg."

"You do have a little accent," he said. "Not much. It's pretty the way you talk, like some movie stars. More French than German though, I think."

She admired his perception. "I lived in France too. I went there when I was ten." Over the mountains with Jürgen, but Jürgen is dead now. He killed himself because he couldn't stand living any more. "I spent the war years in France."

"You were in Europe during the whole war?"

"Yes."

"I lost a brother in the war in Europe, my brother Ed."

She could feel her cheeks and neck drain. "I'm so sorry," she said, swiveling on the stool and touching his sleeve.

"Want to sit at a table?" he asked. "You don't look like the kind of girl who should sit at a bar."

He took the drinks and they went to a table.

"He was the oldest," he said. "Named after my dad. My folks never got over it."

"No."

"You eat first sitting?"

"Second," she said bleakly, thinking of his poor brother, the oldest son, named for his father, dead on a battlefield in Europe.

"Maybe I can see you after dinner."

"That would be nice." After the invasion of Normandy, American cemeteries. His brother Ed. "I've forgotten your name," she said suddenly.

"Bill."

"Oh yes. Henderson."

"Right. Can I get you another Coke?"

"Please. With a piece of lemon."

194

He went to the bar and came back with two fresh drinks.

"How old was he?" she asked.

He looked perplexed. "Who?"

"Your brother."

"Oh. Twenty-two. He was five years older than I. He'd be twenty-six now."

"Did you just graduate?"

"Yeah, Iowa. I'm going to Columbia next year for graduate work. History."

"My father taught history."

The first sitting was announced.

"What do you say we forget dinner and have some sandwiches? They make a good roast beef sandwich here. I got hungry last night and ordered one."

"O.K." She wasn't hungry anyway. She was thinking about his brother.

"What about you? Where do you go to school?"

"I'm starting Pembroke in the fall. I'm a little behind. I had some language problems. I just finished high school." For the first time, it didn't sound shameful.

"Maybe I'll get to see you."

A waiter stopped at the table, and Bill ordered the sandwiches. When the waiter left Bill started talking about history and Columbia and graduate work. She responded only when she had to. She kept seeing the boy, the cemetery, hearing the sound of battle.

She realized suddenly that he had stopped talking, that the sandwiches were finished. People from the first sitting were drifting in, and the band was tuning up. Soon there would be dancing and noise, and she wanted to avoid it, wanted to go somewhere quiet.

"Ready for a walk?" he asked.

"I guess so."

They went out on deck. It was cooler now and starting to get dark. As they traveled eastward, the sun seemed to set sooner. At night they turned their clocks ahead.

They played a game of shuffleboard in the twilight, then started to walk again.

"Cold?" he asked.

"A little."

"Take my jacket."

"Then you'll be cold."

"Doesn't bother me. I'm from Iowa."

"What does one do in Iowa?" she asked.

"One farms," he said, parodying her. "My folks are farmers."

"What do they grow?" Peas? Radishes? Lettuce? Spring vegetables?

"Corn mostly. My brother wanted to farm. Eddy, the one who died." He took his jacket off. "Here, honey," he said. "Put it on."

She wriggled into it. A jacket, a man's warm jacket.

"I haven't talked about Eddy to anyone for a long time. Do you have any brothers or sisters?"

"I was an only child."

"We were very different, but I looked up to him. I was only seventeen when he died. He was already married. Married a girl he went to school with. She's married again now and has a family. We don't see much of her any more. Sometimes I think it's like it never happened."

"I know."

He held her arm as they walked. "A couple of weeks ago they wrote and asked if we wanted his body back. They had sent us a box after he died with his stuff in it."

She stiffened. "I didn't know they did that."

"His uniform, wallet, pictures, that sort of thing. Some of the things in the box were his, and some of them weren't."

She was shaking now inside the large, warm jacket. She had agreed to the sandwiches. She had agreed to Eddy. She hadn't bargained for this.

"The wedding ring was someone else's," Bill said. "And a couple of other things."

"Your parents must have been very upset," she said, keeping her voice even.

"Well, they've decided to bring him home. My mom said she hoped it was Eddy, but it didn't really matter. He was an American boy, and he deserved to be buried in America."

She brushed at her eyes. "Your parents must be very nice people," she said.

"Yeah." They had stopped at the railing, and he had an arm around her. "You ever think in German any more?"

"No. Just the numbers. I still count in German and I do arithmetic in German, but I never do it out loud. I do it in my head so the French won't hear me."

He gave her a puzzled look, and when she didn't answer he touched her neck with his free hand, then let his hand drop, almost accidentally, inside the jacket to touch her breast, to feel its roundness, to rub lightly on the nipple.

Her body tensed with expectation. She had not realized how sensitive she had become, how much she wanted the nerve endings excited, how dearly she craved relief.

"Please don't," she said.

"I'll stop if you mean it. Most girls don't mean it."

"I mean it."

"O.K." He took his hand away and stood close to her so she could feel the little bump, one of those squishy erections that American boys got in cars. One of the boys had told her once what she was supposed to do about it. She had listened in surprise and refused rudely. In America it was right to do things the wrong way.

"I guess I should get you back."

"All right."

"Or we could stay and see the sun rise. You ever see the sun rise before?"

"In Switzerland. It comes up over the mountains." She turned to look at him, this nice American boy whose brother had died in the war. "I'd like very much to see it rise over the ocean."

They lay on a lounge chair, squeezing themselves

together to fit on the narrow mat. She slept on and off, waking finally at the first sign of light. They walked forward, standing at the bow where the wind blew hard and cold, watching it come up, all that light and color wasted on an empty ocean. On both sides of that ocean they slept, the people that she loved, behind her Anton and Ella and Madeleine, and before her Jürgen and all the others, the sacred dead in their mass graves.

Her cabin-mates stirred as she entered. The schoolteacher was already up and dressing herself modestly beneath the covers. Rita opened her eyes and said, "Hi."

Anna waved at the upper berth and started to undress.

"He must be some guy," Rita said sleepily. "To stay out all night with him."

Anna didn't say anything, but it struck her funny. Sometimes things were more upside down than right side up. They would never suspect the truth about her, none of it, what she had done and what she would not do. She laughed.

From the other upper berth the schoolteacher snorted her disapproval. After that morning, she never asked Anna to call her Frieda again.

"You the girl I spent the night with?"

She looked up from her book and felt her cheeks burn. "Hi," she said. It was afternoon, and with the difference in sittings she hadn't run into him earlier.

"Want to try for two?"

"Thank you, no. It was nice to see the sun rise, but it left me very tired."

"Well, we'll do something else then. We can have a drink and dance. There's a guy with a guitar down the hall from me. Plays good music."

"I'm really kind of tired."

"Then I'll get you back early."

She realized with regret that she had misled him. She had been drawn to Eddy, and Bill had become interested in her.

198

She should have said something yesterday, but she had not been aware, not until late at night, and even then, all boys tried, didn't they?

At ten she said she was tired, and he tried to kiss her. She asked him please not to and went to her cabin. Miss Sternberg was in her nightgown reading a book, and the fourth member, Suzanne, was changing into something warm for a stroll on deck. Suzanne said "Hi," but Miss Sternberg kept her face in the book, and Anna didn't bother saying good night when she got into bed.

She awoke in the morning with the rest of them and started to dress. The voyage was one-third over. They were scheduled to land on the ninth day, a small, slow ship chugging its way across a giant ocean. She put her shoes on and stood up to find some clothes as a strange dizzyness hit her, an unaccustomed faintness. The cabin became a newspaper photograph of black dots not close enough together to form distinguishable shapes. She grabbed for Rita's mattress to steady herself and heard Suzanne laugh.

"Someone's seasick," the girlish voice teased.

It wasn't seasickness. Steadied, she sank onto her own bed, curled up, and lay there.

"You'll feel better out on deck," Rita said authoritatively.

"I'm O.K." She lay there until they had left, until she heard the cabin steward next door and knew that theirs was next. She sat up, feeling a little better. The room retained its solid form. She would get some tea and forgo breakfast.

She put her clothes on, got the tea, and carried it to the writing room. Miss Sternberg was already there, papers spread before her.

Anna reached into her bag for her pen and took out instead the little leather calendar book stamped in gold with her initials that Robin gave her every year for New Year's. She turned the pages rapidly. It was four weeks to the day since the last time she had gotten her period. Ordinarily it came a day or two early. Ordinarily it came with cramps.

199

There was nothing ordinary about what had happened this morning. There was no sign of the usual menstrual flow, no pain at all, but she had nearly passed out an hour ago in her cabin, and today was the day. Today.

Her mind did not play childish games, asking questions for which answers were ridiculously obvious and then rejecting them. It settled on her like a brilliant flash, like the sun illuminating a dark ocean: he is going to have a child and it will be mine. She started to shake, so badly that her hand, lying on the dark wood of the desk, moved the paper cup of tea.

"If you're sick, there's a ship's surgeon on board."

She looked up. It was Miss Sternberg, the woman named Frieda. Lotte Kleinberger had known a Frieda. They had called her Friedl, and she had gone to America. She would be alive now.

"I'm all right. Thank you. I'm just fine."

"I just thought I'd tell you." Her look indicated that this was what came of staying out all night, but Miss Sternberg was wrong; it was what came of staying in.

Anna smiled at her private joke. "Thank you. I appreciate it."

Miss Sternberg returned to her letters.

All the rest of it fell upon her in the next moment. Madeleine. College. The cousins.

Ella.

She could not tell him. Not now. She would have to handle it by herself, go somewhere, alone, give birth. Like the Friday he had arrived late at Penn Station, she began planning, taking into account all the contingencies she could think of. Her mind swam with possibilities, with obligations, with questions. She would see him in August. Perhaps then, when they were resting in Switzerland, then she would be able to tell him. He would worry about her, about the things that people always worried about—the shame— but he would be happy. He would be so happy.

It never once occurred to her that it could be something

200

else, that her period might be late for a hundred good reasons—the trip and the excitement and the change in food and exercise, that she might be coming down with grippe, that Miss Sternberg might be right and she should see the doctor. Something had happened, a sign, and she had read it the only way she could. She was sure.

She wrote a brief card to Madeleine, like the other brief cards she had written since Tuesday, and another letter to Anton. She had written him once the first night on board, thanking him for the flowers and saying that she missed him. Now she wrote again, a different kind of letter, with softer words and phrases. She wrote things she had wanted to say but which had never quite come out. He was the one person who understood everything, who knew how she felt, who knew how her body worked better than she. She could say anything to him.

She heard a call for the first sitting, and she finished the letter, mailed it, and went out on deck to walk around. The deck was covered with college kids—card games, shuffleboard, long, earnest discussions between people who had just met and who would never see each other again after next Thursday morning. She floated somewhere above them; she was having Anton's child.

Bill found her after dinner.

"Your roommate said you were under the weather this morning."

"Just my period," she said easily.

"Oh. Uh—sorry, I thought you were sick. Feel up to anything this evening?"

"Not really. I'd just like to rest this weekend."

"O.K."

She kept to herself until Monday, when he reappeared. It was a long voyage in a small, enclosed area. It was harder to avoid people than to find them.

"Where you going after we land?" he asked.

"Through Holland."

"So'm I. You traveling alone?"

201

"For awhile, yes."

"Maybe we'll run into each other."

She didn't answer.

"When're you going to Freiburg?"

His memory surprised her. She had mentioned it only once, the night they met. "In August."

"Probably a nice time to go."

"A very nice time."

She danced with him Monday night and again on Tuesday. Wednesday night, close to midnight, they sailed into Rotterdam harbor.

The lights were magnificent. The decks were crowded with kids itching to move to land and begin travel. The tour groups had all found each other and coalesced, making their arrangements for the following morning.

Anna stood on the deck, tense with excitement, until the ship came to rest at its pier. Bill wanted to kiss her good night, but she refused.

"I don't figure you," he said.

"I'm sorry."

"I'll see you in the morning." His tone was somewhat miffed.

It didn't matter. Tomorrow she was on her own.

She had hoped to sleep well, but she hardly slept at all. The night was full of undreamable dreams and unfadable memories. She checked everything before she lay down, the papers that substituted for a citizen's passport—Bernie had taken care of all that—the yellow card listing in successive illegible lines the required, optional, and totally unnecessary injections she had submitted to in the last few months. To cross a border. She had not crossed a border for three years, and the memory of that last crossing had never left her.

The hours they had sat in that dismal, rotting pier on the Hudson River, waiting to be processed into the Promised Land. Where was that member of Congress now, the one who had expedited their rapid acceptance as immigrants? Was there anything in the world lower than an immigrant to the United States? One after another the other travelers had left as they continued to sit there. No one spoke anything but English. Eventually, Madeleine had cried. Was it possible, Anna had thought, that at this point, having made the crossing, having been shot with preventive medicines for unheard-of diseases, that they could be turned back? Madeleine had a valid French passport, but what did Anna have? She was a J in Germany, an illegal entrant into France, an unwilling traveler to America. She would never see him again. She would never learn this language in which every nuance of tense required another form of the verb. She had let Madeleine pack her suitcase and take her across the ocean. She had not objected. It had simply happened to her.

She got up early, finished packing, and went up on deck. Breakfast was a hurried, frantic affair. At one point she spotted Bill. She knew he was looking for her, but she managed to avoid him. They would go separate ways today, and he would be the better for it.

She stood in line among the confident American citizens, nervously waiting her turn at customs. When it came it was a surprise. The Dutch customs officer was kind and polite; her papers were all in order. In a few minutes she found herself in the sunshine of Rotterdam.

Bernie had selected the hotel, and she knew it was likely to be the best of her stay. She had a small room with its own shower, a luxury she would not permit herself when she left Rotterdam. Inside the room, she went quickly through her mail, dropping the letter from Madeleine on the bed and hastily opening the one from Anton.

It was short, and she read it through quickly, then again, then a third time. He hoped the flowers had arrived. He would miss her. The house in Connecticut would seem very empty now. Probably he would visit Ella more often in June

203

and July. Her lung was responding well, but of course there were still the other problems. The woman who spoke German was trying very hard but with very small success.

There was something incomplete about the letter, something unwritten, a secret withheld. She rubbed her still flat stomach. Her period was six days late now. Whatever his problems, she would make him happy.

She went out walking, following a street guide, stopping for lunch and a rest. In the afternoon she ran into two girls from the ship, girls who had just graduated from college, and she joined them for dinner.

On Friday she went out again, seeking the bombed out center of the city and viewing it as she might view the remains of a dead soldier, of Eddy who had died in her war. She wrote to Robin and then Bernie, telling him how much she appreciated being here, how nice the hotel was. She talked to an old lady on a bench, speaking English, now the lingua franca. The old lady had lived through two wars, but she had had enough; if there was to be another, it would have to be fought without her.

On Saturday morning she stopped at the hotel desk after breakfast to check for mail.

"An express letter," the clerk said, handing it to her.

It was from Anton and she ripped it open as she found a chair in the lobby. The top page brought a shock. It was written in German.

> My dearest Anna,
>   It is with great pain that I write you this letter. I write in German to make it somewhat easier for myself and because it brings me closer to you. All the women I have ever loved have spoken German—my mother, my wife, my little girl, the lovely girl in the farmhouse those days in France. It is hard sometimes to pick out the good days from all the rest, but we have had good ones, many of them, and I shall always remember them.

I am sorry that I will not be able to meet you in Freiburg this summer. Since the last of May I have noticed a deterioration in Ella's condition. The doctors do not entirely agree with me, but I feel they are not prepared for cases like hers. I had deluded myself that when the physical problems were cured, the other problems would similarly cure themselves. It was a sad delusion. I find myself grasping at the bright moments and magnifying them. But they are only isolated moments. I feel that I dare not go so far as across the ocean until there is a more definite sign of improvement. I have therefore canceled my trip indefinitely. If things do not go well, I shall have to send someone in my place in the fall.

You must know that I think about you endlessly, that the memory of our times together makes me very happy. I looked forward to our little holiday in Switzerland as much, I am sure, as you. I am sorry it will not come to be.

I hope you will now reconsider your trip to Freiburg. Whatever we look for, we will not find it in our beginnings. I have never returned to Poland, and while I admire your desire to go back to the place that was once your home, I remain skeptical that the experience will be a good one.

You know that if I were able I would be with you constantly, I would take care of you in the way you need to be taken care of. You know also that I am not able, that I never will be. You are too young and too beautiful to waste all the good years you have ahead of you on my account. In the fall you must go to your college with an open mind and without the repressive chains that I represent.

I am sure that reading this letter will disappoint you as much as writing it has saddened me, but there is still much left of the summer, many places to visit, many people to meet. I hope it will be a good one.

Know that I love you,
Anton

His name was written in large, angular script, the *A* like a sharp black steeple. She put the letter down in her lap, covered her face, and cried. It had been too much to hope for, too much to expect that happiness would remain in her grasp. It had eluded her once, and she had foolishly believed that recapturing it had guaranteed permanent ownership. She felt suddenly moved to call him, to tell him her news which was his news too, but it was Saturday. Probably he was already upstate. Even if he wasn't the shop would not open for hours, and it was too early to wake him. It was too early too in her pregnancy. Switzerland would have been perfect. Now there would be no Switzerland, no summer.

"Hey, you O.K.?"

She raised tearful eyes. The face was familiar. It was blond and full. He was the brother of Eddy, Eddy the young soldier whose wife had married someone else.

"Bill," she said.

"Right. What the hell's the matter? You know, I called twenty hotels before I found where you were staying."

"It's a letter from home, from a friend."

"Bad news?"

"Disappointing. Just very disappointing."

"Let's have a cup of coffee."

"No—thank you—I—"

"Come on." He coaxed gently. "Put the letter away. We'll have some coffee and take a walk. It's a little cloudy out, but I don't think it'll rain. We'll go somewhere, and you'll feel better. You don't have to talk, just take it easy."

He spoke quietly, comfortingly. Maybe he had spoken

this way to his mother once, when he was seventeen, when the news came. The sound of his voice was reassuring. She folded the letter and put it in her bag, stood and went with him. There was something dreamlike about the whole thing. She ordered chocolate instead of coffee. It was rich and warm and delicious. It would nourish her baby. She would have to start to drink milk now, lots of milk. God, why did it have to happen this way? Why couldn't things have gone right for once?

They went out to the street and walked. They had lunch. They went to a museum. The day passed like the cloud overhead, dully, imprecisely. From one hour to the next, she was not sure what she had visited, what they had said to each other.

Finally, they were having dinner. It occurred to her that he had paid for everything all day, that he was only a student like herself, that she must pay her share. She took some guilders from her wallet and offered them to him, but he pushed them gently away.

"Today's on me," he said.

They walked around until it was dark.

"I'm crazy about you," he said. They were somewhere near the ruined heart of the city. "You never let me kiss you the whole week we were on that ship."

"You can kiss me now," she said, speaking from her own ruined heart. She wanted to be kissed. She wanted to be held and touched and aroused and everything that would follow naturally from that. She wanted her lover, but if she couldn't have him, at least she wanted to be loved.

He kissed her chastely. He held open the collar of her blouse and kissed her at the base of her neck, down where the bones parted. He touched her breast. He touched the nipple very deliberately. She trembled. He breathed as though he were racing somewhere.

"Let's go back to your place," he said.

They started walking. She was glad it would be her room because she knew it, because there was a bathroom right there and not down the hall, because it was familiar to her.

They rode up in the ancient clanky cage of an elevator and went into her room. He took off his jacket and touched her breasts. He opened her blouse and reached inside. She had the feeling he was waiting for her to say no, stop, that he was uneasy with a situation in which he was able to move freely.

"Excuse me a minute," she said. She went into the bathroom and opened the cosmetic kit, the case Robin had given her on the ship. Poor Robin! If only she knew the causes she had abetted.

She squeezed the tube hard until the applicator was full, then bent and inserted it. It went in easily. Her body had learned how to ready itself for sex. She had heard at Smith that there were women that needed something extra, a little help, the girl had said, before anything, well, you know what I mean, could get in. Anna had wondered about those women. They must not love very well, or they did not have very good lovers. Her body was still fooled. It was still expecting Anton.

He said, "Hi," when she returned, put his arms around her, held her and kissed her, took her blouse off, then, warily, the bra. He looked at her as though she were something in a museum, some sculpture salvaged from the ruins of a great artistic era. He touched her delicately, as though the curator might come by and slap his hand. Then he took his shirt off and sat down on the bed, pulling her down beside him.

She slipped her shoes off and lay down, making room for him. She knew he would be wondering how far she would let him go. Girls didn't do this sort of thing in Iowa, not nice girls who spend a week with you on board ship and never let you kiss them good night.

He lay down beside her, undid his belt and zipper and lifted her skirt and slip, modestly covering himself. She would not get to see it after all, but she could feel it. His erection was less feeble than she remembered from the ship; tonight it was burgeoning. She pressed herself against him so he would know that she wasn't afraid, that she wanted this. He began to kiss her with great feeling, almost with anguish, and she let herself go, her own misplaced feeling, her own anguish. Suddenly he pulled her pants down with furious haste, reached into his pocket and pulled something out, one of those flat packages with a little oval inside. He tried frantically to rip it open, suddenly said, "Oh shit," dropped it, and went inside her. She could tell that he knew little about satisfying a woman, that he was driven by his own overwhelming needs, but it didn't matter. She was ready to be satisfied, waiting for it, and she held him tightly, hoping finally that it felt as good for him as it did for her.

End of Vol IV

14

It seemed natural that they would travel together. They were both alone. It was cheaper to share a room, and the people who registered them seemed unconcerned about their status. He wanted to go wherever she wanted to go. On Monday they took the train to The Hague, sitting side by side on the hard third-class seats. It was nice to have company, nice to have someone to eat with. He was still a little wary of her. Much about her surprised him. He had lain beside her that first night and admitted his surprise.

"I never slept with a girl who wasn't a virgin. I mean the first time, you know, the first time I slept with her."

She said nothing. There was nothing to say.

"You're different," he said, trying to answer for her.

"Everybody's different."

"Sometimes I think that you're older. Not that you look older, just something I feel."

"I know." It was something she had felt herself, often, even among Robin's friends who were her age and older, something she could not detect in the mirror but which was nevertheless visible, a kind of inherited age, an accumulated age that had nothing to do with time and much to do with experience. She could not talk about it.

She laid an arm over his chest so that he would know she was happy with him even if she couldn't say any of the things he wanted to hear.

They stayed in The Hague only a couple of days and went on to Amsterdam. She loved Amsterdam. Anton had said once it was one of the places he would like to have a shop. She wondered if he knew the city or had only heard about it. She would choose this place too. She could easily live in one of the tall skinny buildings overlooking a canal. Perhaps she would come back here and raise her baby.

They stayed in a little hotel on the Damrak and toured the city, taking the boat through the canals, walking through the great art museum, through shops, old streets with whores in windows, eating in Indonesian restaurants. She tried to pay her share but he accepted it only some of the time.

She thought what a fool Robin was. What would she get out of staying home—a few more kisses on Saturday night? It would never be the same for her if she came with Lenny, even if it was a honeymoon. Already she had begun to talk about dishes and silver and could she get this in England and that in Denmark. It would be a shopping spree in fancy hotels with hot water every night. Something in her life would be forever lost, going alone, roughing it. She would never be able to compare the way she lived with any other way. How would she be able to relish company if she had never been alone? How could she be half of a couple if she had never taken a step as a single person?

They stayed in Amsterdam a week, hiking up and down the canals, sometimes alone, sometimes together, returning to the museum to see a favorite Rembrandt and Vermeer and de Hooch. They visited the Jewish quarter, and Anna hung onto his arm as she read the signs over the shops of the ones who had come back. She knew she wanted him to come with her to Freiburg, but she could not ask it. She could not request a favor for which there was no adequate repayment. They had not talked about the summer. They merely thought aloud in the evening what they would do tomorrow. Then, if there was hot water they showered, and if there wasn't they sponged at the sink. She was an old hand at that; she had lived through a war.

It was already July 9 when they got on a train and traveled

211

to Brussels. They stayed through the weekend and continued on to Paris. Paris was a beautiful shock. Seeing it she realized she had never really known it. What she had known was a small community less like Paris than Great Neck was like New York. Like so many other memories, this one too needed revision.

In Paris she began to get restless. She had scheduled Freiburg for the middle of August because Anton would meet her there. Now there was no longer any rationale for putting it off. She had begun to sleep fitfully, to dream about Freiburg, disturbing dreams that she wanted to put an end to. The relationship with Bill had, by slow, imperceptible degrees, grown out of hand. She had lost her head when the letter came in Rotterdam, and each day she suffered a little more for it. By the end of the week, her period was four weeks overdue and she had no idea how much longer she would continue to feel well. It had to be gotten over with; she had to go now. She knew Bill wanted to see more of France; it was what he had come for. The time had come for them to pursue their separate goals.

She came back to their room in the hotel on the Rue St. Jacques and found him there, reading a book. She had been out buying perfume for Robin and Klara and Madeleine, and for Bill's mother and sister as well.

"I want to go to Germany," she said, putting the packages down and sitting on the edge of the bed. "Why don't you stay in Paris or go on to the south of France? I can't put it off any more. It's gnawing at me."

He looked at her with a sort of quizzical expression he had, an expression that said he was curious but he would never understand her. "What makes you think I want to go anywhere without you?" He said it the way he said everything else, very quietly, all on one even Midwestern level of intonation.

"If you're sure." She said it as though she weren't.

"Can you wait till Monday?"

"I guess."

212

" 'Cause I ran into a guy while I was out, a guy from home. He's with the occupation in Germany, and he's got a car. He'll give me the car for a couple of weeks if I'll pay his way back on the train and enough for him to have a good time in Paris. It's really very reasonable—if two of us use the car."

"If you're sure," she said again.

"Sure I'm sure."

He went out on Sunday afternoon to pick up the car, and she began to pack. After Freiburg she must leave Bill and begin to work out the intricate details of her future. Bernie must be told that she would not attend Pembroke. Madeleine must be told—something. And Anton must know that his child would be born next spring. Maybe she would go to Switzerland by herself, to the Engadine, and sort it all out, write the letters, decide where she would spend the remaining months of her pregnancy.

They left on Monday, driving east, and it was the same road. Mile after mile measured on the map in kilometers, and there were no recognizable landmarks. Three years, and she could no longer find her way. Where had she turned off to spend the night with friends and cousins of Madeleine? What town had she been near when she left the main road for the farmhouse? The debris of war was gone as though there had never been a battle, never so much as a shot. What had become of it all, the tons of steel, the fragments of wasted lives?

She tried several times to tell Bill that this was the last lap of their trip together, but it never came out. Her stomach tightened with every kilometer the old car moved toward the German border. She was no longer sure why she was doing this, except that she had always known that she must. At the end of this long road was a place she had once called home. They had already crossed the Dutch, Belgian, and French borders without difficulty. But this next one, how would she manage this one?

They stopped in the afternoon and spent the night at a pension somewhere east of Chalons, and when she got up in

213

the morning she knew she would reach Germany by evening.

"You're nervous, aren't you?" Bill asked, looking at an uneaten breakfast before her.

She nodded, pushing the food away so she wouldn't have to look at it.

"We don't have to go, you know."

"We don't, but I do."

"Why? What do you have to do this to yourself for? I could go south at Nancy, and we could be in Basel by tonight."

"I just have to do it, Bill. If I don't go now, it'll hang over me, and I'll have to go another time. I want to get it over with."

At Nancy he turned east, and east again at Lunéville. They approached Strasbourg, and her hands got cold, her mouth became dry. Images swirled before her like winter snow and blinded her. She thanked God she hadn't eaten lunch, because she wouldn't have kept it down. How could Jürgen have done that? What terrible thing had they done to him to make him do that? She had had a fantasy about Jürgen, not unlike the fantasy about Anton. He had been so beautiful. She glanced at the driver of the car, Bill from Iowa. There were superficial resemblances, coloring and height. Jürgen had been trimmer, harder, leaner. He had carried her when she had been unable to walk. She needed a man who could carry her.

The car came to a jerky stop.

"Hey, honey, I can't do this to you."

Her mouth was trembling, and she wasn't sure she could speak. "Do what?"

"You're a wreck. I can't take you somewhere you don't really want to go."

She grasped for the energy to speak, for the mechanism that would make it come out right, just a few English words strung together in the right order, her best language really, when you came to think of it.

214

"Please," she said, the voice not functioning properly. "Please don't make me go alone. I want you to come with me." A quick image of herself standing on this road with a bicycle that would not ride. A memory or a prophecy?

The car started up again, and they continued toward Strasbourg.

The Rhine, the great Rhine. It was a trickle next to the Hudson. What had made her think it was so almightily big and powerful? Was that, too, simply part of the enduring myth?

She kept her mouth shut through customs, Bill handing her papers through the window to the uniformed man. They had all been soldiers. One could tell from their age. A few years ago they had been scraped off a road somewhere and cast back to trade one uniform for another.

The uniform stuck his head in the car window and addressed them both: "*Kaffee, Tee, Schokolade, Zucker, Zigaretten?*" Five questions, five chances to do yourself in if he didn't like the way you looked, if he had spotted the invisible *J* in your passport.

She shook her head, and Bill said, "No."

The passports came back with a black stamp, proof that she alone in her family had lived to enter this country once again. Bill started the motor, and they were on their way to Freiburg.

It was such an innocuous town, really, old and very beautiful, peaceful, a place where one might believe that one was safe. Bill found them a room in a better hotel than they had been staying in, zum Bären on Salzstrasse. The room had a private bathroom and hot and cold running water. After they had washed, he took her downstairs to the restaurant and made her order soup. She refused to speak German as three years before she had refused to speak English. Regressing, she thought. Robin would have a field day with that.

The soup was good, and she ate bread with it, good hard dark bread after the French that they were used to. They

215

went up after dinner, and she bathed, put on a clean nightgown, did a small wash, and hung it to dry. Bill opened the windows, and it was pleasant and cool after the heat of the July day.

Bill had gotten a map of the city for her, and she found the section she was looking for at the north end of town beyond the university, the "Musicians' Quarter"—Beethoven Street, Mozart Street—the sensitive, musical Germans.

That night she was glad to have Bill, not because he was someone who happened to be there, but because he was Bill.

She slept poorly and was up early waiting for Bill to awaken.

"You look green," he said when he was awake.

She went to the bathroom and washed, then came out and started to dress.

"You're nineteen, honey," he said. "You've been away from this place for nine years. You've spent the better part of your life somewhere else. Take it easy."

The better part of her life. The better part of her life had been a few weekends in Connecticut in the spring. Imagine being nineteen and thinking that the better part of your life was behind you.

She drank tea with a little sugar, the way Anton did, while Bill ate the rolls and butter and marmalade she could barely look at. They went out into the sunshine afterwards and walked holding hands to the Bertholdsbrunnen on Kaiser-Joseph-Strasse, where they waited for the streetcar that took them north. Through the window she saw Germans on the street in their dowdy postwar clothes, unaware that she was among them, unaware as always.

Okenstrasse.

"We get off here." Out onto the street, and a pause to get her bearings. "This way." A feeling of excitement. They were so near.

Names came back. Hadn't there been a little boy here when she was very young, and hadn't he cut his hand one

216

day, with a lot of blood? Wasn't there a woman around here somewhere who had baked marvelous cookies? What had become of them? What had they done for Max and Lotte when the time came?

Beside her she felt a wispy presence and knew immediately that it was Ella come to walk beside her. She was grateful for her company. Ella knew what it was to search; she had looked in the woods for her children. Today she would help Anna find her parents.

She turned a corner, scarcely seeing where she was going. Her eyes were filled with old images, her mind thick with old sounds. Her heart was doing crazy things, and Ella was telling her to hurry. They would be waiting for her. They had never left. They were simply waiting for her to come home to them.

"You O.K.?"

"Yes." She stopped.

"Is this the one?"

She nodded. The number was right and the appearance was right, but the house had shrunk, as though its fibers had contracted with time. The curtains were wrong, and the door was a different color, but geraniums grew brightly in the window boxes and the tiny rectangle of grass was carefully manicured. They always had time for the important things like grass and flowers. Up there in that top window had been where Max Kleinberger had fixed his clocks and written up his folk tales, read his histories and written the great treatises that no one in the world would ever read.

"That window," she said, "that was my father's study."

Bill looked up. "He had light all day up there."

"Yes, and he burned a lamp half the night sometimes."

She started down the short walk.

"You going in?"

"That's what I came for."

She knocked on the door. A dog barked. She would have to speak German now; there was no longer a choice.

The door opened a crack and she looked eye to eye at a

217

woman with a wide, hard face and crinkly hair the color of straw, bangs across the forehead. The magic of stereotypes was that they were so frighteningly accurate.

"Ja?"

She hung on to Bill's hand. "Excuse me for bothering you," she began politely, cowed by the face and the voice but unable to retreat. "I used to live in this house when I was a little girl. I was passing through Freiburg, and I thought I would like to see it again."

From a distance another female voice called, "What is it, Hilde?"

"Nothing," the woman called back. "You lived here?"

"Yes."

"When was that?" There were vertical lines on the forehead.

"When I was very young."

"Yes, I understand," the woman said impatiently, "but when was it? I've lived here a long time myself."

"Nineteen thirty," Anna said, pulling a year out of her life. "Could I just look around? I won't disturb anything."

"Nineteen thirty." She was a hard looking woman with cool gray eyes. She was figuring it out. This was one of those Jews we thought we had gotten rid of.

"Yes." Nineteen thirty, you bitch. And twenty-nine and twenty-eight. My grandfather bought it for my parents when they got married, my rich, successful grandfather.

The woman turned away. "Hold the dog," she called. "Please come in."

They walked into the living room, the same room where friends had gathered, where Jürgen had played with her, but the smell of pipe smoke was gone. The bookshelves were still there where they had been built into the wall, but there were no books on them. Instead they were cluttered with junky little objects that people without taste found appealing. Crackerjack prizes, Robin called them. She moved into the dining room, replacing the furniture, setting the table with her mother's beautiful dishes. Into the kitch-

218

en. A new stove. Hadn't the Kleinbergers' stove cooked well enough for this Aryan goddess?

From behind her she heard a chime. She looked at her watch. It was ten-thirty. A beautiful chime. Dropping Bill's hand she retraced her steps to locate the source. Into the dining room and then the living room. In a corner where she had not seen it was a tall clock. She went over and touched it, looked at the name, one of the first words she had learned to read.

"That was our clock," she breathed, saying it in German although she had meant it for Bill, who was right behind her. "We kept it in the dining room, but it was ours."

"That's my clock," the woman said sharply. "My husband gave it to me in 1925."

Another woman appeared, a shorter white-haired copy of the Aryan, with some teeth visibly missing.

"Who are they?" she hissed.

The blond woman mumbled something in the other's ear.

"I'd like to go upstairs," Anna said.

"That's not possible."

"Just up to that room on the top floor. My father—"

"That room cannot be opened."

"Come on, honey." Bill touched her shoulder. It was the first time he had spoken.

The woman eyed them. "Where are you from?" she asked.

"We're Americans," Anna said, accepting the label for the first time.

The woman's face changed. Lines appeared, and a red glow shone beneath the surface. Her eyes burned. There was more than anger there; she was seething with hatred.

"Out!" she shouted. "Murderers! Out of my house."

Bill looked totally bewildered. The hidden dog began to bark.

The old woman looked pained. "It's all right, sweetheart," she said to her daughter. "They're going. Please go," she said to the unwanted guests. "Her son was a flier. He fell in forty-four. It was the Americans that did it. Her only son. Hildchen, they're going. Don't take on so."

Without hurrying, Anna took a last look at the clock and followed the old woman to the door. After it closed behind her, she could still hear the dog barking.

She wanted a telephone. She wanted to call New York and tell him—I'm in Freiburg, and the house is empty. They're gone. They're gone! How can I know if they were ever here, if I was ever here?

Inside her she felt a faint pang of hunger. I'm having your child, Anton. Tell me you want your child.

But it was morning in Germany and not yet dawn in America. It was too early to call.

Instead, they took the streetcar to the university, walked until she felt better, and then they had lunch.

"It could have been her clock," Bill said, avoiding mention of the incident which she knew was still troubling him.

"It couldn't. It was in that house when I was born."

"It's not the only clock of its kind ever made."

"Did you feel her loathing?"

"You know," he smiled a little, "I think she felt uncomfortable and put upon. I don't think there was any loathing until the end."

"I'm glad you were there," Anna said.

She persuaded him that she was fine, and he stayed at the university, leaving her alone. She took the streetcar back downtown and wandered around for a while, killing time until she could call. At two she went to the post office, on Eisenbahnstrasse not far from the railroad station, and had them call, giving both numbers at the shop.

The postal clerk who placed the call was old and kindly looking, and she allowed herself to like him a little. He called her after several minutes and said Mr. Peters was not in but they expected him back the next morning.

She thanked him and left. On the street again, she realized how tired she was. She went back to the hotel and went to sleep. Later Bill came back. He had stopped at a book store and bought some books and then picked up some huge chocolate bars. She sat up and devoured half of one, certain that she felt its energy creeping through her veins. When she finished, he got undressed and made love to her. She didn't mind that either. It had been early in their stay in Paris when she had last let him touch her.

In the morning he went back to the university. It was Friday, and they would be gone by the weekend. He wanted to take a last look.

Anna walked by herself, trying to dredge up a feeling of nostalgia, for the town, its cobblestones, its beautiful old buildings, but nostalgia meant love, and there was none. If she had ever doubted that Max Kleinberger had ceased to exist, she doubted it no longer. He and Lotte had disintegrated, and the town had not noted their passing.

At two she went to the post office and placed the call with the same clerk. She waited apprehensively. Where would she begin? There was so much to tell him. It was five weeks today since she had missed her period, and she felt strong and healthy. She knew her mother had lost many babies over many years before Anna had miraculously been born, and she had had that fear, that it would happen to her too, but now she was sure. She knew she would have this baby.

She waited nervously while the connections were made, anxious to hear his voice, to make the final connection. The clerk caught her eye, and she went to the counter. He said her call was ready in the third booth, and she went in and picked up the phone.

"Hello?"

"Hello, yes." It was not quite his voice, but it was no one else's.

"Anton, it's me, Anna."

"Anna." His voice was tight and strained, as though he had only now begun to use it after a long silence. "Where are you?"

"In Freiburg." She tried to keep her own steady.

"Darling child, you shouldn't have gone alone." It was the first time he had called her "child" since forty-five.

"I went to the house." Her voice was thick.

"You must put it behind you now. You must think of other things."

"How are you? Is everything all right?"

There was a long pause during which the line was almost perfectly still. "Ella," he said then. "She wandered away again."

"No." It came out in a raspy whisper.

"Last week. Very far. She went very far away." His voice was shaking. "So far that we looked in all the wrong places."

"But you found her. Anton?" She felt as though she'd been hit and the pain was spreading through her body from the point of impact.

"We found her, yes. It took three days. Her lungs are nearly gone. We don't know—" He was having a terrible time speaking. "We have her in a hospital now," he finished.

The part of her that remained cool in emergencies tried to take hold. She reached into her bag for a tissue and held it to her face. "I can come home," she said. "Would you like me to come home now?"

There was another long silence. "I think—I think we shouldn't see each other again. I think I've been—we have separate lives to lead. It's best that you get on with yours now."

"You don't mean that."

"Yes, yes I do mean it." His voice had recovered some of its usual strength. "We must not see each other again."

"All right."

"It was good of you to call."

She said good-bye and hung up, sat in the booth, stunned, holding her tissue, her back to the glass window on the door. After a few minutes she heard the door open, and she turned to see the elderly clerk.

"Is it bad news?" he asked.

"No, it's nothing, really."

"So young," he said, "to cry your heart out that way."

He offered his hand, and she stood up, settled the bill, and thanked him. Outside she realized she had not stopped to wonder where he had been or what he had done in the war.

She started back to the hotel, walking a corridor of loneliness. Ella had given up. She had searched one time too many, and her lungs were gone. How easy it would be to give up. There had been a time once, in France, after he had left for Switzerland, when she had given up, when she had waited for death or something worse, and he had saved her. He would not save her now. Somehow she had misunderstood everything. She had taken what had not been offered, borrowed what had not been lent. She longed suddenly for Madeleine's presence, ached for her aunt who had brought her safely through a war. Madeleine would understand. What she might not do herself she would forgive in Anna.

But Madeleine was across a great ocean. She turned into Salzstrasse, hurrying. There was a baby inside her, and that baby had to be born. She passed the Augustinermuseum, running now, and came to the hotel. She would go to Switzerland and write her letters, but she had to go alone. She had to leave Bill behind for his own good. His involvement in her troubles must not continue.

She reached the room breathless and packed quickly, anxious to get to the station and board the first train for Switzerland. Just get there tonight and sit and think and begin to write letters.

Letters. She had to leave a note for Bill.

The door opened. She looked up.

"What's wrong?" he said, seeing the suitcase on the bed and looking very disturbed.

"I have to leave."

"Without me?"

"It's better that way."

"You're still upset from yesterday."

"No. Believe me, I just have to go."

"Can't we talk about this?"

"There's nothing to talk about. I was about to write you a letter but there's nothing to say really. It's over, that's all."

"Are you pregnant?"

The question hit her sharply like a slap, disarming her. "Yes," she said very weakly.

"You missed your period last week, didn't you?"

She had told him on the ship, lied to him, and he had remembered. She looked away.

"Why didn't you tell me?"

She bit her lips together, thinking, wanting desperately to say something that was the truth but not the whole truth, something that would allow him to remove himself from this mess, her mess. "I felt it was my responsibility," she said.

He came around the bed and stood next to her, a very placid looking young man, a quiet historian with a slightly troubled face. "Well," he said, "why don't we make it my responsibility too?"

He wanted to marry her. He said it shyly but with an unaccustomed forcefulness.

"It wouldn't work, Bill." She spoke quietly, agelessly, as though she really knew, as though she had had experience with marriage, when really all the experience she had had was with the lack of it. "I need to take care of this myself. You're only asking me because I'm pregnant. You musn't do this to yourself."

"That's not true at all." He pushed the suitcase out of the way and sat down on the bed. "Hell, I would have asked you

224

before the end of the summer anyway." He pulled her gently down on his lap and put his arms around her. "I think we'd make a terrific team."

A team. She could marry him, and they would be a team. She thought about it, sitting securely on his lap, feeling the power of his arms around her. It was all so tempting, this feeling, the idea of a team. Her mother had married a young historian, and it had been a good life, up to a point.

She pulled herself away and stood up. It was colder when you stood alone. Something was lost. "This is a bad time to make a decision like this," she said. "Let me go alone. I'll call you in New York in September. We can talk about it then."

"I won't let you go." He had stood up. "We've gone this far together. We'll go the rest of the way."

She turned away and looked at a pile of books he had picked up in town, cheap cardboard covers and coarse, graying paper. They were written in German. She could read them and talk to him about them. She could be part of his work, part of his achievement. They could be a team.

"You really mean it, don't you?" She had her hand on top of the books, as though she were taking an oath.

"Sure I mean it." He grinned, a big American grin.

Her baby would be legitimate. People would count on their fingers but that wouldn't bother her. She could marry an American, a true-blue American with roots in American soil and a brother who had died defending it. And some of the loneliness would be gone. He was very nice, and he was very fond of her. She would be good to him because he deserved it. She would make them a team.

They returned the car, took a train to Switzerland, and got married. He called his parents, a long trans-Atlantic call from a little Swiss post office, while she waited, turning the new band of Swiss gold on the finger next to Anton's ring. He came out of the little booth rubbing sweat off his face and grinning.

"Mom took it like a trooper," he said. "They're wiring

225

some money so we can have a 'proper honeymoon.' And they think we should try to get a double room on a different ship for coming home. Let's see, and maybe we could come home a little sooner. It looks like Eddy's coming back the end of August and Mom wants me—wants us to be there if that's O.K. with you."

It was O.K. It was fine. The money came, and the amount startled her. Where did farmers get so much money?

She did her own telephoning and writing, and they stayed awhile until the furor abated. Bernie was upset, but Madeleine, as always, understood. There was nothing, of course, that could be done. They were married.

Bill changed the passage home, and they left from France just after the middle of August. Madeleine was to meet them at the dock, and Anna worried her way across the Atlantic. She was still not sure how to calculate a birth date, but she had to be well into her third month by the end of August. There would be no hiding it from her aunt.

But Madeleine surprised her. She hugged Bill with uncharacteristic familiarity, burying herself in his broadness, and while he was somewhere up ahead with the luggage, she slowed down and patted Anna's stomach.

"You're pregnant?"

Anna was floored. "Yes."

"Good. That's wonderful. I'm so glad. Maybe now you'll start to feel like an American."

Anna walked to the car in a daze. After nine years there were still surprises.

226

346

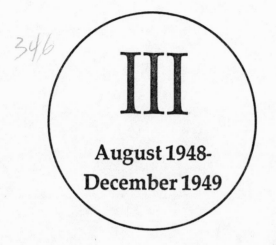

III

August 1948-
December 1949

1

They stayed in her old room at Madeleine's apartment, Bill sleeping on a cot borrowed from Klara. Days they looked for an apartment, finding one at the end of the third full day of searching. They put a deposit down and went back to Madeleine's to discuss it. Madeleine liked the sound of it and drove there with Bill the next morning so she could see it and he could write a check for the first month's rent. Anna stayed behind.

It was the last week of August, a month since she had spoken to Anton, and she had wondered every day since about Ella. She was alone now with the telephone, and she couldn't call, couldn't because he didn't want her to, couldn't because she didn't want to hear the voice, didn't want to ask the question. A certain imminent turbulence inside her had receded slightly below the threshold but could not be banished completely; it even had to be coaxed to recede further.

But there was another number, one that included an open invitation. She dialed and listened for the noncommittal answer at the switchboard.

"Mrs. Morgenstern, please," she said.

A receiver lifted somewhere else. "Mrs. Morgenstern."

"This is Anna Goldfeder. I don't know if you remember me. I spoke to you last winter. You gave me Mr. Pietrovic's address—Mr. Peters. He changed his name."

"Yes, Anna, of course I remember. How nice to hear from you. Have you been able to speak to him?"

229

"Yes. I saw him before the summer. I wanted to ask you something. His wife—Mrs. Peters—she was very ill. I've been away all summer and I wondered— I heard she was in a hospital." She knew she was not being coherent. "I'm afraid to call him." The last sentence had been totally redundant. Her voice had explained it better than the words.

"Yes, I know about his wife." There was a brief silence. "She was very sick."

"I know."

Another silence. "She died in the middle of August."

Anna swallowed. "Thank you."

"I'm so sorry. Did you know her?"

"Yes. I knew her very well. I knew her better than I knew him."

"Many people will miss her. Many people have remembered her very kindly."

"I'm sure they have. Thank you, Mrs. Morgenstern." She hung up and waited in the kitchen for her husband to come home with news of their new apartment.

The way it worked out they would bury Eddy on Labor Day. Labor Day was very late that year, so Bill and Anna went out to Iowa the end of August for their visit. The day after the burial they would return to the east and Bill's classes at Columbia. It was a long train ride with little to see besides farmland during most of the trip. Bill had not told his family about Anna's pregnancy; they had enough to worry about with the burial. But there was no need yet to tell anyone. She had lost weight in Europe and still fit easily in her ordinary clothes.

They read a lot on the train and slept in little berths like those on the ship. For hours at a time Anna looked out the window at ripening fields and thought of Ella. When they were nearly there, Bill started talking about Eddy.

"I hate to see it all start up again," he said. "That was a bad time when he died. The folks were just beside themselves."

"But it's right that he should come home. And it's nice for your mother that she'll have a place to go, something she can touch, and know her son is buried there."

He gave her the wary, questioning look. "That's what Mom said. You'll probably get on well with her."

"I'm sure I will."

"Just do me one favor, Anna. What I told you on the ship, don't let on that you know, O.K.? That it might not be Eddy. Let's just keep that between us."

It didn't bother her to keep the secret, and it wasn't likely ever to come up. They were met at the station by Bill's parents, Ed and Emma, tall, thin people with a warmth that spread like a blanket (and, she thought, might be as superficial as a blanket). But she knew it was a hard time for them, that things would be different later. In Iowa she found out about American farmers and where the money came from. The farm stretched farther than she could see, and the house was large and well furnished.

They spent an uneasy week getting acquainted. Anna helped in the kitchen, learning where everything was kept, how they liked the table set, how they cleaned up after dinner. She met Bill's sisters, one older and married, and one younger, about her own age, and giggly.

At the end of the week the train came, carrying the flag-draped coffin, and they drove to the station and watched as it was unloaded from the last car. Emma had been a wreck all day, looking at her watch every few minutes, fidgeting with her straight, dark hair (now starting to turn gray) pulled back severely into some sort of knot. As the red and white became visible, she covered her mouth and then closed her eyes. Anna turned, put her head on Bill's shoulder, and cried. It was her brother coming home, and the wound, like all death wounds, was eternally fresh.

They followed the hearse sixteen miles to the nearest mortuary, Bill driving now, Ed comforting Emma in the back seat. This was what families were for, to comfort each other when the dead came home. She thought fleetingly of Anton.

231

She had tried so hard not to think of him. After Ella was gone, who had held him when the soldiers came?

The funeral was at ten on Labor Day. She had expected a small, simple family affair, but it turned out to be quite different. Eddy was the first soldier returned to this town, and the town turned out to honor him. Men came in American Legion uniforms, and boy scouts stood looking like miniature soldiers. The high school band came on a bus and played patriotic songs. The minister spoke a few words, then the mayor said something, and finally one of Eddy's teachers said what a fine and intelligent boy he had been, how he had wanted to go away to college to learn how to be a modern, scientific farmer and come back and work the family farm as his father did and as his grandfather had, and his loss was everybody's loss because without farmers, where would everyone be? And when the band had finished and the speeches were over, a boy who had practiced all summer stepped forward and played taps.

It was a moment Anna would never forget—a moment of sunshine and light wind, a moment in which the first feelings of patriotism stirred—the town turning out to honor its son who had died in her war, the band playing after practicing through the hot summer for him, the little boys carrying the heavy American flag. And Ed and Emma standing almost at attention, listening, Emma taking her husband's hand when taps was played.

When it was over, the family dropped rose petals on the long box, and Anna bent and touched it with her whole palm, feeling very close to this boy, this boy who had made her a member of the family.

The townspeople drifted away, but not to their cars. It was a holiday, and Anna saw them, in little family groups, moving through the cemetery, stopping and leaving flowers, people who had grown up in this place, who had buried their loved ones here, lucky people who had a place to lay flowers.

The next morning she and Bill took a train back to New York.

They moved into the little apartment they had found not too far from Madeleine. Anna registered at General Studies at Columbia and rode the train in with Bill three times a week. She took English, American history, and government, and worked furiously, building up a reading list that she would use in the spring when she was no longer a student. Her fellow students were horrified when they realized she was pregnant, and one of her professors suggested "for everybody's good" that she take a leave of absence.

She said, "No, thank you," and continued to report to classes.

At Christmas they went back to Iowa to spend the vacation. She was very pregnant by then, and Emma kept telling her to sit and rest and put her feet up, not to stretch, and not to drink too many liquids. On Christmas day, after the family returned from church, they all went out to the cemetery to lay a wreath. Bill pressed her to stay home but she went, just to see the place in winter, to feel Eddy's presence. His parents were pleased that she came. It was the beginning of a bond.

The baby was born on a terribly cold day in March. It came late according to her actual due date and a little early according to the one she had told Bill and her doctor. She had asked Bill to let her name this one and he could have all the others.

It was a girl, even in the moment of birth a Goldfeder, the dark hair, the cheekbones, the chin—and someone else's eyes. He came to her in her room when they let her out of recovery.

"She's beautiful," he said. "Looks just like you."

"Can we call her Antonia?"

"It's a beautiful name."

"Thanks, Bill."

233

"Go to sleep, honey. I love you."

She closed her eyes and saw him through the window, standing on the road, eyeing the farmhouse with fear and reticence, wondering, after all he had been through, what might possibly wait inside. Now only she knew; he had bidden her to lead her separate life.

In the morning they brought her baby to her, a warm, sweet thing that sucked at her breast blissfully, that blinked large curious eyes and waved tiny hands, and suddenly she didn't know. She didn't know if she could keep this from him forever, or if she should, or if he would want her to. It was such a beautiful baby. What was right and who was there who could tell her?

2

She read like a demon. She read history and government and American novels. When she wasn't reading, she was taking Tonia for walks in the new carriage Ed and Emma had sent, or for rides in the old car Bill had bought. Robin was amazed at what a mother Anna had become.

"I think you went away and sent a double back," she said when she was home for spring vacation.

"I think I sent the double away," Anna said. "The double bothered me. She wanted to go to Pembroke, but I'm very happy here."

Madeleine enjoyed her new role of great-aunt. She baked in advance if she knew they were coming. She played with Tonia although Tonia was still rather too little to be played with. It was a day with cookies and tea when she told Anna the news.

"Richard is leaving. He's been offered a position in California—I can't remember where. It's such a big place, California." She said it as she might describe the weather, pleasant, warm, encouraging.

"Didn't he ask you—" She hated to pry. Neither of them was mother to the other. Still, it was a question one could ask of a close friend. "Doesn't he want you to go with him?"

"Yes, of course he asked me," Madeleine said. She might have been talking about an invitation to the theater. "But of course I can't go."

"Why can't you go?"

"Ah, Anna." Madeleine looked down at her finger, tight in Tonia's grasp. "I have a job here. Who knows what there would be out there. We have our friends here. I can go to France without crossing the whole country first. There's no reason for me to go."

"Isn't Richard a reason?"

"Well, of course, I'm fond of him. He's very good company, but—" Madeleine shrugged off-handedly. He could be replaced. There were other Richards in the ocean. "I've lived here so long," she said. "I'm too old to adjust to a new place."

"You're not too old. You adjust better than I do. You know that."

"Come, don't look so serious. It's nothing. We'll give him a party before he goes, all right?"

She stayed another hour, and they talked about the things they always talked about, the students, the staff, the little scandals. It came time to leave—it was late afternoon, and Tonia had become restless. There was a dinner to put together, a baby to feed and bathe. Bill would be home in an hour. She stood up and started putting baby things into the bag she carried, while Madeleine wrapped Tonia for the ride home.

"Come here," Madeleine said, looking up from the baby. "Let me see that dress."

Anna tugged at it self-consciously and crossed the living room. She hadn't lost enough weight after the birth, and she was nursing. Everything was too tight except Bill's big, comfortable shirts, but Madeleine objected to them. They were all right for single girls, but a married woman—a mother—had to look more refined.

"Turn around," Madeleine said. "Look how it pulls." She lifted the skirt. "It's a good dress. There's plenty of fabric to let out. Drop it off on Saturday and I'll fix it for you."

"Thanks, Madeleine."

Madeleine smiled. "You see? How can I go to California? Who will take care of you?"

* * *

In June there was an enormous party to celebrate Robin's engagement. A tent was set up over the backyard, and tons of food were served. Lenny had given Robin a three-carat diamond. They would marry next June, just after she graduated. Later this month Lenny would start to work for Bernie. It was a perfect match.

Anna wondered often about perfect matches. Mostly when she played with Tonia, when she looked into the now dark eyes that were someone else's, that were Anton's, she wondered with pain how he was, imagined him alone in Connecticut planting the garden—their garden—saw him sleeping in the bed with the brass rail headboard. Sold to the little lady with the big smile. Like Emma's pain for Eddy, this one never quite went away.

Usually she kept away from upper Madison Avenue. But when she went shopping for an engagement present for Robin, she walked there deliberately, staying on the west side, and skittered nervously past the point where his shop stood across the street. Something glittered in the right window as she passed, and something solid shone in the left.

Later in June there was the party for Richard, and then Anna and Bill left for Iowa for the summer. It was a quiet, restful summer. Bill helped Ed during part of each day, and Anna read and helped Emma and took care of Tonia. Anna wrote to a mail-order nursery and ordered some heathers; when they came she and Emma went out to the cemetery and planted them at Eddy's grave. It was pretty there in the summer, and the heathers Anna had chosen would bloom during the cold months when almost nothing else did. Over the summer she and Emma talked and talked, about little things and big things, but not about the one thing Anna longed to talk about, the boy in the cemetery with heather on his grave.

In September they went back, and Bill started his second year at Columbia. They had friends now, other young graduate students preparing for academic careers or for work in Washington. Some of them were married. They visited each other on weekends, bringing their own wine or liquor to dinner, all of them on tight, graduate student budgets.

Tonia was six months old now, rolling over and trying to sit up, her dark hair growing longer, forming tight ringlets around her chubby face. She was a sweet child, easy to please, and Anna enjoyed pleasing her.

In November Anna turned twenty-one. It was a big birthday, Bill told her, and they must celebrate it appropriately. The twelfth was a Saturday, and he invited two other couples out to dinner with them that evening at an expensive French restaurant. Madeleine came to baby-sit, because she enjoyed it, she said (and because Richard wasn't around any more), and because she was more reliable than an ordinary baby sitter would be. Anna and Bill agreed with her reasons and always welcomed her offer. They left the apartment in good spirits; they were off to a celebration.

The restaurant had set up a table for six, and after they had all arrived, they ordered drinks before dinner. She had never learned to drink the kinds of things Americans liked, but Bill ordered her something sweet and she drank it easily, feeling it begin to work on her, to color her cheeks and make her feel a little silly. The other couples brought her small gifts which she unwrapped with pleasure while they waited for their appetizer. They were nice people, friendly and funny and good company on a birthday.

Her pâté came, and she ate it slowly, giving Bill a little taste. He tended to like simpler foods, which was why she enjoyed eating out. She could satisfy her palate without disappointing his.

The soup was rich and spicy, and Bill ordered wine, which they all began to taste. Then the main course came, served with great flair by two waiters. She was about to begin when she looked up, across the table, toward the entrance where a young woman was following a waiter to a table. She was small, dark, and attractive, dressed very elegantly, in her

238

late twenties or perhaps thirty. She looked up with a smile to say something to the man she was with and the man was Anton Pietrovic.

It was as though her heart stopped beating. It was as though her air supply was cut off. He had his hand on the woman's back, and he was listening to her, smiling back at her, answering her. Anna was frozen, watching them, her eyes on his face, such a beautiful face, a face she loved, a face she had never stopped loving.

The waiter turned toward an empty table, and Anton looked up, saw her, stopped momentarily as the woman continued. His hand, which had rested on her back, was still raised. He stood there only a second or two, then turned and joined his companion.

It was like a wave at the ocean. It knocked her down and took her breath away. She had tried so hard to put him aside, to forget, to think of him as an old friend. But now he was there, *here*, and she loved him, loved him more because she had something that was his, a child, and here he was with another woman, a woman ready for marriage and certainly ripe for love. He would have dinner with her and take her back to his apartment. Funny how she had always imagined him alone. It was over a year since Ella died. He would be thirty-eight now. What had made her think there would be no women?

"You O.K.?"

She turned and saw Bill, her young American husband, sitting beside her. "Just a little too much wine, I think. I'll just go and splash some cold water on my face."

"Want me to come along?" It was one of the wives sitting across the table.

"No thanks. I'm fine. I'll be right back."

She got up and made her way to the ladies' room. It was in a small alcove, ladies on the right, men on the left. She was having trouble swallowing. She put her hand on the knob.

"Anna."

239

He was right behind her. She turned and leaned against the wall.

"It's good to see you. I hope you're well."

She nodded.

"Did you know that Ella died?"

"I heard." It was little more than a whisper.

"I thought you would be away at college now."

Her voice responded only minimally. "I didn't go."

"I'm sorry to hear that. I hope—I hope I wasn't at fault."

She shook her head.

"This must be your birthday."

"Yes."

"You look very lovely."

Tears spilled over. She had lived a lifetime of mistakes, her own and other people's, and for none of them had there been a chance to go back, to make a slight correction in the itinerary, to ink out a wrong word.

He touched her arm, then lifted the hand on which she wore the ring he had given her many moons and deaths ago. "You've married," he said, his thumb running over the adjacent rings which symbolized the two unbreakable bonds in her life.

"Yes." Something inside her said, tell him.

He dropped her hand. "I hope you're happy," he said. "You know I mean that."

She nodded. It screamed, TELL HIM.

"Good night, Anna dear."

She turned away and rushed into the ladies' room, locking the door behind her so she could be alone. And she was. Completely alone.

In the car she closed her eyes so that Bill would think she was asleep and not try to talk to her. Where had it all gone wrong? She had done as he had told her—and then he had seen her tonight, and he still cared. It was all there, alive and fresh and frightening.

240

She kept seeing the woman, the small, pretty woman with her easy elegance, the petite, attractive body in the expensive, tasteful dress. The truth cascaded upon her. They slept together. She went to Connecticut with him, and they held each other on the bed with the brass rail headboard. Sold to the little lady with the big smile who has completely misunderstood life. And one day he would marry her, or someone like her. It was well over a year since Ella's death, almost ten years since she had been a wife to him. One day the time came when you made your choice; you lived or you stopped living. You got the answers to your questions, and you lived with them in peace.

He will marry someone and it won't be me.

Oh, God, Jürgen, take me over a mountain. I can't go myself.

Bill parked the car, and they went upstairs. He kept his coat on to take Madeleine home. He insisted that she not drive her own car; he wanted to take her himself, to walk her up to the door of her apartment. How could you hurt someone as kind and sweet as Bill?

She hung her coat up and went into Tonia's room. It was almost a month now since Tonia had been weaned, and Anna missed the nursing more than her baby did. The last physical link between them had been broken.

Tonia lay on her stomach, the blanket half off, her face on its right side, the two middle fingers of her left hand in her mouth. Anna patted her back and pulled the blanket up. What is fair? What is fair to Tonia, to Bill, to Anna? What is fair to Anton?

Who is there to tell me?

Bill wanted to sleep with her. She turned him down. She turned him down the next night too, and the next time he asked. She said she was tired, she said she wasn't feeling well, she said she didn't feel like it. She got her period, and then she didn't have to say anything.

She spent hours each day reading to Tonia, playing with her, talking to her, looking into the dark eyes that were her

241

father's, wondering. She went inside some fragile shell she had never known enclosed her. The scene in the restaurant and the subsequent conversation played themselves out with the monotonous regularity of the last record in a pile, over and over without stopping. He had taken her hand to see if the ring was still there. Seeing her had been as much a shock to him as it had been to her. He had said something once, but perhaps he had meant it only for that moment; perhaps he had spoken out of despair, out of anguish, and then, fallible even as she, he had been unable to change his own itinerary, to ink out the offensive words. Maybe he had needed her to comfort him, but she had listened only to his words and turned around and married someone else to comfort her.

But it was a marriage. She said the words to herself, out loud, in English. A marriage. She had made a promise that day in Switzerland, a vow for life. That promise had given her a place in the Henderson family, a favored spot to stand on while taps sounded. It had provided Tonia with grandparents, aunts, uncles, cousins, a family tree and a family mythology.

She had married him so they could be a team, and they had been, at the beginning. Then Tonia had been born, and things had changed a little. Anna got up from the chair she had curled up in and sat at Bill's desk. It was early December, and already he was working on a paper due in January. She turned the pile of penciled pages to the beginning. They would be a team again; she would make it happen. She read down the page. It was about the eighteenth century. Bill was fascinated with the eighteenth century. He had found his interest and his love early, as a generation ago Max Kleinberger had found his, and Anna admired her husband's as much as she admired her father's. Bill had a pleasant style of writing, easy to read but still very economical. With a pencil she made a slight change in a sentence midway through the page. What was not fair was to make Bill suffer her personal griefs. Surely she had survived much worse than a chance

242

meeting in a restaurant with a man she had not seen in a year and a half.

She turned her attention purposefully to the paper and read it carefully until Tonia awoke. Open at the side of the desk was a book in German with penciled translations and notations filling the margins. Tomorrow she would tackle it. When Tonia was born he had stopped asking her, but she had more time now, felt less tired. One could overcome anything if one tried, and she would try. When she went to get Tonia, she was sure she had begun to feel better.

The next day a letter came from Emma Henderson. She wanted Anna's Aunt Madeleine to join them for Christmas. The invitation pleased Anna. It had not been extended last year. Now Emma felt that Anna was part of the family, and her aunt, by extension, belonged too. Besides, Emma could not bear the thought of someone being alone on Christmas. During the war she and Ed had traveled long distances to pick up soldiers unable to get home for Christmas and had driven them to the farm to spend the day and, if possible, the night. She remembered them all by name, although, except for thank you notes, she had never heard from any of them again.

When Tonia was up, they went to visit Madeleine.

"Bill's mother has invited you for Christmas," she said over tea, while Tonia sat in a high chair Madeleine had bought second hand. "Will you come? It's a big family and they cook a lot and eat a lot and have a lot of fun."

"That's very kind of your mother-in-law," Madeleine said, offering a large cookie to Tonia. "Perhaps another year. You must give me her address. I'll write to her myself to thank her. Gladys has invited me to her parents' house, and she was hurt last year when I didn't go."

"O.K." The little Americanism had intruded itself surreptitiously into her French.

"And I like my church," Madeleine added. Church would, of course, be a problem in Iowa. The nearest Catholic church was quite a distance away, and in bad weather it was a

243

treacherous drive. "Not to mention the weather. It gets very cold, doesn't it?"

"Very. And lots of snow."

"I make too many excuses, don't I?" Madeleine said.

"Of course not. You shouldn't come if you've already promised to visit someone else. There'll be other times." But she knew what Madeleine meant. As Emma Henderson needed to be around people at Christmas time, Madeleine preferred to be alone. She enjoyed the gift-giving and the music, but she wanted it done quietly. The boisterousness of an American Christmas had remained incomprehensible to her and not in the best of taste. Most of all, she wanted to spend a few hours of the day by herself.

"Do you feel better now?" Madeleine asked.

Anna looked at her in surprise. "I haven't been sick."

"No, but since your birthday you haven't seemed—quite yourself. I thought maybe it was too much for you, turning twenty-one." She said it lightly.

"You're right, I didn't feel well for a while. I should have taken two aspirins and gone to bed for a couple of days, the way Klara always says, but," she shrugged and rumpled Tonia's curly hair, "I think those days are gone now."

"We'll go shopping for Christmas presents, and you'll come back to life. Maybe something nice for your mother-in-law."

It was not difficult, during the day, to come back to life. It was a matter of trying, first consciously, then almost from habit, to work at something, read something, cook a good meal, shop carefully for presents. The turbulence must be kept down. Soon it would break up into small pieces, each less dangerous than the whole, and they would dissolve. He had a right to a good life. He had earned it; he deserved it. She would think about other things, and she would forget. Her brain would cooperate.

She renewed her previous warmth toward Bill, and he welcomed it. He was delighted when she handed him notes

244

on the awful German book. He had always known she was smart if she had mastered that language before any other.

But at night she dreamed, crazy disconnected dreams, Jürgen and suitcases and jackets. She awoke not in fear but in anger. She would beat that too, but it would take longer—it would take more cooperation.

With Madeleine she went out and shopped for Christmas presents. She knew them all now, the parents, the sisters, the brother-in-law. She could imagine what they liked, could see their faces light up as they opened Anna's packages. She would make a reputation for herself in the Henderson family as the person who always brought the right thing. Even Eddy would be remembered. She would be worthy of them.

After the presents were bought and Bill had approved of them, Anna wrapped them, letting Tonia play with the leftover ribbons and decorations. She felt better now. It was over a month since she had seen him, two weeks since she had actively begun setting him aside. Bill was more relaxed and Madeleine happier. Even the mirror reflected a positive change.

All the wild fantasies and possibilities of those first days after her birthday had been beaten back. She had kept away from the telephone. She had resisted every temptation to write him a letter. She perceived, gratefully, that it had been an inner strength, not a weakness, that had prevented her from telling him her secret that night in the restaurant. She was Bill's wife now, and she would not disappoint him.

On the day after Bill's last class before Christmas, they left for Iowa. Tonia was nine months old, and she charmed every old lady on the train. There was a strong, happy spirit among the passengers, and Anna felt it and shared it. They were on their way home. In boxes and suitcases, they had gifts for the people they loved most. When they arrived, Emma took Tonia, hugged her, and wouldn't let her go.

The house was filled with friends and relatives and gifts.

There had been crowds like this once at the Kleinbergers', but the Kleinbergers were gone and the crowds were gone. Even the house that had held them was no longer genuine. What was genuine was now here.

The family went to church early on Christmas morning, and Anna stayed in the house with Tonia and made fresh coffee for when they returned. They came in talking and happy, glad to find hot coffee. In a little while, Em would start cooking, and Anna would help, and they would talk together, just the two of them, about Christmases before the war and about Tonia and about Bill.

Anna looked around the kitchen and realized that her mother-in-law was no longer there.

"Where's Em?" she asked.

"Gone to the cemetery, most likely," Ed said, looking up from his newspaper.

Anna got up and went to the back door. The snow was blowing, and through it she could just see Em, bundled up, on her way to the car.

"Em," she called, "wait for me. Em?"

Anna found her coat and boots, wrapped a scarf around her head, and put her gloves on. Out in the garage she picked up the heather she had transported carefully on the train from New York.

"You don't have to come," Emma said as she approached. "I don't mind going myself."

"I want to. If it's O.K."

"Of course it's O.K." Emma smiled. "Climb in."

The wind subsided as they drove, and by the time Emma had parked the jeep there was only a light snow. They got out and walked, each bearing a gift for the dead man. The graves were covered with snow, slanted and angled by the wind that blew unbroken by hills or trees. Emma brushed it carefully away from the new stone, as though it were crumbs on a child's mouth, and laid her wreath on the ground in front of the stone while Anna took her planting fork and tried to dig the frozen earth. She had bought the

246

plant in the fall and nurtured it, forgetting that the Iowa earth would freeze.

"It's nice of you to do that for Eddy," Emma said, bending to brush snow from the other heathers Anna had planted last summer.

"It's the only marked grave in my family." She looked around. There was nothing but snow and headstones, snow everywhere, but it was a friendly place, a place for families to come and lay their flowers, a place to go to remember.

"You lost your parents in the war, didn't you?"

Startled, Anna turned around to face her mother-in-law. They had talked together all last summer, but this was the first time Emma had stepped across the invisible line.

"Yes, I did."

"Do you pray for them—in your faith?"

"I have no faith, Em."

"Sure you do, Anna," with the harsh R of the midwest, "sher," "sher." "We've all got faith in something."

"When did Bill tell you?"

"When you first came to us, the time Eddy came home. He said not to talk about it, it would upset you."

"It upsets me, but I don't mind talking about it."

"There's things we never get over," Emma said. "Not in one year, not in five. Did you know it's likely that's not our Eddy buried here?"

"Bill told me the night we met. He said not to let on, so I never did."

"I guess he thought he was protecting us." Emma bent and moved the wreath unnecessarily. "He's a good boy." Did she see the irony of it, that in trying to protect them he had built a wall between them? "It was a shock when the box came. Some things were Eddy's, some weren't. We talked about it, Ed and me, but I knew I wanted him back. He's an American boy. He's the son of American folks. He deserves to be buried here."

"It's nice you have a place to put a wreath, no matter who he is."

"Yes, it's nice." Emma knelt to fix the heather. She had strong hands, and she managed to wedge it deeper in the earth. "I'll come out the first nice day and fix it." She stood up. "I kept looking for a reason, you know, why my Eddy should have died in that war."

"You can't always find reasons, Em."

"There has to be. When you have faith, there has to be a reason. He would have taken the farm. Bill never wanted it. He just wanted to read and go to school."

"Maybe the girls will take it. A farm should stay in the family. It's not like a store or a factory. It's part of a country. A family shouldn't let it go."

"My goodness," Emma said, "what a nice speech. I never thought to hear you say anything like that."

"I don't know why not."

Emma smiled. "All these months, and I'm just getting to know you."

"Yes."

"Takes time, I suppose. All that time I looked for a reason, afraid I wouldn't find any. I wasn't against the war, you understand. We had to fight it. I know that. I just couldn't see why it had to be my Eddy. And then Bill brought you home last year, and I thought, 'Maybe that's the reason. It was so that Anna could come into our family.'"

A chill, colder than the Iowa winter, passed through Anna. "I'm not the reason, Em. There was a reason for Eddy, but it wasn't me."

"Well, it was my reason. Maybe some day you'll find one for your Mom and Dad."

"They were murdered, Em. It was completely senseless." She shoved her hands in her pockets. That, at least, she had settled in 1945. She turned to Eddy's stone, snow obliterating the dates. "When did he die?"

"In forty-four, in August. It was in France."

Sounds came back, war sounds. You never forget war sounds.

"They all died, all the ones he was with. I guess there was

248

nothing left of his group but a lot of poor bodies, all nice clean American boys from good American homes. You want to go back, Anna? You look chilled."

"I like it here." But her voice sounded hollow.

Emma watched her for a moment. "Is there trouble between you and Bill?"

Anna turned and looked at her in surprise. It was impossible that any vestige of November was still visible. She felt better and looked better than a month ago. She had rededicated herself, and it was all working out. "There's no trouble with Bill," she said and it was true. If there had been trouble, it had been all her own.

"You seem a little different since the summer. Bill too. He kind of tiptoes around you as though he's afraid of setting something off." Emma glanced at her son's stone, then back to her daughter-in-law. "Some troubles last forever. You and I know about that kind. But there's others that come and go. They happen to everyone. It's nothing to be ashamed of. You're part of the family, Anna. You can tell me about it if you think it'll help."

A woman rooted in the land because the land was hers and the land was a farm. A woman who had never been east, west, north, or south of this place. A woman who brought anybody's son home and made him her own.

"Bill isn't Tonia's father," Anna said, looking Em straight in the eye.

Emma Henderson flinched slightly, then stood like a woman listening to taps for her dead son. "Does he know?"

"No. I put it all behind me a long time ago. It was a man from the war. He lost his children and his wife came back— warsick." She made the word up on the spot. It sounded like a good word. If she tried, she would master this language. "She died the summer I was in Europe. There was no reason for it, but he probably felt responsible. I think—it's possible she may have killed herself."

"You poor child."

249

"He said we shouldn't see each other."

"And you didn't tell him."

"No. We went our separate ways. I married Bill, and that was the end of it."

Emma said something, but the wind carried it away.

Anna looked at her questioningly. "I didn't hear you. You said—"

"I said, 'Was it?' Was it the end or have you had second thoughts?"

Just below the threshold the imminent turbulence, but it was her problem, not anyone else's, not her mother-in-law's. They had come to pay their respects to Eddy, not to worry a problem better left quiescent. "No," she said. "I'm Bill's wife. I won't let him down. I won't let anyone down." She kicked at the snow. "I saw him last month. Just for a minute. It was an accident. I never looked for him, Em, and I never will. It left me a little rattled, but I'm all right now." Her voice weakened, then rallied.

"I wonder," Emma said. Her eyes seemed to have sunk into her face. They were all heavy, hers, Anna's, everyone's. She turned and looked away. Beyond the cemetery fence were miles of white fields planted with winter wheat. She and the wheat were hardy. They would survive this winter; they would see spring again. "Maybe there's things that are more important than a promise, even a sacred one. Sure you got rattled when you saw him, Anna." Again the harsh "sher." "It's still inside you. Making promises won't make it go away. Having a man's baby, that's a big, wonderful thing to happen to a person. And then there's Bill. Do you think it's fair to him, not having a wife that's all his? Not having his own baby?"

Anna listened to her without following the thread. It was as though the language had suddenly, after all these years turned against her. "I don't understand," she said.

"He's so young, our Bill." Emma glanced at Eddy's stone. "He isn't any older than Eddy was when he—" Her voice

250

caught. "I wanted so much for my boys. It seems so long ago now. And after Eddy—after Eddy I wanted it double for Bill. You understand that, don't you, Anna?"

Anna nodded.

"I still want him to have it. A woman who's all his. A baby that comes from him." She had looked away and seemed to be talking to herself. "If you're not all his, he's never going to be happy," she said, turning back. "I know you want to do what's right for Bill but you mustn't feel you have to stay with him for his sake, Anna. He's young enough that he'd get over it. When he found himself someone who belonged all to him he'd be happier." She took a few steps through the snow and took Anna's gloved hand in hers. "God knows, I'd miss that baby, but you need to do what's right. Maybe what's best for you would be best for Bill too."

What was best for her. The meaning had suddenly, brilliantly, become clear. For the first time in her life someone was offering her a genuine choice, two possibilities, both equally attainable, stay or go. Bill will be better off if you go. You will never be able to change the past but now, right at this moment, you can change the itinerary of the rest of your life.

Anna looked back to where the jeep was parked. "Would you drive me to the station?" she asked.

"Sure I will. That's what families are for."

She threw clothes into the suitcase, hers and Tonia's. The next train left in an hour and a half and she wanted to make it. It was Christmas Day, Sunday, and no one would be traveling. By the time the rush started on Tuesday, she would be almost home. She was finishing when Bill came in.

"What's going on?" He looked fearful, as though he already knew, as though the question had merely fulfilled a rule of courtesy, not been a request for information.

"I'm going home."

"Why?"

251

"Bill, try to—"

"I asked you a question," he roared. "Why are you going home?"

"I can't explain it," she said shakily, wondering where she would begin if she tried. "Ask your mother. Your mother will tell you."

"My mother?" He looked from her to the suitcase and then around the room. "Are you taking Tonia?" His voice was almost under control.

"Yes."

"Are you leaving me?"

"Yes." She looked at him sorrowfully, then closed her suitcase.

"I won't let you have her," he said.

She stared at him, slid the suitcase off the bed, and picked it up.

"You only married me because of Tonia, didn't you?"

"I married you because of Eddy," she said, and walked out of the room before he could respond.

They rode quietly to the station and kissed when the train came in. Through the window she waved to Emma, holding Tonia near the glass so that her breath misted it. The train pulled away and Anna kept her eyes on her mother-in-law, whom she would never see again, and she knew the time had come to ask Madeleine to tell her the truth.

3

She caught a taxi back to the apartment so that she would disturb no one and no one would know she was home. It felt good to come back, to have all the amenities again after the long uncomfortable trip across the country. When had she stopped thinking of them as luxuries? Perhaps when Tonia was born. There were things that Tonia *needed*; one could not compromise with the needs of a baby, or even question whether they were needs.

After the warm bath and the fresh pajamas, Tonia fell quickly asleep in her familiar crib. The apartment was very quiet, but not with the silence of emptiness. Anna's house would never be empty again; she had a child. In the deepest part of the night, Tonia's breathing broke the stillness. What had her parents' house been like the night she left?

She sat in the living room wearing only her nightgown and thought it out. There were lives that needed to be put in order, and the first of them was hers. There were questions she had to ask and answers she had to hear and learn to live with. There were suitcases to be packed and mountains to cross.

She was up early with her baby. It was Wednesday. It was almost 1950. Mid-century was a good time to pack a suitcase.

The front door opened about eleven, and Bill walked in. Tonia, lying on her stomach in the playpen, saw him and began to bounce around, making flirtatious sounds. He watched her from the door he closed behind him.

Anna walked into the living room and saw him. She felt more pity than she had ever felt for anyone else she had known, more even than for his mother. He was not yet twenty-three, and he had all of this to live with, all these memories.

"I flew," he said, and there was a kind of pride in the words. She knew almost no one who had been on a plane. "I got in last night."

She was holding a dish towel and Tonia's favorite plate.

"My mom told me. She told me everything. You're a bitch, do you know that?"

She watched him almost fearfully as he started toward her. For the first time since she had met him, she was afraid, afraid for herself and for Tonia. She took a step back, away from the line he was walking, a step toward the playpen.

"I'm packing my things," he said, passing her on his way to the bedroom.

She put the dish away and walked to the back of the apartment and stood at the bedroom door.

He opened drawer after drawer and emptied them in huge handfuls. "You could have let me know," he said, anger growing in his voice. "You could have told me last summer. You didn't have to lead me on." He threw his things carelessly into a suitcase, piling them unevenly and mumbling with irritation when it refused to close. He took two cartons from the closet, inverted them, leaving their contents where they spilled on the floor, and began dropping things in—shoes, belts, ties, notebooks. "You were pregnant when you got on that boat, weren't you? You knew it all along and you let me think—" He had a shoe in his hand, and she backed off again, watching him, fearful and fascinated. "It was the guy that wrote you the letter, wasn't it?" He looked more hurt than angry.

"Give me that ring," he ordered suddenly, his hand out expectantly.

She looked down at the two rings on her left hand, the

254

little emerald ring from Anton and the thin band of Swiss gold.

"The wedding ring," he blurted. "You don't deserve to wear it. You lied when you took it from me."

She pulled it off and held it out to him, maintaining her distance. He took it and put it carelessly in the pocket of his pants.

"I'll pick up the furniture when I've got a place of my own, maybe Friday, maybe next week. You can keep the baby stuff."

She knew his threat should horrify her, that probably he had no right to do it, but somehow it didn't matter. They were only things he was taking, things that could be replaced. They weren't people or ideas or memories.

"You know what you are? There are good English words for it, French ones too, I'll bet." He bent the top leaves of the first carton alternately so they closed securely. "I'm taking the car." He said it as though he were waiting for an argument, as though he expected her to plead for it, and then he could use it as another weapon in this fight that he would surely win because she had not contested him. "I'm ashamed you were ever in my family. I'm ashamed you were there when my brother was buried."

My brother, she thought. My brother Eddy. Even after today he'll be my brother. Even when you're not my husband any more.

"I'm leaving." He took the cartons to the front and returned for the suitcase. "My mom said to give you a divorce and let you have Tonia. I think it's a mistake. I don't think people should make things easy for you." He picked up the suitcase, and she followed him. He put it down near the playpen and looked down at Tonia, who was sitting with a Christmas toy and a soggy pretzel. He looked as if he was about to cry. He was so young, and the hurt inflicted on him was such an old hurt.

"You can touch her, Bill," Anna said softly. "She loves

you." It was the first thing she had said since he walked into the apartment.

He knelt and touched the little head with its dark curls, and he sobbed hoarsely. Then he got up, his back still to Anna, and walked to the door with the suitcase, turning finally for a last look. "You never really belonged to me, did you?" he asked.

"I never really belonged to anybody," she said.

He opened the door, shoved the cartons out in the hall, and left.

The phone rang at one o'clock, and Anna put the newspaper down to answer it. Tonia would sleep for another hour and a half.

"Has he left?" It was Madeleine's voice, tight and nervous, speaking French.

"What do you mean?"

"Bill. Is he gone?"

It occurred to her that she had not yet told her aunt she was home. "How do you know?"

"He slept here last night. He called me from the airport."

"He told you?"

"Yes."

But how much? Had he told her everything, that there was a French word to describe Anna? That he wasn't Tonia's father?

"Anna, do you want me to come to see you, or do you want to be alone?"

Anna pulled a kitchen chair closer to the phone and sat down. "Come for dinner," she said.

"It's too much work for you. Bring Tonia and come here."

She bit her lips until they hurt. "Bill took the car."

"Ah, yes. I'll come at four and take you shopping. Then I get to see my little sweetheart while she's awake."

"Thank you, Madeleine."

256

"You thank strangers. You don't thank me."

She hung up and listened to the pounding inside her head, felt it in her chest and arms. There were many accommodations to be made if she was to live alone, and she must learn to make them, buy a market basket to wheel to the store when Tonia outgrew the carriage, find a job. But what could she do? Answer phone calls at a switchboard?

The doorbell rang, and she pushed the chair back under the table and went to answer it. In the hall, looking very unhappy, was Robin.

"Hi. Come in." It was obvious that Robin knew.

"I heard."

"Give me your coat."

"Can you tell me about it?"

"What did you hear?"

"Madeleine called Mom, and I picked up upstairs."

"What did she say?"

"That you and Bill were separating. That Bill had spent the night at her apartment and was on his way over here. It was this morning. Mom cried when she got off the phone."

"That's all she said?"

"Honest to God. I don't even know who's leaving whom."

Anna sat down in the easy chair. "I think we're leaving each other."

"It doesn't make sense."

"Many things don't make sense."

Robin crossed her slender, pretty legs. She was wearing a beige, long-sleeved, cashmere sweater and a matching flannel skirt. As she moved, the ring on her left hand caught the afternoon light, and a flash passed through the room. That diamond could have fed all of Paris for a month during the war. Many things don't make sense.

"There's someone else, isn't there?" Robin asked.

Anna looked away from the ring. "I don't know. It doesn't matter. It's over with Bill."

257

"Lenny was right, wasn't he? Those weekends before you went to Europe."

"Lenny is always right."

"Where did we go wrong, Anna?"

Anna shook her head. The intricacies of family life were not altogether comprehensible. They had brought her here, and now they felt responsible for all the events of her life that derived from that one generous gesture.

"You didn't go wrong, none of you. There are things I have to put in place, decisions I have to make. Nothing your family has ever done for me made me marry Bill or made me leave him. Believe me."

"Will you marry him?" Robin asked. "The other man?"

"I don't know if there is another man." She looked around the living room, which would be bare by next week. "I worry about how your parents will feel. They've been so good to me, so understanding."

Robin stood up. "Don't worry about the family, cousin. Families survive everything. I can take care of Daddy, and Mom's a cinch after that. But you and I have to get something straight." It was hard to tell whether her sternness was genuine or affected. "Whoever he is, he damn well better get a new suit for my wedding."

Madeleine came exactly at four, her face pale and drawn. It made her look old. Her skin was fine and sensitive; it showed little lines that Anna's would never show. Every small burden, every major catastrophe, left its indelible mark. There would be new ones now, a line on the clear forehead, a strand of gray.

They shopped for food, taking turns carrying Tonia, talking about unimportant things, gossip, Madeleine's Christmas. The question came out in the natural course of the conversation.

"Have you heard from Richard?"

They were in the car driving home, Anna at the wheel, Tonia sitting on Madeleine's lap.

"I had a letter before Christmas."

Anna waited. "Is he well?"

"He is thinking of marrying," Madeleine said.

"Is that what he wrote you?"

"That and his work and the weather and the nice place he's staying in."

"He was asking you, Madeleine. That's why he said he was thinking about it. He really wants you, not some silly woman he met last month in California. Don't you see that? He would marry you in a minute if you said yes."

Madeleine adjusted Tonia's knitted hat. "I would have to put my pictures away then, wouldn't I?"

Anna pulled to the curb in front of the apartment and took the key out of the ignition. "You would still have them, even if they're put away."

"No." She leaned over and kissed Tonia's cold red cheek. "It's too late for me. One doesn't have children at my age. One only has memories."

"That's not true."

"We must think of you now. We must see to it that you are happy." But she looked bleak, as though she knew it would have to get worse before anything got better, before anyone could be happy.

They fed Tonia and bathed her and put her to bed, had their dinner and did the dishes together the way they had when they first moved into their apartment. There had been great joy then. Anna had chosen to live with her aunt and take her name, and although there was still much reliance on the cousins, the two of them had maintained their unity. Tonight the unity was still there, but the joy was gone.

"Do you want to come back to the apartment?" Madeleine asked.

"You mean to live?"

"I would love to have you—both of you."

"You're so good to me."

Madeleine looked away. "Was it a mistake to leave France?" She looked almost gray.

"It was the best thing that ever happened to me, Madeleine."

"But nothing has worked out right."

"It will now."

"If I can do anything— You know I'll do anything you want me to."

"You can tell me something." She felt herself tense with a morbid anticipation. "I've always been afraid to ask, but I have to know now. I have to know where I'm going. It's about my father."

Madeleine had almost stopped breathing. She sat on the sofa where Robin had sat this afternoon, but there was no glitter now, no flash of diamonds.

"You always knew what went on in my family. Josef used to tell you. My father didn't say good-bye to me the day I left."

"It's over ten years ago," Madeleine said in a strained voice. "You can't remember what happened. You were only a child."

"But I do, and I know that you know why."

Madeleine moved her hand. "So much was happening in those times. I can't remember everything."

"Please, Madeleine."

Madeleine twisted her hands. "I knew you would ask one day," she said. "I remember how you waited for them when you came to me, and I knew they would never come. Josef asked them a hundred times to leave. Lotte would have gone, but Max said no."

It was funny to hear Madeleine refer to them by their first names. She had always called them "your mother" and "your father." It had never occurred to Anna that Madeleine had thought of them as her in-laws, like Ed and Emma and the group in Iowa.

"The nice German who brought you to France told me—" She frowned. "What was his name?"

"Jürgen."

"Ah yes." She didn't attempt to pronounce his name.

Even now she pronounced Josef in the French way. "Max was furious when the German said you should go. He forbade it. It was Lotte's decision."

"I see."

Madeleine smiled. "You go your own way too, don't you? You really are a Goldfeder, aren't you?"

"I suppose I am." She could still remember the day before, the raised voices. They had never raised their voices to each other, and she had not understood. Then, in the morning, Jürgen had come, and Max Kleinberger had not been around. He had been in the little room on the top floor. Had he watched through the window as she left? she wondered. Or had he been too stubborn? You really are a Goldfeder.

"We never heard from him," Madeleine said. "I thought he would contact us after the war. He might have been able to tell us something about Max and Lotte."

"He died, Madeleine."

"What? How do you know?"

"I met someone the summer I was in Europe who knew his sister. He committed suicide in 1943."

Madeleine whispered something and crossed herself. "How terrible," she said. She looked very pale.

"I've always thought he must have done it when they took my parents away."

Madeleine shivered. "I try to forget," she said, "but the memories are all around me."

Like the pictures she would never put away. Like Anton's dreams. Anton. Always in the front of her thoughts, Anton.

Madeleine had stood up. "You must try to forgive him," she said. "He loved you, and he didn't want to let you go."

Anna walked her to the car and came back, showered, and got into bed. The fatigue of the day added to the accumulated fatigue of the long train trip, so she fell asleep quickly, but there was no rest. The oldest dream came back and haunted her sleep, Jürgen coming to the house that sunny

September morning and taking her by the hand, the knapsack on his back. Her mother cried, and Jürgen led Anna out the front door, down the walk to the street. She was a child again, and Jürgen grew a little beard. She was afraid because after a while they didn't speak German any more; she couldn't understand anyone, and she had to keep quiet. But he could be trusted. He got her to France, to Aunt Madeleine, who was Uncle Josef's wife, and when he said goodbye he said it in that special way the Germans have that means forever.

A baby cried, and the dream ended as Anna awoke with a start. She put her hand out and said, "Bill," and then she remembered; there was no Bill any more. She listened for the sound that would make her leave her bed, but there was none. Her baby was sleeping. She turned over and slept, and it came back, Jürgen and the knapsack and her mother crying. Why again? She had lived it. Wasn't that enough? Was there something she had to see, some little detail that had escaped her all these years?

She turned over, wanting to sleep but not wanting to go through it all again, but there it was, Jürgen with the knapsack, her mother crying, the front door opening before her, and the short walk to the street. But this time she stopped and looked back, up to that window on the top floor. There he was, her father, smiling above his beard, waving to her. Dream or memory? She would never know, but she waved back, just to make sure he knew that she forgave him.

When she got up in the morning, as soon as Tonia was fed and dressed, she called Madeleine and asked her to come and stay with Tonia tonight and could she please borrow the car?

262

4

There were two columns of Peterses in the Manhattan
phone book that she kept in the apartment, but only one of
them, A.R. Peters on West 99th Street, had the ACademy
phone number that matched the one he had given her a year
and a half before. She waited until Tonia was napping, took
the suitcase out of the closet, and opened it on the bed. The
time had come. She would pack her most precious possessions and take them with her. There was really very little to
choose from. The furniture was no longer hers, and the car
was gone. Even the gold ring had been taken from her finger. Among what was left she would find those things that
were essential to her life. Whatever happened—where had
she heard that before? —she would start a new life, she and
Tonia. She had left Germany and France, and now she
would leave this place, these memories.

She opened drawers and moved her hands questioningly
through their contents. Slips, stockings, underclothes,
sweaters, blouses. There was nothing of value, nothing
without which she could not survive. On one wrist was the
watch Robin had given her for her seventeenth birthday; on
the other the silver charm bracelet with additions from
home and abroad. On her left hand was Anton's ring. There
was no other jewelry. She closed the drawers, one after the
other, taking nothing, and went to the closet. A dress, a
skirt, another few of each. She pulled the hangers along the
rod like a disgruntled customer in a department store. Noth-

ing appealed to her. Nothing was necessary. Life would go on with none of the things in the closet.

At the end of the rack her hand felt the jacket. She slipped it off the hanger and brought it out into the light of the bedroom. It was soft from wear, but the fabric was still sturdy. It would keep the rain off you; it would warm you. She folded it tenderly and laid it in the bottom of the empty suitcase. Wherever she went—whatever happened—it would remind her that once something important had happened to her, and that memory would sustain her as the clothes in the closet and in the drawers would not.

She walked around the apartment, searching for irreplaceable objects, but there was nothing else. Max Kleinberger's book was still in Madeleine's apartment, and it was safe there. Poor Max, to have found out too late.

Had Jürgen brought word back from France? she wondered. Surely he must have. He had lived another four years. He must have let Lotte know that her daughter was safe, that she had made the right decision. You really are a Goldfeder.

When Tonia was up, she made a simple dinner. Madeleine arrived at five and saw the suitcase.

"You're not coming back tonight?"

"Yes, later. I just—need to have the suitcase with me."

"You're going to see a man?"

"Yes."

It was a strange conversation. Anna tried to imagine Robin and Klara talking about the same thing. Klara would have forbidden; Robin, enraged, would have screamed. She had misunderstood that too. There is nothing quite like a mother and a daughter. There are no substitutes in life, no perfect imitations. What is lost is lost forever. What is not yet lost must at all costs be preserved.

It was dark when she left. The winter solstice had occurred only a week ago, and the days were depressingly short. She dressed after Tonia was in bed and put her warm coat on. From a drawer in the kitchen she took a thick envelope and dropped it in her bag.

"You're almost as old now as I was when you came to me." Madeleine was watching her from the kitchen door.

"You were too young for such a responsibility."

"By the time you came my young days were over. Are yours over too now?"

She was at the door, smoothing her gloves on. "I don't know." (I was only young one day of my life, when I licked an ice cream cone.) "I suppose they are. I think they were over a long time ago, and I didn't know it."

"Come back safe, Anna."

She went down to the car and put the suitcase in the back seat. It was very cold, but the streets were cleaned of snow, and the car started easily. The tank was full. Madeleine had been thoughtful, as always. She drove west toward New York, picking up parkways where she could. There would be many highways built soon, Bernie said. Going into New York by car would be a breeze. Long Island would fill up because driving would be so easy.

She kept the radio off, trying to think what she would say. The words came, and they were always wrong. They sounded foolish and unconvincing and miserably trite, what you would expect from a Hollywood musical. What she wanted to say was something that transcended what they felt for each other—Lenny and Robin felt the same thing, anyone and anyone felt the same thing. But she and Anton meant something to each other, something that was tied up with Madeleine and Jürgen and Eddy, with Lotte and Max.

She crossed the Triboro Bridge, found 125th Street, and continued west. It was a part of New York she did not know. Dark-skinned people lived here. It was an odd country, the United States. Once it had pained her that she could not understand it, but now she wondered if any one individual really could.

Left on Broadway under the elevated train. Down past Columbia where she had studied, pregnant, for one semester at the start of her marriage, her poor, ill-fated marriage. At 107th Street Broadway veered off to the left, but she continued straight and came onto West End Avenue. She was very nervous now, as nervous as she had been that day on Madison Avenue when he had gotten out of the cab, as nervous as the day she had walked up to the front door of the house in Freiburg that was no longer hers. One Hundred Third Street. She slowed down. One Hundredth. She looked for a place to park, turning and turning again. He might not be home. He might have someone with him. He might have married in the month since she saw him. He might have meant it on the phone when she spoke to him from Freiburg; I think we shouldn't see each other again.

Lights went on in a car at the curb, and Anna stopped. The car pulled out and drove away. She backed neatly in and turned off the motor. She had arrived.

She locked the car and carried the suitcase through the cold wind that blew from the Hudson, looking for 99th Street and, when she found it, for the building. It was between West End and Riverside Drive, the entrance well lighted. She pushed open the door and inspected the names next to the black buttons. Peters. But there was no way through the inner door without a key, unless she wanted to ring. She looked around, saw someone coming from the elevator, and slipped in as he walked out. She took the elevator up, watching the floor numbers pass through the window. Something that transcends how we feel about each other.

It stopped abruptly, and the inner door slid noisily open. She pushed the outer door and walked down the corridor. Music greeted her, piano music, something she recognized. It was Beethoven, and it was coming from his apartment. Anton was home listening to music.

She put the suitcase down and waited. It went on without interruption. It came from a long-playing record with all the

266

richness of a concert hall. She listened until the movement was over, until there was a moment of silence. Then she rang the bell.

The music began again, a lock turned, and the door opened. She looked at him without saying anything. He was surprised, but not happy surprised. He was frightened surprised. After a moment, he stood back and opened the door wider.

She picked up the suitcase and put it just inside the door against the wall. He looked at it as if it were an uninvited guest. She walked into a good-sized foyer ending in a wrought iron rail and two steps down to a sunken living room. On either side of the foyer there was a clock, one tall and heavy, a deep mahogany, the other a lighter wood and a lower, slenderer build.

"Give me your coat," he said.

"I can't stay." She took the coat off and folded it over the railing. "I packed it myself," she said.

He looked at the uninvited suitcase. He was wearing a white shirt, open, without a tie, deep blue pants with a velvety look about them, and slippers. In one hand he held an open pair of glasses.

"Many things have changed," he said.

"Nothing has changed."

"You're a married woman."

"I left him."

He smiled very slightly. "On my account?"

"No, on mine. It was a mistake. I married him for a lot of wrong reasons. It wasn't fair to anyone."

"We do many things we shouldn't have done."

"But *we* didn't."

He looked away, folded the glasses, and slipped them into his shirt pocket. "I don't know."

"Is that all it was then—a few weekends in Connecticut that shouldn't have happened and a couple of days somewhere in France?"

267

He shook his head, but she had no idea what he was negating, whether it was what she had said or something else, something unspeakable.

"You were so good to her, Anton. I hope I could be that good to someone myself. You never put anything ahead of her. When she needed you, you were always there. Always. She was lucky to have you. I think she knew how lucky she was."

He shook his head again. He had not looked at her for several minutes.

"You don't know why she went away in the woods, but I do. I know because I did the same thing myself. She was looking for something, the way I was, something that wasn't there, but she couldn't be sure. I wish now I hadn't gone, but I had to go. I think—I think until the moment that door opened, I thought they would be there."

He looked very tired now, as though the war had chosen this moment to take its entire toll. "I shouldn't have let it happen," he said.

"You did everything you could. There was nothing else. I had to knock on that door."

The music had stopped, and she had dropped her voice.

"I live with it every day," he said.

"We live with everything every day. My aunt still keeps her pictures . . ." Lovely pictures, Madeleine, but not forever. Don't you understand? "You came to me a long time ago. It was the night you came back from Switzerland, do you remember? You said you wanted to take me to my family. You told me who my family was. I want to take you to yours now. You and I are family. No one else ever will be for me." It was the thing she had been trying to say, the thing that transcended the other love. It was what made you cross an ocean to knock on a door, or bring a boy home who might not be yours, or walk in woods that were too deep and too cold, but something might be waiting at the end of it.

"I feel that," he said. "You know I feel it. I would like to believe it too."

268

They had not moved since she had dropped her coat over the railing. Without the music, it was very still. Dust would settle over them soon.

Somewhere behind him a phone rang. He waited until after the second ring. Then he said, "Excuse me," and went into the room adjoining the living room.

You can always tell when a man is talking to a woman. There is a different sound to the voice, a different cadence to the speech. It was someone he knew well, a call he had been expecting, or one he should have made himself. She heard only scraps, unfinished phrases.

"Yes, I know . . . Yes . . . I was reading . . . I don't think I can . . . No . . . very difficult . . ." There was a long pause with only an occasional barely audible syllable. Then, "Yes, it seems so . . . unfortunate . . . perhaps at lunch . . . sorry that . . ."

Behind her the clock made a brief whirring sound, the strike mechanism readying itself. She heard the telephone hung up, and then there was absolute quiet. She wondered if she should go to him or wait, and how one made such a decision. A minute passed, then another. It was time to leave, time to gather up her things and go. It was over.

He came out of the kitchen. "Will you stay here tonight?" he asked.

She put her coat back down. "I can't."

The slender clock behind her struck the half-hour, and the great one across the foyer echoed with its own hollow gong. From a distant room a high-pitched chime sounded twice. She tried to keep her lips from quivering while the tears spilled. She had not observed the apartment well enough to describe it, but it had the feel of home.

"I'll have to shut the strikes off if they bother you so." He came across the foyer and brushed her cheek with a finger.

"Don't do that. It's really very nice. I've never stopped missing it." She reached down into her bag and pulled out the envelope. "Come and sit down with me. I have something to show you."

269

She took his hand, holding it too tightly, stopped at the steps to the living room, and sat on the top one. The step was just wide enough for two people, and when he sat down they were very close. She handed him the envelope.

"It's for you, Anton."

He opened it and pulled them out, the pictures Bill had taken each month of little Antonia Henderson, the one on top marked "Two Days," a grinning Anna in her hospital bed nursing a tiny, dark-haired infant.

"You have a child," he said, his voice full of surprise, full of shock.

"A little girl."

He put the top picture precariously on his knee and looked at the next one, marked "One Month," then the next, "Two Months," then the next.

"She's beautiful," he murmured and turned to the next picture.

She knew the exact moment when he measured the number he had seen against the number that remained even as her own heartbeat picked up.

"Anna—"

The early pictures slid from his knee and fell softly to the carpeted floor, and he flipped rapidly through the rest of them, a dealer in a card game with incalculable stakes, stopping at the last one, Anna's daughter, Tonia, "Nine Months," the big smile, the fat cheeks, the unmanageable dark ringlets of hair framing the little face. She could see the uncontrolled movement in his hand, heard him swallow.

"She's mine," he said hoarsely.

"Yes."

He sat staring at the picture, the eyes which could be no one else's but his. Then he put his arms around her, tightly so that she could scarcely breathe, tightly so she would know she was his, forever now a part of his family.

Through the window a man in khaki, a deserter without a belt, a number on his arm. I have never wanted anything in the world except to belong to this man.

270

He kept his left hand still tightly around her, stretched, and reached into his pocket with the right, taking out a handkerchief and using it on his face. "I had no idea," he said. "You must have been very frightened that summer."

"I wasn't. I was very happy."

"Where is she?"

"With Madeleine."

"Come with me. I'll have to change my clothes."

He took her into a bedroom, a double bed made without a spread, a pair of black shoes on the floor next to it. He sat, put the shoes on, unbuttoned the shirt, and took it off.

"Does your husband know?"

"Only since I left him."

He took a shirt out of a drawer, tore off the paper, and pulled the cardboard out. She turned to the mirror, an old, round, ornate mirror hanging over the dresser, and watched him in it as he dressed. He buttoned the shirt and turned to the mirror, glancing from his own reflection to hers.

"You're not sixteen any more," he said to her image.

"I never was. But I want her to be. I want to see it happen."

He kissed her cheek and got a jacket from the closet, and they went out into the foyer. At the door he picked up the suitcase. "It's empty," he said with surprise.

It seemed a little foolish now. "When it came right down to it, I had nothing to pack. There's nothing I need really. Except—I have the jacket in there, the one you gave me. With the zipper."

He put the suitcase down. "Perhaps we can put it away now," he said quietly. "I have a closet in Connecticut. It will be quite safe. There's no need to have it around every day any more, is there? Will you let me put it away?"

"Yes, if you'd like." She watched him put it in the closet behind the coats and close the door.

Auf Wiedersehen, Jürgen.

Auf Wiedersehen, Anna. Leb wohl, Kind.

In the elevator she fished in her bag for the key to the car.

"We'd better take my car. It's Madeleine's, and she should have it back. Bill took ours. He's sending for the furniture." The elevator stopped, and they walked out into the lobby. "I really have nothing."

He held the door for her and took her arm when they were outside. "Perhaps you'll spend some of my money now," he said. "I found all the bills I had given you when I got back to Connecticut. It wasn't necessary, you know. I never kept an accounting."

She reached up and kissed him.

He put his arm around her shoulder. "Will you wake her up for me when we get there?"

"Yes. But just this once. I'm a very strict mother."

"I'm sure you are."

"I don't take any nonsense from her."

"I can tell that from looking at you. I can see you don't take nonsense from anyone. Perhaps you'll both benefit from having a rather easy-going man take care of you." He stopped. "Where's your car, Anna?"

"I don't know." She looked down the street, lined on both sides with rows of cars that were all black in the night like Hegelian cows. "I don't remember where I parked it."

"Then we'll take mine. We'll get your aunt's tomorrow."

He opened the door, let her in, went around to the street side, and started up the motor.

"The Triboro Bridge," she said, the words coming out smoothly, almost without an accent.

He made a U-turn and started up West End Avenue. After a block he reached out and turned on the heater. She felt a rush of warm air, taking away the cold of the winter night. It was the reason people got married, to be warm at night.

"Don't fall asleep," he said. "You're the only person who can tell me how to get home."

"I won't fall asleep." It was what she had always known. She was the only one. Tonight she would take him home.

Acknowledgments

In the course of the research this novel required, many people in many organizations selflessly donated their time and expertise on my behalf. When, on occasion, their own investigations failed to turn up the information I had requested, they offered leads which often proved fruitful and always were interesting. Because of their help, and even more because of the courtesy and kindness they showed me, I would like to thank the following in the order in which I contacted them:

The American Jewish Committee; the Army Quartermaster Corps at the Pentagon; the Division of Military History at the Smithsonian Institution, especially Dr. Donald Kloster; the United States Army Center of Military History, especially Miss Mary Haynes and Mr. Moreau Chambers; and the National Archives, especially Dr. George Chalou, Assistant Branch Chief of the General Reference Branch.

In addition, there were many people, some of whom I know well, some who are friends of friends, who contributed priceless recollections that I could not have matched without them. In particular I would like to thank Mr. Peter Fieger and my friends Sigrid and Helmut Klotzsch, and Gitta and Robert Tabory.

SYRELL ROGOVIN LEAHY

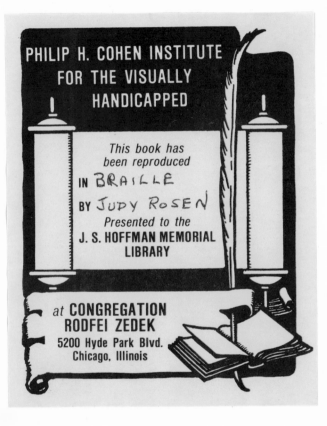

PHILIP H. COHEN INSTITUTE
FOR THE VISUALLY
HANDICAPPED

This book has
been reproduced
IN BRAILLE
BY JUDY ROSEN
Presented to the
J. S. HOFFMAN MEMORIAL
LIBRARY

at CONGREGATION
RODFEI ZEDEK
5200 Hyde Park Blvd.
Chicago, Illinois